Sometimes These Things Happen

Virginia Watson

To Chris,
Enjoy the Read!
Cheers, Virginia

This is a work of fiction. All of the characters, organizations, and events portrayed in this novel are either products of the author's imagination or are used fictitiously.

Aphrodite's Mermaid Productions. P.O. Box 496, Washington, VA 22747. For more information please visit www.vwatsonwriter.com or email vwatsonwriter@gmail.com

Edited by Sound Pig Productions Studio
Cover Photo by Virginia Watson
Cover Artwork by David Evans

ISBN 978-0-578-26226-0
First Edition: February 2022

Dedicated to sweet Bill, my inspiration.

"Poor Flopsey! Never called me mother and now she's dead."

Paraphrased from Monty Python's Flying Circus.

Chapter One

It was well past my usual time to leave. My shoulder muscles screamed for relief as I had been sitting like a pretzel for over two and a half hours. It was late and I was tired. I sat up a bit more, hoping that the exhaustion would somehow magically disappear with a straightened spine. My last paper to grade was an especially wordy one entitled, "Home and Hearth - Artifacts From the Battlefield of Culloden."

I rested my chin on my stiff hand and began reading the droll, opening paragraph which turned into many pages of the same boring content. My eyes burned red and my hand went numb. I decided to try to bring my hand back to life and shook it hard. Quite unexpectedly, my elbow collided with a large and rusty key from the mid-1700s, knocking the protective paper wrapper off it. The paper flew as an old dungeon key ignited with my silly bone and a faint impression of a granite stone floor, mixed with the smell of pungent red wine, cut through my sleepy haze and began to take shape. This was not what I wanted at all. I bit the inside of my lip, trying to use the pain as a way to stay in the present. But like marching soldiers the images bubbled up, one after the other, and soon my oak desk got muzzy and faded away. My world was replaced by a series of three-dimensional, full-color memories, that spun off the eighteenth-century key and there was nothing that I could do about it.

The year 1745 surrounded me. Ancient coldness from a worn, gray floor seeped into the bottom of my mud-caked boots and drained the warmth away from my feet. A transparent tissue paper covered my reality, smothering my perceptions of the present. The Scottish lady's world pushed mine under as our hands became one. I could feel her wrist grow limp as the rusty key that had been used in my lecture, now hung heavy in her hand. Its squared-off bottom had a sharp edge that was entangled in a wisp of a white-lacy cuff. The frustration that it caused the nervous woman was vividly perceptible to me. Her paralyzing terror crept down my spine and mingled with the frostiness that had settled on top of my feet. I sucked in a long breath and heard heavy steps bounding down the damp passageway. The lumbering footsteps drowned out the rapid rhythm of my own heartbeat. I was caught in life experiences from long ago. This frightful world was now mixed with mine whether I wanted it or not.

"Stop, stop!" he called out. The muscular sentry was sprinting down a long, darkened hall. His torturous thoughts hung heavy with each crashing boot heel that pounded the rough stone. Closer, he was getting too close! I shuddered. She froze. I felt her sensation of not being able to move, although a desire to move was frantic within me. With this new anxiety pressed close to my face, I became overwhelmed by her fears. Cascading tears burned her eyes, leaving them blinded. She was lost in indecision.

The guard rounded the corner. I could feel the heat of the guard's breath. Sweat flew as he lunged towards her slender arm. A large oily puddle made the smooth rock next to her treacherous. He met it and slipped on the wet slab, cursing as his feet went out from under him. The lady took that moment, and wasted more precious seconds by still puzzling over which of the two dark corridors would lead her to safety. I mentally screamed, *Just move!* But she continued to debate her choice, absolutely stuck in her mental sludge. At long last, she made a decision to turn to the left. The guard's large, scarred hand reached out and grabbed the key that she had been clutching, tearing the lace flounce as her panicked cry echoed down to the castle's keep. I was terrified for her and struggled now with my own fear. I pushed back at the memories that had stormed into my current world by touching the old key. Their emotions lingered and clung to me. I endeavored to shake it off by a yoga technique to bring peace of mind. I expanded my lungs fully, feeling the air go deep into my belly, slowly releasing it out. I counted nine more controlled breaths in and out. Soon my heartbeat went from an antelope being chased by a lion, to a sleepy cat. I could feel the solidity of my old oak desk once again and smell the fragrant bunch of fresh-cut, butter-yellow daffodils on the windowsill. My fear departed. I was back in the present.

I mulled it over; this was once again another unwanted glimpse of someone else's life that had now, unwillingly, become part of mine when I shared that wretched memory. Predictably, the event was a traumatic one that would leave me shaken for hours even though the experience was less than two minutes long. These events never seemed to be a kitten playing in the sunshine, or a drag queen with a great act that I was able to see and share; instead, it had been my experience that the more intense and gruesome the emotion had been in the incident, then the more likely that memory would be stuck to the objects around the person and so transferable to me. And so, I picked up the bothersome eighteenth-century key that had once been held by Ms. Lacey Indecisive, and flung it back into the Archeology Department's cardboard box where it belonged. I wished that I could put all of my "unusual abilities" into the same box, wrap it up with a big red ribbon and toss it in with the rest.

"Professor MacGregor, there's a visitor here for you," I heard the loud, baritone voice call out. "It's someone with a badge, or so Tim said. Do you want me to have them come down here?" He paused as he tugged on the end of his Viking style pony-tail, waiting for me to respond.

I recognized the voice as Sean, one of my undergraduates. He had taken on the role of my earnest helper and the defender of all of my break times. For the last year he did everything that he could to make sure that I had whatever I needed; a pen that would write, a cup of scalding hot coffee from Shenandoah Joe, even some pretty good jokes now and then. I decided that Sean would make someone a well-educated, thoughtful and stable husband. He'd also be most happy with a couple of children clinging to his back for a ride; this is how I saw his future.

Thinking about Sean and about the type of woman that would probably choose him, made me think of the string of husbands that my mother chose. Sean was very unlike the four or five husbands, I refused to remember the exact count, that my mother had ensnared and married.

I looked over my tall stack of musty books, past Sean's concerned look, and with a lingering disappointment about the memory of my mother, mixed with the realization of what was about to occur, I became irritated, not with him, just the situation that I found myself in once again.

I had had enough of the FBI's demands. I knew that someone was here from the Bureau with an unsolved crime. They would attempt to manipulate me into agreeing to help with this often described as, one-last-case. I was weary of being the FBI's go-to-freak. This was not my lifetime's ambition. I did not appreciate hearing the news from one of the agents that I was referred to as "Professor Freak" when they spoke to each other. No one had actually said it around me, but they thought it often enough and it was all too easy for me to hear. I knew that my name came up only during times of desperation, so they must be pretty desperate to call me after our last encounter. I decided that after that time, I would most likely never hear from the Bureau again. At least, I hoped that would be the case. I had shared thinly veiled insults with the Not-So-Special-Agent-In-Charge that ended in a boisterous fight, or as the report said, "A divergent opinion as to a logical summation." I wondered what that bureaucratic vernacular meant. There was one thing that I was certain about though, the box next to my name on his report must have had a check mark in it that said, *Talk to Never*. No psychic abilities were necessary to know that fact.

"Thanks Sean, I'll go see whoever it is. I'd rather not have anyone see how messy it is here." I grinned at him, while I put my tired feet back into my worn Dubarry boots, stuffing my dark-olive linen trousers down the long, brown-suede shaft. I left the sanctuary of my quiet, small and messy office, stepping through a stream of brilliant sunlight, wondering what their gimmick would be this time.

"Professor MacGregor?" She called out to me as soon as I had popped into the hallway. The attractive, young agent had on a bright red suit with three-inch pumps to match. She didn't look like the usual federal type. She captured the look of a high-fashion model. This agent had the type of beauty that was hypnotic; stellar complexion, shiny auburn hair that had not one split end and which framed her symmetrical face flawlessly, with arms and legs that seemed related to a gazelle. All in all, she was model perfect.

Then Agent Sexton, yes, it was Sexton, I thought, flashed a beauty-contestant, award-winning smile, that could have been used as a super power. I had never seen anything like her come out of Quantico before, but I had learned years ago that things were often quite different from what they seemed, especially if the federal government was involved.

She squeezed past the last bunch of coeds that were giggling their way down the pristine white hall and now stood a few feet away from me. The Agent extended her perfectly manicured hand. My hand, with its ragged cuticles from pulling up some of the Pavilion Garden's abundant crop of weeds, soon neared the woven, rose-gold ring on her right index finger. It was then that I could sense that she was not playing by the rules. The beauty contest winner had something unspoken for me.

I hesitated just a half-second too long before I started to withdraw my hand from hers. Special Agent Sexton noticed the small motion of me pulling away. As quick as she could, she grabbed my hand and with a kung-fu hold, firmly shook it.

The vision popped open as soon as I touched the ring. The room was poorly lit; dark stains crawled up from the floor onto the cracked walls. I saw a man sitting stiffly in a wooden chair behind a desk. He was breathing hard and I felt that he was anxiously waiting for something or someone. His anxiety about waiting pervaded the memory, eating up all of the nooks and crannies. My stomach involuntarily began doing back flips as I saw a woman standing in front of him. She pulled out a revolver from her purse and shot him in the center of his forehead. I could feel the clamminess of her hand, as she let go of the gun. The gun and a ring clattered down to the cement floor. His head jolted backwards and then his body slumped forward and crashed onto the desk, spewing blood on the blotter like a broken water fountain. Blood covered what was left of his head and dripped down, decorating the unwanted gun and ring. Like a panicked deer, she took off.

I pulled my hand away from the agent's hand, and from that

ring. Steading myself, I leaned on the spotless white wall and saw that she was scrutinizing me. Her eyes squinted almost closed. Agent Sexton was desperate to see what I had just seen by staring at my eyes! I must admit that this was a new twist. I guess that she thought that I worked just like a DVD player; just pop in the disc and watch the movie. Little did she know that she really didn't want to be able to see what I saw, or feel what I felt.

"Professor MacGregor, I am Special Agent Colleen Sexton," she said with as much authority as she could project, as she straightened herself to stand even taller.

"Yeah, I got your name coming down the hall, and that was a rotten memory that you shoved me into,"I snarled. I had just gotten through one terrifying glimpse of a Scottish dungeon failed escape and now this! I was vexed.

I never mentioned having any type of unusual abilities with most people, but with the Feds, the secret was out. This one I found particularly irritating because of the amount of manipulating fairy-dust that I knew would soon be sprinkled on me by, as I had just dubbed her, Miss-no-splint-ends-at-all. So I decided it was okay to put her in her place and righteously storm off, but then, I opted to be kind and give her another chance. After all, I knew that the tale of Miss Lacey Indecisive had rankled me like a festering sore.

"Well,... what did you see? Anything?" Colleen Sexton was pushy, and I just realized, she was about six feet tall sans shoes. Wow, now that's a tall woman! I wondered why she was wearing such high heels? My focus was stuck on those heels. I felt mesmerized by the red of the blood and the red of her outfit.

Colleen cleared her throat. "So, I would like to verify what information you got from that ring."

Her words lit my raw nerves like a match tossed on gasoline. I viewed my options and chose my first one again, leave. I was half way back to my office when I heard her call down the hallway, "She's ten years old, the same age that you were when you were abducted."

And as Agent Sexton had planned, her clearly spoken and sterile words made my knees go weak and my stomach began to ache. I came to a dead stop. My boots squealed on the waxed floor as I turned to face her. I watched two coeds, now not giggling, turn towards our public event to see what would be said next. Even on such a large campus as the University of Virginia, there could never be enough fodder about professors to ignore it when things so easily flew by your ears. This could be a high ranking post on Snapchat, Instagram or Twitter. For them to miss something this potentially salacious would be a true waste in their opinions. And because I was the youngest professor on campus, any and all gossip of my doings were a hot commodity.

I pointed towards my office and began marching towards the partially open door. She got it, and followed me down the hall, her heels clicking sharply behind me, a further annoyance. As I closed my door, Agent Sexton took a seat and pulled out the newest iPad. She opened up a file and handed it to me. I was now going down the familiar path to my own horror show through this little girl. I did not want to go.

The story stared out at me in a digital display of the mundane turning into terror; the girl's photograph, the parking lot where she was kidnapped, and various shots of the mall and of her house. Copious pages of witness interviews took up the bulk of the information but it was the gruesome expression on the deceased undercover policeman that made my pulse quicken. His throat had been torn open by a large throwing knife. The next photo was of the mother's bloodied camel-colored cashmere coat. She had been standing next to him, so most of his throat splattered on it along with a great fountain of his blood, making this season's choicest piece in classic camel look more like last season's edgy leopard.

I made myself look at the vacation photos of the family. These were the worst for me to view. They were the photos of her and her family in happier times. The collective joy on their faces seemed to slam up against the evil of the current situation, making the horror of the event unforgettable. The juxtaposition made me shudder.

I pushed on and read the agent's account of the occurrence, the lists of potential suspects, and scanned the summary of the massive amounts of what was to me, useless data that had been compiled and carefully entered into the report. The FBI had been trying to find her for four days! There was not one lead that had panned out. I looked up at Agent Sexton and asked her what I already knew.

"You have nothing? Not a clue on who took her? Statistically, she is already dead. Why did you wait so long to come to me?" But I knew that answer too. I was the last stop on the Bureau's train to Wits End. And they had to go to that station, as this little girl was Jennifer Stark. She was the daughter of the Director of the Federal Bureau of Investigation.

She paused, took a deep breath and started the sales pitch. "Professor MacGregor, may I call you Tess?"

Okay, so a big *no* to that one I decided. I never liked the way they try to disarm you by using your given name. It was an old tactic used for years by door-to-door salesmen, and I wasn't buying it. "You may call me Professor MacGregor," I told her. There, the line was drawn.

Agent Sexton was not a stupid person and she put the best, All-American Federal Agent, here-to-save-the-world-glow on her checks, and went on with the rest of the rehearsed pitch. "Professor, I have asked that we, the FBI, explore all leads that are possible to us, and I knew about you. SSA Robert Ashwood, one of the agents that found you when you were abducted, well, he was my mentor at the Academy. He told me that you had special abilities in helping people so I brought your name up and got the go-ahead." She placed both hands back in her lap and rested her case.

I felt trapped. Anywhere but here, was where I wanted to be. I looked down at my desk and noticed the faint scent of Chanel No. 5 that clung to Agent Sexton. It reminded me of mother and the countless cocktail parties that she went to nightly, even just a week after I was back home from my ordeal. I could still see her dressed in her glamour magazine clothes, with polished nails, and wafting perfume that enveloped all of her distant goodbyes and left me crying in a dark room.

"Huh, I guess you have the whole story then," I paused and I felt my feet go cold again. It was not because of the old Scottish key this time. The chill was a natural by-product of my memories of being snatched, alone, and naked on a cold floor. The terror rose from my core, draining the blood from my extremities and just for a second, I felt ten years old again with no one to help me. I involuntarily shook ever so slightly.

She closed her notebook and the magnetic snap brought me back to the present. "So are you interested? Will you assist us?" she asked me with a subtle irritation that she tried to suppress. Agent Sexton wasn't used to having to ask for much of anything, ever.

"How far away is it?" I asked as a way of delaying the inevitable.

"Not so far, it's near Washington. The helicopter is close by so you'd be at Quantico in about fifteen minutes. You could be back in time for dinner." She made it sound like it was just a pleasant stop-over to see the Wizard of Oz for a brief tete-a-tete and then back to Kansas. I looked down at my well-worn boots that were still caked with a bit of dirt from the garden and thought about Jennifer Stark, and a mad man that was now in control.

I could tell that Colleen was pleased with herself. She saw that I took the bait just by reading my body language. She got up from the chair and looked down at my worried countenance and smirked just a bit.

My response was to let out a long sigh. I was resigned to this now and I contemplated about the last time, the last case, and how it was so tiring for me. That ordeal seemed to go on forever, and the 'vic,' as they like to say, the woman, died. I felt so useless. All of my special abilities were no more effective than parlor tricks during that case. I looked down at the floor thinking about Jennifer Stark, all alone and terrified.

"I must be back by 7 p.m., no later." I was drawing another boundary line; although I knew that I would stay as late as they needed me. "I need to stop by my apartment first. You are not the pilot, are you?" I asked her while looking at her three inch heels.

Chapter Two

Soon I was in their helicopter and feeling slightly ill as the low-flying craft danced over the jammed traffic on Route 95. My stomach held onto an annoyance that was now physical. I knew that my upset stomach's roots were found in my psyche; it was my mother, the original pain. Just before I jumped into my uncomfortable airborne seat, she had texted me with another frivolous complaint about her very expensive, luggage. Her wayward emotions all seemed to be about her possessions, never relationships. I could see that mother was enchanted with her new husband's bank account. Her desires were endless, one new Chanel bag followed another; just as one new husband's bank account was greater than the one before.

She garnered a multitude of European accents that she could perfectly mimic, as she twirled her way around the globe. Mother seemed to find eligible and wealthy men in every five star resort. I pictured her following the trail of Alexander the Great. She would follow a yellow dotted line on a large wall map to different capitals, each capital represented by a large diamond headed pin. Mother was represented by a towering crimson stiletto heel that would unwaveringly follow this dotted line to the next resort to plunder whatever was there to be had. Alexander the Great had determination and wisdom, mother had her own glib style made up of glamour magazine tips and wish trips to expensive perfume and make-up counters. Hmm, it was amazing what she could catch with that! But none of those relationships approached anything that anyone would consider lasting or with merit according to my sensibilities.

But then, my view on the world was most certainly conservative; an unwavering attempt by me to find the normalcy that holding on to the status quo promised. Contrary to me, mother danced in the wind, floating from one champagne adventure to the next, always landing squarely on her stiletto heels with more diamonds encircling her fingers. I didn't have one diamond; mother often pointed this out. Thinking about that my stomach took one more flip.

We touched down at Quantico in time for me to see a line of Marines execute their close-order drill moves. That was always an impressive sight. They practiced for months to be able to move as one person. Just as I felt spellbound by their motion, the helicopter door opened and a blast of strong wind hit my face, my blond hair flew wildly around my head and left me looking like a straw man.

"Tess MacGregor, great to see you again." John belted out to be heard over the din of the chopper blades as they slowed down. He offered his large hand to me. I gladly took it and looking at his handsome face, and not at what was below me, I landed squarely in a guard dog's excrement.

Lovely, I thought. If that doesn't show that I am paying too much attention to him, what would? John's blazing good looks and friendly smile could be the government's secret weapon against me if only they knew. I was over the patriotic riff and the years of stories of dire consequences that the agents formulated so well in all of their talks. In fact, all that the FBI needed to do was to send John, and I would follow him anywhere. Thinking this, my cheeks turned a crimson red. I could feel the flush as it moved down my neck, I really did need to find someone, I reminded myself once again.

"Good to see you too," I gushed as a large grin uncontrollably covered my face. John smiled back and I thought that I would melt into the earth or possibly jump up and kiss his neck. Thankfully I did neither.

Soon we stood inside the complex on shiny white marble floors that glowed from the sunlight that was reflected through the large windows. We walked past the round, eight-foot Federal Bureau of Investigation logo that commanded the center of the wide hallway's floor. The design was chocolate brown with gold lettering. The circle showed no signs of wear. It would seem that no one stood on it, just near it, for a tourist photo. This was an unspoken sacred spot in the building.

We continued down the long hall and passed through a double-glass doorway to my often desired location. I had finally made it to the hallowed elevator. At least, this is how I thought of it. This was the elevator that went all the way down to the steel encased room. I knew that all the top level, most important cases and people, were taken there.

The stainless-steel elevator had two armed guards; big brutish men, or at least that was what they liked to put out to the world. I picked up a passing thought from one of them about his daughter's favorite song. He began to mentally hum it. Nice tune about jumping up and then reach, reach for the stars. I guess that he wasn't so brutish after all. They were both in charge of security for getting on the elevator and were carefully checking the four men's passes that were ahead of us in line.

The humming guard squinted down at me and said to John, "Mhmm." He then gave a nod while the slender, tall guard noted something down on the computer. After several years wondering what it might be like to be allowed to go down deep into the earth and discover what mysteries were there, I got an *mhmm.*This was not the way that I had scripted it in my fantasies at all.

We travelled with the four other men who all seemed quite uninteresting to me. They had squared-off shoulders, locked in place from the amount of tension that was present in their neck and shoulder muscles. They stood stiffly, draped in black suits, taking only shallow breaths with empty minds, no cheery songs there.

Down we went to where I had perceived the mysterious steel room. I knew that this held a SCIF, a Sensitive Compartmented Information Facility. Here is where one would go if you wanted to protect your confidential conversations, the live, or the digital types. No unwanted signal could escape, and none could enter, at least that is what they thought. My perceptions were things that could not be measured by today's scientific community, so no one knew that my senses could penetrate steel and even a SCIF. This was not a problem for me and I would never tell them.

With a soft bounce the elevator came to a halt and the doors opened up to a brightly lit hallway that was humming with the brain-numbing sounds of fluorescent lights. The hallway reminded me of a Hollywood version of the CIA. I pictured Tom Cruise being chased down the hallway with the theme to Mission Impossible now drowning out the hum from the bad lights. Staring at John, the closest man that resembled a Hollywood star that I knew, I began to mentally wander and hum the MI theme song. I was off in my own world again, oblivious to the flashing red lights that now filled the hallway to warn that I was present, and that I was not cleared for top security of any kind. But barring the red lights, the rules would be broken for this one mission in a very quiet way.

My imagination was a world filled with comfort for me. I slipped into it easily and thought of the time that mother informed me, after one of many mandatory school conferences over my "adventures," that is how mother would phrase it, that the school psychologist said that I had a tendency to mentally wander and that this was a response to my overloaded perceptions. Although it was a given that the next breath would contain that these perceptions, whether "real or imagined," could be "cured" with a drug, the one right thing that mother did, was to not buy that cure. She insisted that, "I was to remain drug free to explore my own individuality, wherever that led." *Many thanks to mom*, I thought to myself, and for once I meant that without heaping on sarcasm.

"Tess, come this way," John half whispered to me. While I was lost in my own thoughts, I had not been keeping up with everyone else in our procession.

"Sorry, I'll pay more attention," I whispered back. I stopped humming and followed John into the cold steel room.

There was another ID check and the same questions to make sure that I did not have any digital device on my person. I knew not to bring any, John had warned me earlier. Since I was not given a pass, I surmised that John must be my pass. I also realized that it had been decided that my name was not one that should go on an official guest pass. As far as the official record went, I was not here officially with everyone else. I was, once again, the unmentionable freak in the room.

The door opened. I saw a spacious room that was dominated by luxurious curtains that lined the far wall. I concluded that an interior designer had put them up to give the illusion of windows. They were a navy blue velvet and quite thick. A magnificent oak table took up most of the room. It was a neat rectangle with square wooden light towers built into each corner of the table. The towers stood three feet above the top of the table, and were done in an attractive mission oak style. Admiring the design, I saw a dongle was attached to the lights. I looked closer, the lights were LED and outfitted with cutting-edge technology of Li-Fi, an interesting technology that allows the internet to transmit data very rapidly using light instead of radio frequencies. One of my Scottish friends had helped develop it, and was busy trying to sell it to Verizon. These fancy aluminum Li-Fi dongles were not available to the general public, in fact, my friend said that would be three years away. But here they were.

I wondered what other clandestine toys were embedded in the luxurious surroundings. I suspiciously scanned the computers that were set flat in the table in front of each of the deluxe chestnut-brown leather chairs. Many possibilities of a very dark and secret tech world lurked in those flat screens. I did not want to contemplate that yet so I gazed down at an enormous, hand-woven, forest-green oriental rug that the oak table sat on. The sheen of the green silk fibers set off the navy velvet curtains and honey-colored oak beautifully. Feeling somewhat now like an interior designer, I decided that this was a beautiful and expensive room that embraced no life at all. None.

"Please sit here Professor MacGregor." Supervisory Special Agent Eastman gave me a thin smile and motioned me to have a seat. Reluctantly I left John's side and went to my assigned place. I watched as John left and a new person came in the door. The man was the last one to enter. He was very tall, blond, and had ice blue eyes. His suit was a better quality than that of the other men, and he walked in like he knew it.

I had joined a task force composed of a very elite group of eleven men and one woman, me. They were a mix of FBI mostly, two men from the HRT, the Hostage Rescue Team, and another two men of unknown origins, and a new alphabet group that I had never heard of before, the NGA. The National

Geospatial-Intelligence Agency's geeky guy sat two chairs down from me. He kept adjusting his glasses up and down his nose and it was obvious to me that he was most uncomfortable in a room that was filled with sharks. The scientist's name was Howard. He had a bad sinus condition. I became quickly bored with Howard's odd nasal noises and put my attention on the tall blond. He was a most mysterious man. I did not know which ABC group he belonged to yet but I was confident that I could find out.

I looked at the faces around the table and wondered what was I really doing here. The man across from me looked into my eyes, quickly looked down, and then set his tense gaze on top of his briefcase so that he would not have to acknowledge me. The other men around the table were not much better, except for Howard. At least he had no ill will pointed in my direction. Howard was so worried about his sinus cavity that he neglected me all together. This was not a healthy place for me to visit, much less hold hands with these guys as they recited the Pledge of Federal Allegiance. There was not one person that I felt a connection with, until there was a loud commotion outside the door. After much cacophony, the door opened and a Charlottesville Police Detective that I knew, walked in.

"Yes, I am sure that I am supposed to be here." He growled and then shoved a piece of paper into the guard's face. The guard stepped aside and watched him suspiciously as he entered the room.

Detective Ed Kravitz was all smiles, standing as tall as he could make himself stretch. He had enough attitude to swim with the sharks. He found an empty seat and filled it up. I had seen him for the first time just about a month ago, when I met my sister, Libby, in the parking lot at the station. She had briefly introduced us. It was comforting to see him here. Ed was, after all, nice to look at, and I am sure that he felt that having a soul was a job prerequisite. A nice plus point for me after looking at the misfit cadre of heroes. There was just something about him that made me want to linger longer over his features, more so than a polite person would do. But casting my eyes quietly around the room once more, confirmed that no one here had any angst about being polite, I could keep resting my eyes on Ed.

The blond man in the good suit moved closer. I took my eyes off of my new fascination and saw that the Agent that I had dubbed Mystery Man, was standing across from me. This time I carefully took him in. He stood about six-foot-four and had blond hair, like my own, but his eyes were ice blue. Blondie must be about 40 years old. I just realized that I had picked up no name from him. Actually, I got not much from him at all. I could only pick up what I could see with my own green eyes, no psychic connection was made. Blondie seemed to hover around the table, not wanting to sit and stare at the computer screen as the rest of the men did. He stood with his muscular frame rigid against the back wall and casually surveyed the room.

"I want to thank Professor MacGregor for joining us today and to acknowledge that Detective Kravitz is here, representing Charlottesville PD," said SSA Eastman from the top of the table.

I stopped listening to SSA Eric Eastman at that point and shifted my attention to the information about Jennifer. There were just too many distractions for me between Ed and trying to decipher Mystery Man.

The computer screen was very responsive and so it was easy to wade through the plethora of information. I knew from experience that I would not be useful acting like a detective, as I had no training in the field. I was there for my unusual abilities, no one here needed me to pretend to be a psychic Sherlock Holmes. I skipped over all of the gathered facts and interviews. I read only the synopsis and looked at the photos again. I needed to see an image of Jennifer. This would help me establish a connection with her. I became lost in her soft, honey colored curls, brown eyes and crooked smile. She had thick eyebrows and a cute nose. I got a faint aroma of butterscotch looking at her. She appeared to be a happy little girl. I got the sense that she liked cereal. Specifically, she enjoyed Trix Cereal, the kind that had a nice sugary, fruity taste.

"Hmm, that's odd, why would I be getting the taste of cereal from a photo?" I wondered aloud. Then I realized that the tip of my shoe was barely touching a box that had been put close to my chair.

"Professor MacGregor, would you like to view these items from Jennifer in the back room? The lighting is better there." I looked up startled, it was the Mystery Man.

"Hello, I'm Stefan Hannigan," he announced to me. Then Agent Hannigan flashed me with his dazzling blue eyes and let loose one sunshine bright smile. I lost my train of thought for a just a second and wondered if those tactics were honed from being handsome all of his life. I looked closer still. His features were truly chiseled. I had read about men with dimpled chins and thick brows laying on sculpted cheekbones defined by full red lips, but that was usually only described in a romance novel or used in a Paco Rabanne underwear ad. Men like that didn't really exist, at least not in my world.

"And you are with whom? Doing what?" I prompted him, my curiosity peaked uncontrollably.

"I am involved in this case on behalf of the Government, and I am here to assist you in whatever you need in order to do the best job possible. I apologize for the ambiguity but I have recently been assigned to head my part of the Task Force and I am uncertain about what I can discuss." He paused just long enough, waiting for me to say okay and let it go. Agent Stefan

Hannigan did not know me, I was not the let-it-go-easy type of woman.

"Unless you can come up with something a little bit more definite than the government, I may get lost in the generality of my impressions." I dug my heels in and watched to see what he would do next. There was no physical reaction that I could see. His muscular shoulders remained relaxed and so did his face. Next, he looked directly through me, not at me, and Agent Hannigan seemed to put on an emotional cloak. I took it as a sign that he would be even more distant.

Just as I became comfortable with my decision, he beamed another melting smile my way. Agent Hannigan was enjoying the game after all. "All right, I am with the FBI, the CARD team." He could see that I was a bit puzzled and deciphered the message, "The Child Abduction Rapid Deployment, CARD." I could detect a hint of suppressed laughter in his voice as well.

Funny, but he did seem emotionally and analytically distant to my psychic probes; unlike the vast majority of people that I interacted with every day. Most folk were as easy to read as the Sunday comics. Sadly for me, almost none of them were as entertaining as the comics. Looking straight into his eyes I realized that I might be mesmerized by his vital type of self-confidence, and the blond hair that went with his obvious Viking ancestry. I had always been a fool for blond men, it was a known weakness. And this man was noteworthy; he would make any woman take notice of him no matter what their age. I watched his leg muscles spring easily into action. I could feel the strength within him. He was intoxicating to my perceptions and I enjoyed it.

He pushed open the thick glass door that had wires embedded in it, while I cautiously entered the well-lit back room. Special Agent Hannigan placed the box on the table, with latex gloves on top, and motioned for me to sit next to it.

The SCIF had no sounds, nothing that wasn't made by us; no lights humming, no water pipes making noise overhead, no creaky furniture, nothing, I briefly thought that this was an electronic tomb and that thought made my skin crawl.

"Professor MacGregor," he looked faintly worried. "Can I get you water?"

"Yes, that would be nice." I gave him a half grin and watched him as he went back to the main room. I could relax a bit better now that I was alone.

The box held bits of Jennifer's world. Before I touched any evidence, I put on the required gloves; then, I pulled out a small flowered pillow, about 12 inches square. The pillow had been kept in their car for her. The little purple and blue pansies on it were interwoven with an ivy design. The pillow gave off a relaxed, cozy feeling of falling asleep on it. The next item that I touched was an open box of Trix. Well, that explains the sugary goodness. Next, I held her diary. It had a copy of a Degas ballet dancer on the cover and a smeared chocolate spot on the lower right corner. I got the thought of work, or no, not work, it was homework. She was concerned about her homework assignment. Next was a chocolate candy wrapper under the notebook. I presumed that it must be the chocolate that had helped make the smear on her book. I stopped myself from reaching for it when I saw the blue bunny. I had read that the bunny had been with her at the time of her abduction and that her abductor had thrown it out the window as he sped away. I twitched uncontrollably, for no reason, and then I felt the wrapper give off a faint impression. It was just a glimpse of a big man throwing away the bunny and I could see she had this chocolate wrapper stuffed under the bunny's collar. I guessed that she was hiding her chocolate snack from her mother.

The bunny was Mr. Hoppy. Wherever she went, Hoppy went too. I delayed picking him up, I knew that touching this item would bring me close to her hopes and sorrows that now would be topped off by the ultimate horror of being snatched away from the safety of her family. Knowing that if someone, especially a child, kept an object with them for most of their waking hours, that object would be most easily read so it would have the greatest emotional punch. It had been my experience that the events would tumble off quickly; many memories, both good and bad, and in this case, all with a child's vibrancy stuck to them. All of them would be spinning and dancing towards me and this is what I would need to decipher. I would have to separate her emotion of horror from her perceptions of the event. I did not relish the expectation of what I was soon to feel around me.

I looked back out to the main room and saw that Agent Hannigan was in a deep discussion with another agent. I took this as my cue to touch Hoppy.

I placed my palm on the top of the bunny's head and pulled him up by his long, blue ears. Hoppy had many miles on him. I guessed that she did not give him up very often for a bath, if ever. I put my right hand around his neck and held him close to me, as Jennifer would have done. The fear spun off of him like a tornado, and left me reeling in the storm of her responses.

The turbulent scene played out in the same sequence that the report stated. Dark shadows towering over her, people moving quickly away, her mother's shriek, a sensation of being lost and floating. The only thing different was that I was seeing it fly by from her ten-year old viewpoint. Deciphering her image storm, I could see her looking up at the late afternoon sky and then to her mother's face. She was a bit bored and tired of shopping and so she had quietly clutched Mr. Hoppy to her chest and quickly walked away into the crowd.

Jennifer had noticed a fat sparrow pulling out french fries from the red container that was on the edge of the parking lot.

She decided that it would be nice to introduce Hoppy to the small bird. Jennifer increased her gait and stayed focused on the chestnut-brown sparrow.

The tall man had his attention on her. He reached out and snatched Jennifer's hand as she hurried by. She looked up at him, not knowing who the stranger was. She knew that it wasn't Daddy. He knew it too. He grinned menacingly down at his new prize and pulled the little girl with the crooked smile closer.

"Hey, hey you, get away from her!" The woman's voice was at a panicked pitch. Her mom alarm had gone off and she quickly spotted her daughter who was holding a stranger's hand.

He swiveled his head in her direction. His dirty hair fell across his eyes and momentarily blocked his view of the assembling crowd that was forming behind Jennifer's mother. She stood forty feet away from him, next to her cream Mercedes Benz.

The monster, as Jennifer knew that he was a monster, delighted in feeling the hysteria heighten. He imagined that he could smell her fear, he thought that he could even taste it. Jennifer felt his satisfaction and panicked.

Her fear drenched most of the perceptions that formed these memories. I could feel that she closed her eyes as he raised her hand up, as if he was offering to take her back. She did not want to look at the crazy man. She didn't want to feel the crazy man.

"Jennifer, Jennifer!" Her mother pleaded, as the little girl stood frozen in place.

He decided to give the press something to talk about. After all, he reasoned, they had been wanting to talk to him for years! He covertly pulled out his newly bought Randall-Made Model One Fighting Knife, that he had purchased from a pawn shop far away from his home. Tossing his waving hand high, he pretended again that he was trying to get her mother's attention as he was bringing Jennifer back to her, but his twisted smirk gave another message.

Kathleen Elizabeth Tyler Stark knew in an instant that this man wanted to kill someone, maybe her child. Time seemed to move in a sticky fashion. Her fears were like glue on everything that she saw or heard.

"No, what do you want? Don't, don't ..." she called out. Tears began to spill uncontrollably from the attractive woman. Her breathing stopped as the blade glinted in the last of the sunlight. Kathleen could see now that he had a knife. She felt a muscular hand grab her bicep to stop her from running straight on to what Al felt would be a certain death.

Al was an armed undercover policeman, one of Charlottesville's best, who was a scant second away from charging the crazy guy with the little girl. Al had not moved yet, but the mad man could see that he would.

The monster didn't hesitate, he threw the knife at Al's throat and hit his mark. Deep crimson blood spurted on the mother's camel-colored coat as she howled with horror. He was dead before she stopped screaming.

Most of the crowd stepped back. A few began to run towards the mall for cover, others dove down to the pavement. The armed man was now the center of attention and the mob consensus was that he was a terrorist that could have a hidden gun. Everyone seemed to have a gun these days.

Jennifer's eyes were wide open. She kicked him in the shins as he struggled to reel in his catch. He put his large hand over her mouth, punched her in the stomach, and began humming a song that she knew, thanks to Dad's classic rock station, Sympathy For The Devil.

It was easy for him to toss the daughter of the Director of the FBI into his nondescript silver Honda Civic, as she was in a stupor. He pitched his gloves on the dashboard, started the car and slipped into obscurity with a new toy to play with.

"Things are looking up baby doll!" He pronounced to Jennifer as she cried into the top of the bunny's head. Giving her a wide grin, he wrenched Mr. Hoppy out of her hands and tossed him out the window.

The last of her horror let go of me, as I slumped onto the cold, white table.

Chapter Three

"I told you many times, she was squirming against him. He had on a heavy coat, seems like it was dark brown with black buttons. His shoes and gloves were black leather, expensive, maybe Italian or Irish? He didn't seem to tense much as Jennifer struggled to get away so he probably is larger than an average man. From her perspective, he's huge. It could be that he is just very muscular; it is hard to give you an exact height because to Jennifer he was very tall, tall and menacing. And his hair that I can see underneath the fedora looks unwashed to me. He's caucasian, didn't notice any wrinkles. That is it! I have no other things to say about this. There is nothing new to add. There is not one thing left that I haven't said at least ten times!" I opened my eyes and tried to focus on the room again. Red indentations stayed visible on my forehead from my knuckles digging into my skull. Enough was enough! Shouldn't they be satisfied! I focused on the agent's nose so that I could glare better.

I needed some time alone, preferably with a very large glass of a California Cabernet Sauvignon. Going over this incident for over three hours, with several agents, had stirred up my own carefully hidden fears from my past. I could feel myself slowly starting to unravel with the pressure of having to duplicate her horror each time I went over her thoughts. In vain, I wished that there was another way for me to see through her moments and get the perceptions of who he was. I just couldn't clearly make out his face. Most of the time she had her eyes closed, or she was crying, or his stringy, dirty hair was hanging down in front of his face. This was impossible and I was tired of trying to do the impossible.

"What about the bunny? You didn't mention the bunny this time."

Agent Hannigan gave the other agent, who was from the Hostage and Rescue Team, a slightly dirty look. He did not like the other agent. I saw that there must have been competition in their past. Both were good looking, one blond, the other a brunette and from different agencies within the FBI. In some ways the HRT Agent could have been a smaller version of Superman, while Hannigan was Thor come to life. It gave me a small bit of comfort imagining cartoon super heroes. Too bad they weren't real.

"So just tell me, and we can get off this, and wrap it up. What about the rabbit? What did she think as he tore it from her grip? You must be able to see something there." The HRT Agent was unrelenting.

"The monster, Jennifer thinks of him that way, she calls him that in her mind." That was a new part to the puzzle that I regretted saying as it would mean more time being grilled. I did not know how much longer I could continue and remain civil.

"That's new, isn't that new?" The HRT Agent was at last satisfied, he had managed to get a new piece of information. But this piece of information meant nothing. I doubt if he could look up Mr. Monster in any of his data bases.

"Good, let's end this for the present." Hannigan proclaimed.

"So, he looked at her, grabbed the bunny, rolled down the window and threw it out. The end?" The HRT agent asked in an exasperated tone; he demanded more.

I had put on my own personal brakes, as I intended to not run head-on into my own horror train that night. I could feel Agent Hannigan preparing to jump on the HRT Agent if he requested one more go through. He could tell that I was used up and my abilities were being clouded over by my own physical and mental exhaustion. I deduced that Stefan was a master at reading body language. He gave an intense look at the other agent to signal that we were done. Superman conceded.

"Thanks, thanks Professor MacGregor." The number two man from the Hostage and Rescue Team said. I guess that he was hungry and tired too, and he must have realized that there was nothing left that would be said tonight other than an uncomfortable stand off with Hannigan. The agent pushed himself up from the table with his left hand, grabbing his bag with the other, and left with his meager scrap of news. Agent Hannigan was directly behind him, tapping him on the shoulder once they were both through the thick glass door.

I looked down and touched Mr. Hoppy's long blue ear one last time and wished that I could touch Jennifer and let her know that it would be okay; let her know that the good guys were coming soon and that all she needed to do was to let me know where she was. I could hear her voice if only she was able to speak to me, but she wasn't able to talk to me or anyone else. My weighty thoughts tamped down any hope, telling me that statistically she was dead.

As I left the much awaited mysterious SCIF and the deluxe steel room, I contemplated that some things can never be as wonderful as what your imagination can turn them into being. Some things are better left in the box with the ribbon securely tied. My journey's end was to a cold, dead room that was filled with hours of worry, stuffed with criminal memories, and I was now certain that not one of my Mission Impossible exhilarations of Hollywood heroics, was felt there ever.

"Professor MacGregor, Thank you for everything, I know that was not easy for you." I could feel Agent Hannigan near me, I could faintly smell his expensive cologne as he held open the door for me one more time.

"Yes, I hope that the description of the car and the vague sketch helps." I smiled and headed for the elevator. We were up in just three-seconds flat. It reminded me of being in my scuba gear and needing to get to the surface in order to pass the PADI test. You could always get up in 3 seconds as long as you stayed in the 66 foot depth range. But with my luck, it wasn't in the warm waters of the blue Caribbean where I dove to pass my exam. No, it was in a cold, muddy rock quarry in Pennsylvania. My mask was quickly obscured with bottom silt which made eyesight impossible when I had to take off and then put back on my mask. I used my third sight to see through the mud. The mantra that I said to not panic and remain calm was , Up in three! It wasn't graceful, but it did work. I used this mantra again to leave the Federal gloom. Wishing that I could shake off her horror and my nightmares as easily as bottom silt.

Agent Hannigan was stopped by one of the guards. I guess that he was needed to sign me out, then I was free to wander outside on my own. I nodded goodnight and pushed open the glass door.

The temperature had dropped. The cold air woke me up and I felt refreshed just leaving the building. I looked around for John and found Detective Kravitz instead.

"Hey, ah you're Policewoman MacGregor's sis, right?" The Brooklyn accent was not a deal-breaker but almost, to my Southern sensibilities. Just hearing him made me want to throw out a random, *Well, butter my butt and call me a biscuit*, but I managed to reign in that impulse.

I nodded and he smiled. He was handsome after all, not like the god Thor, but there was just something about him that I liked. "Yes, Abigail is my baby sister."

"Since we're headed the same way, I thought that we could ride back together," he said.

"Sounds nice but I think that I have a helicopter waiting, somewhere..." I started to look about, wondering more intently where John was.

"Something funny about that," he said. "I told the big guy that he could take off. He had some big date or something, so I said that I would escort you home. I mean, we're both going to Charlottesville. Made him happy, I didn't think that you'd mind."

Interesting, I could tell that he was lying about John having a date. "I see." I scanned the horizon one more time wishing that John would appear and the pushy detective would leave me alone. I was in no condition for any type of prodding.

"Okay, which car is yours?" I asked as I resigned myself to not seeing movie handsome John one more time.

My response elicited a very big smile as he pointed to a somewhat menacing car that ate up the darkness. "That baby is mine." He was beaming.

We walked over to his baby and he tapped the orange hood with his right palm. "So, you're into cars?" he asked me.

"No, not really." I started to reach for the door but Detective Kravitz had more to say as he walked over to my side of the car..

"Well, you are lookin' at one of the modern wonders to come out of 1974, the last of the true muscle cars. She is a real piece of history. A one of a kind, that's my baby. She's a 74 Pontiac Trans Am SD455," he exclaimed. "Look." Ed turned and pointed at a large silhouette of a black bird that looked like it was enveloped in yellow and an orange flame design. "That's the Screaming Chicken," he nodded his head while making that announcement proudly to me. I had nothing to say about it as I knew nothing about muscles cars. All I could think of to comment on was what might turn out to be an insignificant mark on the chicken.

"What does the SD stand for?" That was a weak question on my part but at least it showed that I was listening.

"Yeah sure," he bobbed his head again, "it means Super Duty, like push that long clutch pedal all the way down to the floor, wiggle it into first gear and then whammo! away you fly!" He gave me a grin and then winked as he opened the door for me to climb into his cherished ride.

I had no idea what he meant but I got in.

The road we took, was quiet and dark. Since he asked, I opted to go the back way. I didn't want to see the bright headlights coming at me on the big road. I needed as much calm around me as possible to get my past ghosts gone. Detective Kravitz seemed to sense that saying nothing would be a blessed relief for me so he said very little. I was not in the mood to fill up the car with senseless chatter. I looked over at him - he was lost in the sound of his car's engine and I saw that he was as comfortable in the quiet as I was. The quiet before a storm, I thought with a sense of foreboding.

Chapter Four

As the orange Trans Am hummed down the country roads, Special Agent, Jack White, was nearing the end of his snooping. He had been working in Tess's place for about three hours.

Tess's apartment was very large. It was located in an old warehouse section of Charlottesville that was now taken over by various types of artists. The rooms had 12 foot ceilings and sizable windows. Her windows though, were not original. She had replaced the old drafty ones with large, two-paned, very expensive windows that were a snap to open and clean. There was one large room that was separated into smaller compartments by half-walls that went up 8 feet or so. The one exception was the mermaid-themed bathroom. It was closed in for privacy except for the immense jacuzzi, which spilled out into the large bedroom. The agent noted that she must have come from money. No young professor would be living this lifestyle without some type of help. Everything in the apartment was top-of-the-line, from the Viking oven to authentic Oriental rugs. Not one piece of furniture was from Ikea. Jack knew that because most of his household was bought from that big box store.

He went through all of her paperwork and found nothing significant. He checked every book for notes or hidden papers and found nothing. He opened her Mac, hacked the password with help from a top-secret FBI device, and copied the hard drive onto his jump drive.

Pushing aside some rather large dust bunnies under the antique iron bed, he found a large, gray portfolio that was bursting at its seams. Stuffed inside were photos of ancient relics from the Bronze Age up through the Renaissance. There were sketches of old buildings and also botanical colored-pencil drawings that she had made. The botanicals had hand-written notes down the side saying what the plant was, how to use it medicinally, and on some, what color of dye could be made from it. He thought that the sketch of lovage was especially nice, with a flourish of quick sketches of a soup bowl with a scribble of a potato and leek soup recipe crammed down the bottom edge of the page. She had a few postcards. Jack perused them quite casually, not really thinking that anything of value would be found. Just as he was closing the album a sketch tumbled out with the back side up. Scribbled on the back, "A drawing from my 1620 memory." He thought that the hand writing looked like Tess's but not being a handwriting expert, he pulled back on that assumption. Flipping the card over was an old watercolor of some type of fruit with a bird that looked like a robin sitting alone on a branch. He looked at the back of the card and saw that it was from the Bodleian Library, University of Oxford, the drawing was The Mussule plum, from Tradescant's Orchard. *Pretty fancy living*, Jack said to himself as he wondered why he was there, investigating someone who clearly held no threat to anyone that he could discern. Jack decided that it was just another job that he would only see the corners, he never would get to know the main text on the page.

The last item rescued from the dusty floor was a small, cornflower blue booklet. He could tell that it was handmade, the papers felt thick, substantial. The title page was Libby's Lives. The booklet was like an old-fashioned flip booklet. You flipped the pages fast enough and you got a type of moving picture. There were drawings of a girl touching a gravestone, and then crying. She ran towards a stone one-story cottage with a thatched roof. As she opened the door to the cottage it became a modern bungalow with a television set on the wall. "Weird. Guess this goes with the sketch." Jack puzzled aloud as he snapped pictures of the book's contents and then put it back in place. He studied the photo he had taken of the stacked up books and envelopes that were covered in dust before he disturbed all of the items under her bed, and so was able to put everything back exactly the way that they were before; even the dust bunnies were tucked in the identical places.

Agent White felt his phone vibrate. "Yes, I am still here. I am just about finished. No, I haven't found anything like that." Then he stopped talking for a minute and said, "So she just left with that detective? Doesn't matter. I'll be out of here in five minutes. I'll text when it's done. Yep." He put his phone back in his pocket as his stomach growled.

Jack White was quite sure that no one saw him enter her apartment. And he knew that only one person had seen him leave. He was also positive that the story he gave to one of the residents about being an electrician who was called for an emergency fix, was believed. Feeling confident that his ability to lie for the good of the country was working, Jack slipped into his black Mazda, dreaming about dinner, as he jumped into the light traffic heading north on Route 29 towards Washington, DC in the cool spring night.

Chapter Five

Charlottesville, Virginia was a moderately big Southern town. Even though it had been around since Thomas Jefferson's time, it was still not really a big city. It just didn't have the right trappings. You could feel safe in all but a very few iffy streets, and it wasn't until the last few years or so, that the larger chain stores had started their invasions. There was only one true mall and it had less than forty stores. The one thing that Charlottesville did have, was an abundance of charm. There were many stately homes that were surrounded by graceful gardens that seemed to have something blooming year round. Fountains, ornamental brick walkways, fancy-scrolled black iron gates, mock Greek goddess statues and a picturesque willow tree shading a Monet like pond, these were the welcoming sights down prestigious Rugby Road.

The University of Virginia, Jefferson's most proud accomplishment in his eyes, dominated the town with its classical architecture, 200 year old oak trees, and the constant supply of creative talent and youthful vigor from its 20,000 students. There was a happy mix of old money, new money, almost got enough money, to no money at all. Everyone seemed to fit into the city in some vital way. The radio dial was filled with progressive/alternative programs and several classical stations, as well as WXTJ, the University's radio station.

C'ville, as it was called by the locals, was so laid-back in its hip intellectual culture, that the Republicans even took on a decidedly Democratic feel. You couldn't spot them just by looking at them, the way you could in DC. After two-hundred years of instilling a gentile culture in every institution that mattered, Charlottesville was as welcoming as a warm Southern breeze on a cold spring morning.

One of the last holdovers from the good-old-boy, Southern-town type mentality, was the Police Department. The police acted as if the evils of the modern world for the most part had passed them by. In many cases they had been right. But their antiquated way of running things would soon be a thing of ancient memories.

The Charlottesville Police Department was contained in a small, two-story, red-brick building. It was constructed with a tight budget in the 1960s and was built on a side street off of the main walking area. Today the walking street was the hippest spot in C'ville. Although the station was close to the absolute coolness, of well-heeled shops and elegant dining, it was not part of that map. Instead, it had its own despondent atmosphere. As a member of the City Council once said, "An adequate structure filled with the promise of might." No one really knew what she meant, but it was one of the few compliments ever bestowed on it. Well, maybe it wasn't actually a compliment but it wasn't a hateful remark. There were certainly enough of those!

The double glass doors, eternally smudged by something or someone, both had Charlottesville Police Department etched on them. Someone wanted to make sure that whoever crossed through those doors knew precisely where they were. The dirty, black and canary-yellow fallout-shelter sign was the cheeriest part of the crumbling brick facade.

Officer Kravitz had just walked up from the parking lot. He looked disheveled and distracted as his partner, Princey, briskly walked down the white-walled hallway on the way to his desk, making it there before Ed. Princey usually was the early one, believing that the early bird really did get the perp. He had a very welcoming wife to go home to and a good supper waiting most nights. This made a most happy life that left him with an ever present bounce in his step.

Detective Kravitz was a well-known night owl and bachelor, who often stayed late at work. His best thinking would happen once he was left alone. But last night the gang of clueless detectives had cornered him with a long list of what he called, *Just fix the damn thing*, requests. Detective Kravitz was a digital whiz and all the old dinosaurs knew that and took advantage of it. Ed rubbed the sleep from his eyes and plopped down at his desk.

"Hey, Ed." Princey gave him a smile while looking over his steaming cup of coffee. "Any new revelations from the FBI?"

"Yeah, well, we lowly types got a few breadcrumbs. Being as one of our own saved the Director's wife and so got blown away, they had to put up with me." Kravitz turned and glanced down at the stack of papers that was placed center on his desk. "Humph." He ignored the pile and walked closer to his partner's desk, and plopped down on the corner. Ed bent down close to Princey's right ear to tell him what he just deduced to be true about this case. He was sure that no one else knew it. Not the fancy Feds with their high-tech ways, much bigger budget, and college degrees that lead to masters. Nope, he knew something that all of them hadn't a clue about yet. Ed had made it a late night dive into the entire stack of data having to do with Jennifer Stark. He read it all and put the pieces together well after two in the morning. Ed's eyes crinkled up at the corners as he told him in a whispered tone,"The perp, you've chased him before."

Princey kept still, not even taking a deep breath while waiting for the next sentence to form. The smell of coffee filled in the empty space.

"You know, he's the one that took all of those little girls, about 20 years ago." Kravitz's voice got a wee bit louder with each word as his cadence picked up."I figured it out when I saw Officer MacGregor's sister there and after I chewed through every god damn report; each page packed with no real clues, only BS data that mostly went nowhere. Truly, just a bridge to nowhere. Stupid bureaucrats, but you already know. So back to Tess MacGregor. You remember her? She works at UVA, a professor or something. Blond, green eyes, ah, smart, cute, and she scuba dives. Remember her?"

He looked up at Kravitz, the smile was now in his eyes. "Yes, I do remember her. She was there?" he asked incredulously.

"Yep," Ed shifted his weight. "Seeing her made the dots connect." He paused for a bit of dramatic effect. "You see, I read the side notes to all of the reports and one captured my imagination, you might say. One note had been scribbled down quickly, and must have gotten wet because you needed to be a detective to decipher it. You know, I just realized that the guy probably didn't want to write it, he must have been afraid of the consequences, so he made his handwriting messy. Huh, well, I figured it out." He flipped opened his small notepad and read the revelation out loud. "The neighbor, Mrs. Bintliff, said, "Jennifer Stark was a nice, quiet girl but she seemed to be a little odd, a bit prescient, I had to look that word up. I bet almost no one could have picked out the blurred letters and then known what that word was. How bout you, did you ever hear of it? Of course you probably did, you worked the original case! I remember early on, your advice to me about staying with what your instincts tell you to do but just layer it in with a-by-the-book sandwich. That took some time for me to figure out what exactly you meant, but I got it now, and I think it applies to this situation. I am sure that you agree? Right? Right."

Princey kept his smile in place and asked, "Are you going to answer all of my questions for me? If so, maybe you are prescient as well."

Kravitz, shot off, "Well, maybe I am. But I can tell you that he's back and he's collecting psychic girls again. I am sure that no one else has detected this yet and I don't think that they will. I have never been in a room that was filled wall to wall with zombie stiffs! Not a single individual thought between them. Just having Tess in that room made them all squirm, I could feel it." Ed spit out that sentiment, took a pause to squelch down his anger and then continued. "And then I heard why she was there - she's psychic and she is gonna help them out. Right? Huh! They wanted nothing to do with her. All except for maybe one guy. Some rich looking bastard, real tall, expensive clothes, Italian leather shoes, expensive cologne. I mean, how many feds who aren't appointees have that? He's the first one I've seen. He was definitely checking her out." Ed seemed to growl.

Princey pivoted around. "He could just come from money. It does happen." His eyes grew big, he sincerely meant that.

"If you had the cash, wouldn't you wanna be some nice safe tax lawyer or just play polo all day long?" Ed asked with a dollop of sarcasm placed on each syllable . "Oh yeah, you do have the scratch." He winked at Princey as it gave him great joy to push that button. Princey's wife, Rosslyn, was from a wealthy family that owned most of Lafayette, Alabama and the timber that grew in the thousand or so acres just outside of town. This made it possible for his family to enjoy expensive vacations and afforded their two boys enrollment in an exclusive private school that was an institution with the affluent in Charlottesville, Blue Hill.

"Might be an adrenaline thing. This guy might need the high that the chase gives. I haven't thought of that case for a very long while. But it wasn't 20 years ago, it was 23 years ago now. "

William Noble, or Princey, the nickname that he was anointed with in sixth grade stayed with him his entire adult life. Brian Cully, his best friend when he was in sixth grade, deciphered that since he was a Noble, William could be a prince, as he then decided that *he* was the king. King Brian didn't stick, but the tag, Princey, did. He grew into his name as well. At six foot, six inches tall, he almost always could see over everyone else's head. This unnerved the criminals that he chased, and it made women look up to him as though he was their knight in shining armor - which was similar enough to a prince for his liking. He had a gorgeous smile that made up for his rather large ears and a pleasant demeanor under almost any circumstance. He knew not to bring up religion, politics or any experiences about being a homicide detective when in polite company. And especially not when he had to be around his wife's art gallery crowd, as he teased her. These were the people that didn't just go to the gallery, they owned the paintings and sculptures that belonged in an art museum. Her best friend, Leila, had a John Singer Sargeant painting that hung in her living room. Princey was worried that it may give Rosslyn ideas. They had agreed early on in the marriage that the majority of their expenses would be paid by his job, her money was for investments, education and vacations. Of course what she bought on vacation, the jewelry, furniture, and designer clothes for both of them, that was acceptable. This, she had skillfully negotiated over the years. He drew the line when she wanted to go to a Ferrari dealership just on the outskirts of Charleston. He made her laugh, as he often did, when he told her "You are going to make it look like I am on the take! Who is going to believe me that you are this beautiful and rich too? That is one of my best secrets, girl!" He convinced her that the Ferrari would make a great retirement present and then sealed the deal with a messy kiss that made Rosslyn want even more. He wore a broad smile whenever he thought about her.

Princey had learned much about the human psyche doing his job. With years of knowledge, it was a simple task to question others and get the information that he needed while making them feel quite safe. Simple, he learned, was the best way to go about detecting and living. He reflected now that he wished he had been wiser during his first case. The smile dropped off his face. He recalled that only one of the girls made it back intact, more or less. And now that little girl, grown-up, was on the team to investigate the man that may have kidnapped her. He wondered if Tess suspected.

"So what are we going to do about this, Detective Kravitz?" Princey asked him. But in this case he did not need to ask, Princey could read the tea leaves. He knew that Ed's dislike for anything federal would mean that he was going to keep this a family secret. He also decided that Ed must have a thing for Tess, or why would he notice and dislike someone else's attention on the girl.

"Whaddya think we're gonna do?" The Brooklyn accent was most pronounced now. "Maybe I should get a horse's head and throw it in that rich fed's bed, that would give him something else to notice, wouldn't it?" Ed snickered; he loved their gangster banter.

"Sounds good to me!" Princey laughed and stood up, his long legs were stiff and he was feeling restless. He walked over to the hallway and looked around. There were just the usual people walking by. He saw Mercer, from the Theft & Fraud Squad hurrying by, he was probably on his way to smoke by the look of stress that made his forehead tight and moist. He smelled a stale milk odor come from the blur as he went by. He turned his thoughts back to Tess.

"You do know about Professor MacGregor, her past, right?" He asked as he turned to face Ed. Princey realized that his partner might know a bit of her story, but not the entirety of it. He put down the burnt, half cup of coffee. "She was the only one that lived. He let her go. We never really found out why. Oh, he didn't spare her any of what he did to the other little girls. He just did not kill her."

"Huh, you mean Tess, ah, Professor MacGregor, was kidnapped by him? Why didn't she tell me? I didn't know that any of those girls lived. Jesus." Kravitz developed a more personal hatred for the scum as he sat down heavily on his well-worn chair, making a loud squeak. He thought about the ride back to Charlottesville with Tess and recalled her face. Now he knew the origin of her nightmare. "We have to do something, he might go after her now, now that the feds have put her on this case. You know, get the fish that got away. I have to tell her... now. And we gotta get him."

"Yeah." Princey looked over to his cup of coffee that was now lukewarm and felt the back of his neck, trying to rub away the stress of the past, that was now sitting on the back of his neck in the present.

Chapter Six

It was a glorious Saturday far from Quantico's horrors. I was off the hook with the FBI until I had passed their latest security check. An FBI agent called and curtly informed me that Special Agent Hannigan said that this had to be done before I could be brought further into the case. I was a bit bewildered as I thought that I had been checked out every which way possible over the years, but I was wrong about that, and it further proved to me, that you never knew what the feds might do.

Today, I intended to enjoy my morning and make myself pull away from my own dark experiences so that I could better see Jennifer's life. It was good to breathe a bit in my own bright world of the Goose Creek Farmer's Market on a crowded May morning.

"Libby, I really do love these zinnias." I said to her over my shoulder. "Oh look, heirloom purple Cherokee tomatoes! Maybe we could just get a tiny bit of herbs? And look at this!" I exclaimed as I moved away from my sister's side to go to a large bouquet of dark and light pink peonies. The scent was intoxicating to me as I bent down and grabbed a bunch, cold water streamed down my jeans as I straighten up and pulled the newly picked bunch to my nose.

Predictably, I went straight for the flowers and herbs, while Libby looked for the fresh Amish desserts. She was hoping to find the perfect chocolate. It was a life long quest that I am sure she wished would never end.

This was my way to let go, throw all of my senses into a garden, even if it was not a true garden but only a farmers market. I was a reluctant city dweller. My large apartment stood as a monument to urban renewal. It had been a run down cigar factory that became a well-heeled, and some might say, posh, residence and artist enclave on the Rivanna River. The sunlight freely streamed in my southern facing, double-paned glass windows, enabling flourishing thyme, chives, rosemary and a bay tree all to thrive. The bay I had babied from an eight inch plant to a four feet tall beauty. My basils were varied and well pinched. If I could just rig a way to grow garlic, my windowsill garden would be complete.

I spied Libby. I lugged my overflowing market basket, it's straps now digging into my aching right shoulder, as I made my way across the scorching pavement. The hot sun hit the wide brim of my straw hat making a large shadow on the asphalt. "Why do they decide to put a farmer's market in a parking lot? Couldn't someone choose a park?" I said aloud, as I crinkled my nose and stepped on a large unknown bug. I looked for the next tent of shade and ignored the smooshed and smelly insect.

Here, I was blissfully giddy and lost in the colors and smells of the herbs and flowers. I had recently read that some special people could smell colors. I wondered what scents I would give to a prism of light waves. That thought delightfully stayed present with me as my straw bag soon was bursting with more of the freshest plants that the market had to offer. It was easy as pie to grab away at joy that only cost a little over four dollars a plant. Deciding that it was time to take my haul back to the car, I sauntered over to Libby to see if she was done with her shopping.

She was shielding her phone from the light, stepping into a tent, her back turned to the sampling of lavender and balsam, hand-made soaps and creams. I could feel her squirming the way she did when mom was looking for her and she didn't want to be found. I walked over wondering what would most likely spoil our day together.

"Yes, you got me." Libby unshielded her eyes and looked directly at me. It's the station. Seems that my day off is..."

I abruptly cut her off. "No, not this time! Can't they just give you one day off? What about dinner at Bocce's?" My nostrils flared, I could feel the flush of blood pulse up my neck and to my cheeks. She noticed. My defiance was easy as I did not have to talk to her boss or suffer any consequences.

She irritatedly put her phone in her back pocket. "So not all of us have a big fancy degree that lets us have a big fancy job like you do." Libby used this as her fall-back argument ever since I had completed my doctorate degree.

"It's your birthday. Couldn't you just once say that your phone was dead and not answer?" I knew that this would be vetoed but I said it anyway."What is it?" I demanded, as I gave her my older sister stance, my right hip and shoulder thrown up and tipped a bit forward in a subtle aggressive move. She was most familiar with that move, and so, not impressed.

"It's blowin' up a storm. Detective Kravitz wants me to find you, and bring you down to the station. Said that I should, *Grab you by the hair if needed.* Guess he must have a good reason. Something that you haven't told me?"

I began to protest, but Libby was ready for that. Before the first words left my mouth I felt a force nudge me. I looked over my left shoulder expecting to see someone or something there.

Nothing was there. I instinctively looked for Libby's reaction, she had none.

"Libby, did you feel that?" I raised my sunglasses up to the top of my head to get a better look around. She did the same and soon we were both scanning the tents and the crowded walkways that were filled with buckets of cut flowers and apple crates that were stacked on top of each other, their tops overflowing with fresh vegetables and breads.

My sister's hand went to the top of her gun, her fingers just resting on the cold metal. I felt a chill start at the top of my spine and travel down both legs. "There!" I spotted what I thought was the source of my anxiety. A dirty guy had stumbled in from the surrounding woods. He had a red rose in his teeth! "Typical," I said to her aloud, and then sent the thought to her of red representing love, passion, but probably it meant blood with this guy. But who was this guy? Libby was as still as a statue and then became a blur.

She was almost over to him before I realized it. She smiled, brightly, as she approached and asked, "How's it going?" I felt her hand was still resting on the gun. The dangerous gun. She was not afraid of anything.

The man began to chomp on the rose stem. I think that he was eating it! Libby's puzzled face showed a lack of any true alarm to me. She just was wondering if he was gonna eat the bloom; me too. And with that last thought, he took the blossom and put it behind his ear, tipped his head to Libby and left, melting back into the brown of the scrubby woodland's edge muttering about finding a lost rabbit.

She looked over at me, shrugging her shoulders and making a small frown. I was the more psychic one by far, but Libby could read body language better than me, and she did have a knack for knowing if something was truly dangerous or just in the weird zone. This man, she had put in the weird zone. I trusted her judgment. But I wished that the chill would leave my spine. Breathing better, I still had an urge to look over my shoulder that I could not shake.

We put our new-found herbs, flowers, and chocolate into a large basket that lived in the back of my car and off we went.

I pushed the smudge-laden glass door and followed Libby to Detective Kravitz's office.

"Professor MacGregor" I heard him call. His head appeared around the corner up the hallway.

"I'm here Detective Kravitz." He gave me a short wave, turned around to whoever he was talking to, said a couple more words and then walked toward us in a cloud of worry that I saw surrounded him. I tugged at Libby, did she see this too? Her silent reply to me was *yes*.

A very tall man was soon following Detective Kravitz. We paraded into the office. He sat down on a chair opposite me. The tall man smiled with his eyes, a very reassuring feeling was conveyed. I instantly trusted him, odd as I wasn't that trusting a person.

"Professor MacGregor, I am Detective Noble." He easily reached over and took my small hand in his very large one and shook it. He gave me a nice smile. Maybe I should know him? It seemed as if he knew me.

Detective Kravitz sat on the edge of his desk. I was unsure at who would start, so I blundered in first.

"It is nice to meet you Detective Noble. Have we met somewhere, maybe at the museum?" He looked like a man that knew fine art to me. That elicited a smile from him but no words. He started to lean a bit closer.

"Tess, " Libby whispered in my ear, "I probably should leave. Angeline has a question and I know that you are in good hands here." Angeline was Libby's partner now for the last two years. She straightened up and started to walk away.

"Stick around Officer MacGregor. I think that you need to know this also." Detective Kravitz called to her and then motioned for her to sit down. The gray worry cloud hung close to his chest. Ed was unsure of how to start, normally he would just blurt out bad news. He learned that it never got any better by holding it in. Princey felt his unease and threw him a welcomed lifejacket.

"We know that you are working on the kidnapping of Jennifer Stark. Professor MacGregor," he paused briefly and continued,"This case may be closer to you than you may realize." He gave me another warm smile. Now I was worried too, how could this possibly be any more personal for me? I had once been kidnapped when I was ten years old also.

Ed couldn't take it any longer, the worry storm took him away. He would not be held back by the barriers of social niceties."Listen Professor MacGregor, it's the same guy that took you. The same evil bastard. I know that maybe this seems, ah, seems like it doesn't add up, but it does. Look, the girl he took is psychic, just like you. He has started collecting them again. And Detective Noble was on the first case, and he agrees with me."

Oh, so that's how I know him? I thought to myself. He is the one that I think picked me off the cold floor and wrapped me in a blanket? I furrowed my brows and looked into his eyes. He was. He saved me. I would never forget the feeling of someone good holding me once again. His arms picked me up as I attempted to bury myself in his chest. His goodness washed some of the dirt off my reluctant consciousness. My teeth chattered and I wanted to scream but couldn't. I had learned what evil felt like and he pulled me from that evil. Since then, I had been trying unsuccessfully to forget that feeling my entire adult life. And here I was with my hero, and now, I even knew his name.

"Are you sure?" Libby urgently asked him.

I sat, dumbstruck unable to form questions. I was being pulled like a piece of taffy by two distinctly different feelings, a joyous disbelief that my childhood hero was sitting right next to me and the utter fear of facing the man that ruined me, the one who tried to eat my soul. It was too much, I folded inwards not letting one teardrop fall. I learned this skill being around that monster too. The monster that never went away.

Princey saw that I was diving into a deep emotional hole. He put his large, warm-hand out again and just placed it on my cold one. It was exactly the right thing to do. I lifted my eyes and met his, grateful again to my hero. "Tess, do you mind if I call you Tess?"

"No," a breathy response slipped out.

"You call me Princey, okay? We, me and Detective Kravitz, Ed, well, we believe that there is a high possibility that this is the same perpetrator that caused you and the other girls, great harm." He was careful not to use the ugly words rape or murder. I appreciated that we kept on the higher ground. I felt myself sinking and I didn't need to hear words of violence that would push me further down into my abyss.

"She is also psychic?" Libby was putting the pieces together for me. "Did her parents tell you?"

This personal mess was now much, much too personal. My out-of-control thoughts were racing too fast for me to keep up with. I felt like I was watching a bear chase a fawn with no safe way to save it. Bile bubbled up from my stomach.

"I looked at the Agent's hand-written notes." Ed precisely articulated each word to put an added significance into their meaning, knocking out the Brooklyn accent, and then continued, "He found that the lady next door said that the girl was strange, maybe prescient. He had sloppy writing and it was blurred, must have gotten wet. Anyway, I don't think that anyone else bothered to do that, look at his notes, I mean, they all had their noses glued to those flat screens." Ed looked over to Princey, he gave him a small nod.

It felt as if everyone was waiting to see how I would react. I was too busy spinning in my uncontrolled emotional whirlwind. Then on my endless horizon of low, heavy, gray shrouds, the clouds cleared and I knew that they were right. I did not want this knowledge, but the more I tried to push away those thoughts, the louder they became. I had to face it, I had to face him. The evil seemed to kick at my reality, coming back from a deep hole, but I held on tight and this time I looked back, straight into my abyss. My vision blurred and then went into a clear focus as my world became an orderly place again.

I sat up straight in the cold wooden chair. "Then there's hope." I proclaimed.

This was not what anyone expected to hear, but Libby understood; there was hope for me to overcome my nightmare and fully take my life back.

Chapter Seven

The old iron gate was heavy as he pushed it open. Green English ivy grew thick in the rich dirt. It blanketed the side of the hill and wound up the trunk of a large white oak tree. The day was turning into night very quietly. He preferred things that were quiet. It helped him to feel and smell if there were no distractions. The twilight made the color leave the world and that was a comfort for him as well. The monster travelled further along the chalky darkness, along the disappearing brick walk that snaked its way towards the vintage carriage house.

The 150 year old carriage house stood straight, made of solid brick from Virginia clay. It was two stories tall. The large double doors were once forest green and their ornate iron hinges that were originally painted black, had softened to a weathered gray. The window's creamy white shutters had lead-tainted paint that crumbled off, leaving traces below.

On the north side of the building, one of the lower shutters hung precariously on bent pins. Wind had knocked a large wild grape vine against this shutter's hinge. The constant thumping scared the little girl inside. Each time it hit the shutter, she was sure that the monster had come back to eat her.

Earlier that day, Jennifer had watched him eat a rat with the most horror that she had ever felt in her ten years of life. Just like the rat, she thought about him biting into her belly. It was more than she could tolerate. Her young mind was at the breaking point and Jennifer knew that she would end up just like the rat. She could see things before they happened in the world. Her cognizant perceptions had not been tested though. Her abilities stood at odds to her parents view on the world. The Starks were Catholic with a capital C. That left no room at all for the supernatural and specifically, for her personal spiritual abilities to exist. To her parents, the only gifts that one could have would be God given. She was told many times that telepathy did not exist and certainly if it did, it was not from God. None of her abilities were good, or nice, or belonged in her parents outlook of the world. Since they were bad, then Jennifer concluded that she must be bad too. That's why she was here. As she sat with her desolate thoughts, Jennifer wondered if her bunny, Hoppy, would die when she did. If his eyes would close forever. The vine slammed against the shutter, pulling her out of an imagined horror and throwing her into her living nightmare. Jennifer began to cry. Tears fell on the cold cement floor as her small cries echoed in the vacant building.

Louis wanted to be with Jennifer all day. He couldn't believe that his doll was happily waiting for him. After an invigorating day in the bushes at the Goose Creek Farmer's Market admiring his first girl, Tess, he delighted in the knowledge that he had a new bright and shiny penny waiting for him at home and soon that she would meet Tess. He'd have them both! How fabulous it was to have his life, Louis decided.

On the way home he bought all that his heart desired at the Quickie Mart. Louis had made several good buys; a baguette for

$1.69, brie cheese for only $2.99, and a bunch of spent, white daisies that were just a dollar. Overall, life was the best that it had been in a long time. The monster pulled out his bonus card for the cashier. She took it, scanned it and then shot the groceries in a bag like an NBA player hitting only net. This just confirmed his sunny outlook until Louis sensed that the bitch behind him was staring at his ass. He thought of Frank Zappa's "Hot Rats" and began to shake his ass just a bit while humming. His pleasure was annoying the bitch because she couldn't touch it. There wasn't anything else that he could do about it there, it was too public. So he thought about selling her a used car. He liked selling used cars to used people. He knew that they are old and decaying, and that they tasted funny. He loved the unused ones; little girls that were still innocent and believed in Cinderella and faeries. They could speak to him in their own way and he could hear them when others could not. He was always alert for the special ones. Thinking about that now put an extra wide smile on his clean shaven face as he continued down the overgrown brick path to Jennifer.

He stopped to listen to the last of the cicadas in the tall weeds. He wondered if bugs could cry as loudly as people could and then remembered the screams that he had caused. Nope, he decided that the bugs were quieter and not as satisfying.

Louis was his not his given name but it was the name that he went by. He thought that his government name was too commonplace, it was a name for a cretin and not grand enough for him. He chose Louis. Louis was the name of kings and it suited him altogether. Louis Lanzac had just that right amount of je ne sais quoi to it! He adored himself and that name.

The monster was hungry for food and for Jennifer. He strode to the front door, took out the heavy key chain and let himself in. Louis put down his bags and got out the perishables; eggs, milk, broccoli, lettuce, meats and brie cheese and put them in the refrigerator. The monster made a show for her with the French baguette, twirling it in front of his stomach and then pretending to eat it mid-air. Next, he took out the day's newspaper and scanned for his story. He absolutely loved his story. He found a partial telling in the metro section on page two. It was just a small mention, girl missing, but he knew that it would grow much bigger as his collection grew and especially when the reporters found out just who this snatched prize was. Most certainly it would make it above the fold tomorrow.

Jennifer sat shivering in the middle of the floor. Her hands were bound behind her back and her feet were tied together. She was so cold.

Louis turned around and said, "Hello my little doll. So good to see you! I hope that you are hungry tonight. I have liver for diner." The smile he gave her sent a line of goosebumps down her bare arms.

Jennifer said nothing. She held back her tears. She had practiced not crying the last two hours before he came home. Jennifer was sure that she could do it, almost sure anyway.

He flung out a mental rope around her mind. She sat squirming, attempting to escape from his torture, but the pressure grew more deliberate as Louis ate up each inch of space that before had held her resolve.

The monster walked over, grinning and clutching a large pair of kitchen shears. He bent down over her small body and stroked her long auburn hair. Her chin was warm to him, as he held her face in his massive hand. Looking directly into her eyes, he took the scissors and cut her tree frog t-shirt down the center front. Jennifer gasped. She had never been partially naked in front of any man except her dad or the doctor. This was an unexpected horror. Jennifer just thought that he would bite into her, clothes and all. Her heart beat was ready to burst through her chest as she made herself think. Jennifer reasoned that he had to take off her clothes before he cooked her, as it looked like that was his plan now. She was being prepped for dinner just the way her mother's housekeeper, Violet, would cook corn beef. That was the only thing that made sense, and she was desperate to make any thought make sense. No one would want to eat clothes, she reasoned.

Louis cut off her blue denim skirt leaving her in a pair of yellow flowered underpants. Very slowly he cut those off as well. His broken face, now appeared to be split in half, like a tortured Picasso painting, conveying his sardonic countenance. His doll sat rigidly on the bare floor, eyes shut tight, naked and waiting for him to eat her liver.

Jennifer could feel his presence inside her head. It made a pressure start at the center top of her skull and radiate out to the sides, above both ears. She dropped her shoulders down towards the dirty floor and tightened her elbows as if she was readying herself for a blow. Louis never physically touched her. This made the waiting interminable, as she could feel his mind but not feel his hands on her. The monster's intention cut through her mental fog. It made her believe that there was nowhere to go. She felt a scream start at the back of her throat and travel up to her mouth and abruptly stop there. Jennifer was too afraid to scream. Louis could feel her absolute terror and it gave him what he wanted. Pleasure radiated from him and fed his rotten craving. Her mental anguish poured into his being, making him strong and firm. Louis did not want this to be over too soon. He made himself pull away from her mind. Just as he unhooked, she fainted. The connection was severed. Jennifer fell into his lap like a broken toy. Louis lost his desire and became enraged. He entered her mind again but no one was there. She had escaped in a slumber drenched by fear.

Disgustedly, he tossed the flaccid body onto a lumpy, green velvet chair that smelled of accumulated rat urine. He arranged his doll so she would not fall, and then went to get a towel to cover her up. Louis always enjoyed the special dread felt by others when they sat naked, waiting for him to take off the last of their covering, a thin armor to his evil. Removing that last defense was a delicious high like savoring the best dark chocolate. He realized that he was mentally eating her and that made him happy again.

Louis walked over to the dusty desk in the back corner of the room and switched on his computer. He was in a mood for a little visual stimulation to help him create even greater depravity. He had bookmarked his favorite site, torture.com. There he was at home with his peers and wannabes. It seemed so in vogue now, a predilection for creating pain for oneself or for others. But Louis had had this fascination for as long as he could remember. It started with neighborhood cats and progressed to the neighborhood's little girls. He could always find willing ones. Since he had one now, he decided to get his digital camera and send a picture of Jennifer to his on-line entourage. They would surely love to see Jennifer, see her *before* he menacingly thought. Yes, it was definitely a before picture, as this website specialty was in photos of tortured or dead bodies. Dead, mutilated corpses from all over the world could be seen there. It was a cornucopia of victims put up as inspiration for the ghouls that roamed the site. Anonymize software coupled with being buried deep into the bowels of the dark web, made the users believe that no one could track them or their misdeeds. The only justice that ruled here had to do with cold cash. How many levels did you want access to? Or could you skip the bitcoin and put up great content that you proved you owned. Louis documented his events, and so was at the top of this heap. He deemed that the best photos were the naked dead that had not yet been reported, forensic photos were number two. But he preferred the fresh meat, nothing topped them.

He put in the url, his password and thumb print and read the eerie greeting. The site explained that its presence was why the internet was invented - To circumvent stupid laws from around the planet!

"Yes, fucking assholes!" Louis said loudly to wake up Jennifer, but her eyes remained shut, as her soul floated away in despair.

The monster started to relax. He watched each pixel form on the screen as though he was receiving messages from God. It was a new mutilated corpse. He thought that by the way it was positioned that it was probably from a friend of his, Julio. He had that signature that was so easy for Louis to discern. Louis believed that lovers would always recognize each other's touch.

Julio was in love with Louis and Louis wished for the day that he would taste him. They had emailed each other about a possible romantic rendezvous in New York City. Plans were made to go the delightful Pastis Bistro, or possibly get a suite at the Muse. These were all sweet dreams wrapped in a shared demonic craze for dead bodies.

"The deader the better!" That was the post that Julio made once and it spoke to Louis as no other ones did. He messaged him as soon as he read it.

Louis breathed in the anguish of Julio's photo and resolved to meet him soon. It was time for his embrace.

The monster poured over image after image for hours. Fortunately for Jennifer he went to sleep there and slept the sleep of the dead.

Chapter Eight

Libby was off duty. She went to her locker and sat down on the metal bench. Her partner, Angeline, was already seated and was in one of her notable puckish moods.

"I can't wait to take these things off!" Libby chided as she unlaced the heavy black, steel-toe boot on her right foot and gingerly placed it on the floor.

"Oh come on now, don't you like walking around with cement bricks on your feet girl? Maybe most of the fashionistas don't have this, huh? Just us! And we are so exclusive, a club of what, five policewomen now? And we're the supermodels of that bunch! Can't you just see us strutting down the runway!" Angeline began to pose as she mimicked a model.

"Yeah, love that shuffle, drag, shuffle down the runway! Makes me fit in with Chief Townsend's parade of old farts!" Libby retorted. They both laughed, it was good to get off duty.

Libby kicked off the left shoe and undid her heavy, black leather belt. "I can breathe again! After so much Mexican food at lunch that's a miracle! How many burritos did you eat?" She eyed Angeline. "Guess I should be happy that we are parting company before those refried beans hit!"

"Say what?" Angeline said with big attitude as she snapped her fingers and made her mocking, I-am-fed-up-with-you, face. "I think that you had a bigger plate than I did!" She retorted, while wagging her finger at her.

Libby snickered. Their laughter now was heard echoing down the hallway, all the way to the antiquated coffee maker. This surprised none of the officers waiting for their soon to be burnt-flavored coffee to brew, as both women were known to share a twisted sense of humor. And they were also both known, and resented by some, as superior tech geeks. A small group of grumblers didn't think much of computers or the people who used them adeptly, and if you were a woman and you also could run circles around them with your computer expertise, why that was good reason to not make eye contact or even say hello in their books. Smart women have been subject to suspicion down through history and it seemed as though a few high placed officers of the Charlottesville P. D. kept that part of history alive.

Libby finished getting dressed. She was most comfortable in blue jeans and her over-sized, cream, hand-knitted fisherman's sweater from Ireland. She reached for her top-of-the-line iPhone, digging around in an old, much-loved, leather backpack that she used as her purse. "Lets see if she got my text, and if she got it, did she read it, and if she read it, would she remember tonight or not?" she wistfully questioned. Even though they had just seen each other a scant few hours ago that day, Libby was accustomed to Tess being the stereotypical ditzy professor and forgetting their appointments. "Hey, she remembered!" Libby's delighted tones made Angeline smile. The text from Tess confirmed Libby's birthday celebration at Bocce's. It also meant that she was still not cleared by the FBI or tonight would be off.

"Good, you two haven't had much time to spend together this year. You be nice to her this time, okay?" Angeline's request was given with a motherly look on her face. Having two children, she was an expert on this look.

"Yeah, yeah." There was no use for Libby to argue this point. "Tess did get the blowback from my frustrations earlier today. It's just that she's got a big important job with lots of pay and great benefits and I just run around after bad guys on a *good day*, even out at the farmers market! Hmm, maybe that's not so bad after all, I get to chase the bad guys and carry a gun!" Libby grinned as she put her Glock in the backpack.

They walked down the hallway together, Libby noticed that Detective Kravitz was still at his desk and lost in his own cyber world. He was the only other one in the station that could outmatch her and Angeline's tech skills. She left him alone as he chased down the digital road to the monster. She felt his attention was riveted and smelled the traces of illegal cigar smoke that seemed to appear there at night only.

"Okay, I gotta run. Jeremy is taking the kids to my sister's place and we are heading off for a nice long weekend. Alone. Imagine that, some time alone with my big stud!" Angeline's happiness was infectious.

Libby turned around and playfully punched her in the arm, "Go ahead and rub it in, your big stud!"

"If you just went to a few parties, or college events or somethin', maybe one of your mother's ..." Angeline was quickly cut off.

"Mother's? You do remember me, right? I am the one with the world-class vacant mother which really meant no mother, no mother for any of my needs. Now I am supposed to go to her events? And believe me they are all staged events! That's something that even Tess and I agree on. Mother is a manipulative, social climbing, stranger." Libby's exasperation exploded like a fireworks display.

Angeline bobbed her head a few times in agreement, and thought about the last time she mentioned Libby's mother. She decided that that was probably a mistake also, and to not do it again. Libby had deep issues with her mother and Angeline had no way to solve them. She had better things to think about tonight.

The women stepped out into the night air. The sun had already set an hour ago. Angeline was off for her romantic weekend and Libby was just off. She sensed that something wasn't right but decided to ignore it. Libby felt that her annoyance was caused from voices in her past. She had many demons from long ago, most of them had to do with not saving Tess from the monster; these she kept mostly suppressed but memories would pop out at the strangest times. Libby shuddered a tiny bit and then made herself think of the wonderful seafood pasta topped with fresh Genovese basil and sun-dried tomatoes that she would order at Cafe Bocce. Birthdays were a wonderful diversion from everyday worries.

"Bye Angie, see you Monday." She said, as she waved her good-bye.

Libby got into her red Toyota 4 Runner and popped in a CD. She drove down Monticello Avenue with the stereo cranked as loud as it could go without distortion. She loved being surrounded by sound. Frank Turner's guitar filled the air around her. She didn't look or act much like a cop now. She cracked the window down a bit to let the cool evening air in as she sped down the curvy road, oblivious that she was being followed.

Crossing under Interstate Route 64 she was now headed south down Route 20. It was a lovely single lane road in the daylight. Many of the landed gentry lived down that way. They had their fifty acres or so, and expensive horses with four-board fences stained black with creosote. There were plenty of rolling hills and just as many private schools with calming names - Blue Hill, Jefferson Academy, and Chisholm, to name a few. But in the black night, this was a lonely, winding country road with no one around and gated houses that were far from the highway. The eeriness closed unknowingly around her.

The twenty minute drive to Scottsville was just barely enough time to hear her favorite song, "The Way I Tend To Be." It was just beginning to play when her right front tire blew, just as she was on a curve. Libby tightened her grip on the steering wheel and released her foot from the gas pedal. Everything was under control and then it wasn't. In less than a second, a tire veered off the road, hitting a large protruding rock. She desperately tried to right the boxy vehicle as it went its own way and not hers. Her hands lost their grip, flailing uselessly in space. Her forehead smacked the steering wheel hard and the song quit playing.

The man that had been shadowing her, pulled his car close to her rear bumper. He left the motor running and partially closed the door so that the interior light would go out. A heavy coat with black fedora hat made his silhouette loom large. Wearing a new pair of gloves, the stranger went over to the blown tire and removed his expertly aimed dart. Breathing heavily, his gloved hand reached for the door handle when he heard another car coming down the quiet road. The man bent down and quickly moved out of sight. Like a ghost vanishing into nothing, he and his car folded into the darkness.

I hated being late. I flew down the road knowing that if I wasn't seated with a menu in hand, Libby would make a stink about it, as she was perpetually late for all our appointments and would complain about each time that her big sister was running late. She probably would be early, I reasoned, as tonight's dinner was to celebrate her birthday, and I was picking up the check. Knowing that, she would bring her tremendous appetite with her and would want time to have a full, four or five-course meal. Hopefully, she would not wear her uniform to dinner or at least hide the gun. I brooded about this as it was hard to pry her out of that safety shell she wore. It was then, rounding one of the curviest curves, that I got a glimpse of a red SUV. I was still fully engaged with my own worries about Libby's habits that I disliked, lost in what my yoga teacher calls "monkey chatter." Then, half a second later, my mind finally registered what I had just seen - that was Libby's car! I awkwardly turned my huge boat like car around in a driveway that was two minutes down the road. I sped back to her SUV and saw that it was dangerously perched on a large rock making it so it could easily fall further into the deep ditch, landing her upside down.

I pulled close to her car and saw a dim trail of red tail lights streaking back to Charlottesville. Odd, I didn't remember seeing anyone pass me. I slammed the heavy door shut and jumped out. It took three long steps to get to the driver's side. I saw Libby's head was bent over the steering wheel. The bitter taste of bile began to rise in my mouth, my response to this emergency was an overload of adrenaline. Now shaking, I got out my phone and fumbled with it as I attempted to use it as a flashlight. "Libby, Libby!" I bellowed through the glass of her window. There was no response from her limp silhouette. I strained to see inside. Blood streamed down her forehead. I wanted to get her out and wipe away the blood but I knew that I couldn't safely move her. I dialed 911. The dispatcher was a friend of Libby's, and so were the EMTs that arrived in what must be record time. They got her neck in a brace and gently untangled her from the car. I moved out of the way as they closed the ambulance door and sped up the black, snake-like road.

Abigail Lucy MacGregor was admitted into Martha Jefferson Hospital. After filling out a stack of forms, I plopped down on a light blue sofa and thought that light blue was not a good choice for sick people to sit on as it would show too many stains. I was nervous, I did not wait well. I was feeling miserable. I stupidly added to that by calling mother.

The phone rang four times before she picked it up. "Bon jour." She said, after putting down a glass of champagne - I was sure that it was champagne, as that was her nightly companion. I was twelve years old when mother explained that a lady should have nicely manicured hands, wrists adorned with diamonds and she should be gently holding a champagne flute, preferably a Waterford or Baccarat crystal flute, at every social occasion. Most nights involved a party or a gathering, as she preferred to call it. I grew up watching as she elegantly sipped her champagne. Years later I realized that it wasn't about the alcohol for her; she was studiously projecting the image of a successful woman and that is what always mattered to her. As she often said, "It isn't who you are, it's who you think you are, that matters my dear, as that is how the world will see you." Regrettably for mother, I didn't care for tall, skinny crystal glasses, I preferred hand-thrown coffee mugs. Our worlds were light-years apart.

I looked down at the floor, wishing that I could melt away. "Hi mom, Tess... It's Libby," I took a deep breath and spit out the rest of the story as fast as I could. "She was in a car accident. Her tire blew and she went off the road. She was on her way to Scottsville, and I .."

"What, what did you say? Accident?" Her voice was filled with mother terror.

"Yes, an accident. I think that she hit her head on the steering wheel. She's in with the doctors now," I glumly stated. "But she's with Doc Campbell and he's..."

Mother began wailing in earnest, "Oh my baby, my baby!" I heard the champagne flute hit the floor.

My shoulders tightened and my hips locked in place, while I waited for her emotional bomb to go off. No matter what, it would always come down to this between us. I was more "psychic," and "older," so I was "RESPONSIBLE." Yep, she was going to have to spit this out any second now. It was welling up inside her stomach and she couldn't hold in her emotional vomit much longer. Mother, I decided, would never really be responsible for Libby, it was up to me.

"Mom, I see Doc Campbell. Let me find out what happened. I'll get back to you." I cut off my phone before the atmosphere could get more toxic between us.

Doctor Campbell was a family friend and had been our physician for many years. He even knew our father, and since that was the number one husband, most in her circle didn't know him. He saw me approaching and took both of my hands in his. "Tess, she will be fine. Just a nice big bump on the forehead. It is a mild concussion."

"Thank goodness, I just can't believe how lucky she is. I am so relieved that you're here."

" I was teaching tonight and I heard that a policewoman had been brought in. It didn't take long to find out that it was Libby." He had a calming influence. "I want to keep her here overnight though, make sure that nothing else comes up. You know, play it safe." He smiled and I felt my shoulders relax a bit. "But you know her and as soon as she wakes up, she will want out of here. So you'll help me to convince her to stay, that's your job."

"So you mean to say the dinner at Bocces is right out for tonight?" I teasingly asked him.

He nodded in the affirmative and then we both laughed. It was a break-the-tension type of laugh.

"Mom is waiting for me to call with the news. So, I can tell her that Libby will have the usual headache, nausea and an appointment with a chiropractor in the near future, right? Her baby won't turn green, or have any necessary appendages fall off, and hopefully, she can still bear children, correct?" I was in the silly zone as this was my way of coping with stress.

"You should be able to ask her yourself soon. Remember the last time she was admitted? When she wakes up she'll be demanding her freedom like William Wallace in Braveheart." Doc rolled his eyes for dramatic effect when he said freedom. Libby could be such a royal pain. "I think that you can safely tell Mrs. ..." and then he paused.

"Yes, its her fourth or fifth marriage and I sometimes forget her last name as well. It is Dupree or Devarouix? Something French that starts with a 'D.'" My tone was getting quite cynical, as it often did when I spoke about her.

Doc Campbell just looked at me with a knowing twinkle in his eyes and said, "Just tell your mother that her youngest daughter will be all right after having a righteous headache for a couple of days."

"Thank you for taking care of her." I replied.

"You're welcome, I wouldn't want to have it any other way. You've got my number, so call me if you need me, okay?" He turned around and went through the double doors, towards the emergency room.

Hesitantly, I picked up my phone and called back. Mother, after rambling about who was to blame, was in a low-moan mode concerning the quality of Libby's care. "Mom, you know that Martha Jefferson is an excellent hospital so don't say that it's inferior. Please, don't presume the worst!" I was exasperated. I had had no dinner and now I get mother as my dessert.

"Tess, we have made an endowment at the University, a sizable endowment. Libby belongs there." Instead of saying UVA, like any normal person would, mother has now personalized it, as if was hers alone. The muscles in my shoulders grew tight again. "She will be treated with special attention and the proper concern for her welfare will be shown because of my generous gift. I will call Doctor Fitzsimmons and arrange for an immediate transfer." This was her pronouncement on the state of what should be in the world, as opposed to what was.

She took a breath so I jumped into the fray. "Mother you are not calling anyone. Doctor Campbell has taken care of us for years! Libby is in fine hands here, surrounded by friends." Mother didn't care for this comment.

Her voice was on the brink of hysteria again. She was beginning to lose her faux French accent or maybe I was just noticing a new counterfeit accent aborning. Was it an Irish one creeping in now? Mom was so reptilian. She could mimic any accent and she seemed to take on whatever accent that was around her that had the most money. It was a wealth gauge. All I had to do was listen to her speak for a while and then I would know who was the wealthiest person around her. Guess the new French hubby was as loaded as Libby and I had speculated last spring, as the French accent was remaining strong with her.

"Darling, Tess, you must be the responsible one and see that your baby..." Her sentence was drowned out by a sudden flurry of motion and sound coming from the double doors. I couldn't hear what mother was saying anymore. The doors burst open. The nurses were frantically scurrying around and one rather large one, who resembled a professional linebacker, seemed to be acting like a barricade.

"Ah for fuck's sake!" A female voice bellowed out above the din.

I didn't have to to look to know that Libby was awake now and making a run for her freedom. Seems like she intended to keep that dinner appointment after all.

"Tess, Tess, what is that shouting about? Should you call the police? I told you that my baby girl needs to be in a safe, nurturing, prestigious institution. This place obviously ..."

I cut her off. I couldn't stand her snobbish droning any longer. "Mom, that is Libby making all the noise. I have to go." I turned off my phone and found my screaming sister.

"You always knew how to make an entrance Libby! Let's see if you can make a more dignified exit, okay?" I squeezed my way in between the wall of nurses, and grabbed my sister's elbow giving her the look that if she tried anything with me, I would be able to inflict more pain than she could stand. We had tortured one another for several years around puberty so she knew that look meant trouble.

Libby made a much quieter retreat back to bed. She was still in the hallway of the emergency area. No one had assigned her a room so she thought that she could leave. At least, that was her weak story.

"Tess, I really don't feel all that bad. I would heal much better at home, in my own bed. I just can't be here." Libby was trying her best to rationalize her way out of the hospital.

"Look kid," I always called her kid when I needed some leverage, "I need you to stay here tonight so Doc Campbell doesn't fire us as patients. I promised him that you would cooperate." I let out a deep sigh and waited for the next volley.

"Okay." That is all she said. I couldn't believe it. Libby never gives up that easily with me. I then watched incredulously as she climbed back into bed, pulling the sheet over her shoulders.

That was when I first wanted to go and touch her car. I looked over at Libby to tell her about my plan and that is when I could see that she was wrapped in gossamer gray shadow. It hung around her like a spider's web. She was very frightened. How stupid of me not to notice until now!

I went over to the bed and touched her arm. "Libby, I'm going to stay here tonight with you. I'll arrange it and be right back." She gave me a soft smile and closed her eyes. She knew something was wrong and once I stopped reacting to the situation, I could sense it too.

Chapter Nine

Detective Kravitz liked it when everyone had gone home, at least everyone within earshot. He thought best when it was night quiet. That was his made-up term and it meant that special time before his mother would call to check up on his dining habits and after the day shift was over. Night shift was a slow ease into the worst of evil. He liked that shift.

There were always so many layers of things to think through that it was difficult to keep them all juggled if you had some guy sitting near you bitching about how his wife doesn't look like she did twenty years ago. Ed was fed up with simple minded co-workers. But tonight he didn't want to fill up his mind with stupid complaints or hear about who would be drafted in the NBA. Tonight he wanted to ride the dragon. That was another one of his made-up terms, meaning that all of the little pieces of data that were swirling in his mind would be forming a creature, a dragon specifically, that he could grab ahold of and ride until a new realization about a case was made. The dragon was sometimes hell to hold onto, but this mental ritual always worked for him.

Ed pulled out one of his illegal cigars and sat in his comfortable self-made smog. He smiled, his dragon should be smoking any minute. But try as he might, the beast was going nowhere. Ed's thoughts were glued on Hannigan. He subconsciously thought of him as a rival for Tess and he had not yet spotted his desire for her. And so he consciously hated and distrusted Hannigan using an old prejudice of his instead. Ed distrusted the majority of the privileged college educated pricks, as he relished calling them, particularly Federal ones. He was sure that Hannigan went to a school that had a name that anyone would recognize; maybe Columbia, or Stanford, or Yale, someplace that he could never afford to attend. He visualized him in his neatly pressed suit, shiny black shoes that probably never showed any wear and then he recalled the jingle of Hannigan's huge silver key chain as he strode by. He pictured him again, as he got it out of his pocket and tossed it around a few times during the meeting at the SCIF. He noticed that Hannigan did it in front of Tess, probably just to get her attention so that she could see that he must have some kind of car to rate that kind of a key chain. Ed believed that often it was the little items that someone had or did, that spoke the loudest about who they were. Good detectives noticed the small details and Ed knew that he may not be wealthy, but he was a good detective. He noticed the details. Well, most of the details except for his new fascination for Tess.

Ed got out his personal laptop and began to go to work in earnest. Tess had called five minutes ago and told him that she was with Libby at the hospital. There had been a car accident and Libby would be out of commission for a while and she was staying by her side for a day or so.

"Wonder how that went over with the Feds? Bet they don't give her a break longer than tonight, if that." Ed spit out his sarcasm to an empty office.

He took a big drag on the cigar and enjoyed watching the smoke swirl. Ed decided that Hannigan had lied about Jennifer just being a random kidnapping and wondered what other lies he had heard. He put his attention back on what he considered was the heart of the case and re-read the file on the Psycho Psychic, as the Charlottesville Daily Progress had dubbed him more than 23 years ago. There was virtually no information on him, except that he was Caucasian, maybe 18 or 25 years old and he was big. That was all that a ten year old Tess could say. After the kidnapping she retreated into her own world and that world held no monsters that she would discuss. She did like bunnies, she must have liked them a lot, he decided, as one report made a big to-do about it. He wondered if she ever really came out of that bunny world.

Ed read more of the files. His head hurt. Elusive thoughts circled around. He felt like he was in a burning room with nothing there to put out the fire. There were just too many photos of dead girls taken at different angles, all in color and most close-up. He was pushing himself to see the faces of each one of the victims - there were nine total. Pathologist reports explained with scientific detachment, the exact steps and causes of all the injuries that lead to these nine deaths. The autopsy reports were succinct and each validated that the crimes were linked to one perpetrator. The crime scenes had not been compromised and anything that could be dusted or a gel lift used on - was. The cause of death was the same for each girl, and they all were kept alive a week to ten days before being strangled. All of them were raped; all were tortured. The images were shadows that probably never fully left Princey's mind. He read all about the horror except for Tess. He wasn't ready to read the details of her torture quite yet.

Ed's hatred was bordering on poetic. He felt the dragon lash at him with a split tongue and in an instant the pieces fell together in an unexpected collision. "It's Libby, she's involved in this, he wants to get her next! This asshole knows that Libby is psychic! Why didn't I know that?" He was talking to himself and enjoying the performance. His cigar was flying around like an orchestra conductor's baton. That truth put more of the puzzle together for him and Ed saw that what seemed to be, to him and others on the force, written off as woman's intuition was more than just that. He knew that she solved cases quick. Hell, all the males in the department must be vaguely, at least, aware of that. She had showed many of them up a time or two.

"Strange it was never something that I can recall anyone mentioning, but I get it now! Libby must be so psychic that she has to keep it under her hat all the time," Ed told his computer. He reasoned that she had to make up stories about how she had noticed this or that when no one else had. But now he realized that her secret weapon was being a psychic; must be a family affair he decided. "That's why she figures cases out when we were all standing around scratching our asses!" He pontificated joyously to no one. His dragon was back.

"Bzzt, bzzt!" Ed 's head swiveled as he stared at his phone. He hesitated to pick it up. He was sure that Libby must have felt his revelation about her and she was on the phone. He eyed it suspiciously. The phone kept ringing. He picked it up.

"Edgar, you took so long, are you all right dear? Do you have some indigestion or something like that?" The old woman's voice cracked.

"No Ma, I'm just peachy keen. Never felt better, okay?" Edgar shifted his feet around waiting for his mother to mentally pat his head.

"Why yes, my sweets, I am happy to hear that you are doing so well tonight, Are you coming home for dinner? Or should I package it up and let you heat it up when you get home?" His mom, Rose, was still taking care of him after thirty-two years. It was the one job that she was good at and she didn't intend to ever give it up.

"Ma, I think that I will get a bite before I go home. Okay?" Ed didn't want a repeat of matzo ball soup for tonight's dinner.

"What kind of meal is that? You don't expect me to tell you that it is fine for you, my son, to eat a bunch of fried Southern stuff, that will clog up your arteries and keep you up all night with gas, do you?" His mom meant Southern shit, but she never cursed. Her meaning was clear enough to him though.

"Okay, I will be home in a while. Not sure when, but I will be happy to have healthy food from you, okay?" Ed knew when to give up and go along with mom, and now was the time.

Rose, satisfied that she had again saved her son from an early grave, was happy to hang up. She believed that she was lucky to have her son. Her husband had been dead for five long years. A lot had changed after dad's death and Ed knew that it was time to pry his mom out of her New York City neighborhood and get her to go south to live with him. Rose soon liked Ed's new home more than her Brooklyn brownstone, but she would never admit to that! She had made a big stink about moving to Virginia, and in hindsight, realized that in Virginia, she had a large garden, a huge kitchen, and best of all - her son to order around again. Mentally counting all of the non-stick pans she had hanging up in the kitchen, she contentedly padded her way down the hall and back to bed.

Ed looked at his watch and thought about stopping by Aunt Sarah's Pancake House on his way home. He could stomach another matzo ball soup if he could fill up on a burger and fries first. His phone rang again. Ed thought that Rose had some more words of wisdom for him and this time he grabbed the receiver after the first ring.

"Hey ma, did you forget something? Need me to pick up something from the store?"

"Edgar?" The male voice asked him.

"Yeah, who else would answer this phone?" His hunger was now impacting his social skills but that didn't deter the man on the other end of the line.

"Its Josef, my friend!" The German accent was clearly heard this time.

"Josef? Great to hear from you! Isn't it after midnight there? Is everything okay?"

"Ja, all okay here. Ed, I read the internal security feed, saw that the FBI Director's daughter was kidnapped. Well, I've been doing researching for Bundestag on sex trafficking, horrid stuff. I found a site buried deep in the dark web, have you heard of torture.com?"

"No, can't say that I know that one. Sounds like another cesspool." He put down his spent cigar.

Josef went on to explain what one of the most depraved sites on the internet was about and that it's newest victim could be Jennifer Stark. The line between them sizzled.

He opened the photo from Josef and there she was. This was the worst nightmare that he could imagine. "Can you find her? Can you trace it back to the source? Oh hell, I know you can, how long will it take?" Ed was no longer thinking about his mother, or his dinner, as he pressured Josef Dornbach to make this his number one priority, leaving the Bundestag in the dust for a while.

"Its going to take quite a while to figure this out. Their specialty is anonymizing and hiding all the big money people that support it. I caught wind that she was on the site from a fairly reliable source at Interpol, and now you have verified that my friend, but there still is much for me to do."

"She is only ten years old." Kravitz thought of Tess again, being 10 years old and was thankful that this site didn't exist when she was snatched.

Josef thought of his own daughter, Uta, and said "We will get him. I will let you know, richtig?"

"Richtig," Ed growled back.

And just like that, one of the best computer minds had joined the hunt for Louis and one of the best detectives now held his smoking dragon by the tail.

Chapter Ten

Ed got his coat and headed out just before the morning shift was due in the station. He stopped by Aunt Sarah's Pancake House on his way out of town. There, he decided to skip the hamburger and get morning food. He wolfed down his usual five-stack of pancakes and drowned them in make-believe maple syrup. He had four deliciously greasy sausages on the side. He chugged down about a quart of coffee and kept thinking of his mother the entire time. Guilt drove him to call her before he was done with the meal and let her know that this was going to be an extra long day too.

Ed had gotten no sleep the night before. It was around 7:30 in the morning when Josef finally called to say that this was really quite a Satan's knot and that it would take even more time before he could unravel it. Kravitz couldn't justify biding his time anymore so he called the Feds and let them know about the torture.com tip.

Kravitz had arrived in the doorway to the FBI's SIOC, Strategic Information and Operation Center, just barely being held back by a young agent. He had been kept waiting there for fifteen minutes by "His Royal Highness Hannigan," as Ed called him. His eyes were red and tired. The blurry world numbed his perceptions, as exhaustion took away his best Brooklyn manners.

"Hey Hannigan, remember me? I am the one that gave you your lead," Detective Kravitz raised the volume of each word to the man standing center front of the large computer screen. Ed couldn't take the wait one second longer.

Agent Hannigan, seeing that there was no other option, looked at the guard and motioned for Kravitz to be let in. Standing next to him, Kravitz was uncomfortably aware of how much he needed a shower.

"So Detective Kravitz, you have known about this site for a while, haven't you?" Hannigan sharply accused him.

Ed looked vacantly past him and onto the computer screen that took up most the back wall. It was fascinating to him to watch the way the bytes could be tracked on their tour around cyberspace. The amount of decoding software in operation was mind-boggling to him. *If only we had something like this, I wouldn't have to be here with my hat in my hand,* he thought.

The computers made no sounds as they ruled out one access point after another. There were a roomful of agents all working on the problem. One of them had downloaded Jennifer's photo and put it dead center in the large eight foot by ten foot screen. The photo dominated the room and the overwhelming motivation for the agents came from Jennifer's eyes; the look of complete terror was unmistakable. There was no doubt that it was her.

"Do you wish a shower and a place to clean up, Detective Kravitz?" Hannigan asked with false cheer.

Now he was just being nasty, Ed thought. "Nope, I'm as fresh as a daisy," Kravitz spit out, and then scowled at Hannigan's shiny shoes.

"Just thought that you would like some private time to

collect your thoughts and get refreshed, but I can see that you are at your best now, why, aren't you?" Hannigan caustically added.

The words seemed to tumble out the side of his mouth. Nothing ever was straightforward with this snake. Ed was just micro-seconds away from pretending that he was in the World Wrestling Federation when one of the cyber cops got excited. "Sir, I think that I've got something here!"

Hannigan was there in a few steps. Kravitz was right behind him, breathless, but still not missing a thing. He got a glimpse of the monitor before Hannigan bent over and purposefully blocked the screen.

"That's her location, more or less. At least that is where she is in cyberspace or was last night. You see that trail there," the technician pointed at the screen to a stream of numbers and symbols that meant nothing to Hannigan. "That is the connection that he utilized to get to the anonymizer. It came right through Iceland to this point here sir." The overworked programmer grabbed a pencil and began to fidget with it to keep his hands off the keyboard. Kravitz was bobbing up and down behind them, desperate to get a look. He did a two-step to get over to the right side of Hannigan and then muscled his way to the front.

Kravitz stared at the monitor and said loudly, "'Bullshit, that guy is NOT in Iceland. Anyone can use a VPN. Come on, that IP address is hidden behind the VPN server. You must know better than that!"

Hannigan ignored his outburst. "Do you think that you could link this to other military installations?" Hannigan asked quite drolly as he stretched his chest muscles under the fine Italian suit.

"Could be possible, yes. All I would need are links for collecting information from the Air Force and this would be faster. Might take five or more hours to complete without them. Hard to say, sir." The computer geek was now thinking about his pension, or lack of it, if he couldn't deliver what he was promising in the time frame that he promised. This was about the Director's daughter after all. Sweat formed under the nose bridge of his yellow-tinted glasses.

Kravitz got it, military installations. Does that mean that the Director's little girl was snatched by some military psychic pervert? He ruled that out before the complete thought was formed as utter bunk. Realizing that he would get nothing from Hannigan, Ed happily sat in his orange Trans Am, listening to classic Rock, heading for home.

Ed's sleep was short, but he felt refreshed and ready to be on the hunt again. The station was noisy on Mondays. That was the time it would be decided who would be working on the following weekend. Kravitz wondered why all the problems of the world had to be solved before that decision could be made. Princey, seated with his second hot cup of coffee, just wished for some peace and quiet. He heard a bellowing voice say that Officer MacGregor was on sick leave so somebody had to step up and work that weekend for her. Maybe she'd be back but no guarantee on that one. No one was eager to lose their precious weekend.

"Hey, Princey, you got any extra printer paper over there?" Kravitz called out and balanced his chair on two legs while reaching over with one arm extended behind his head to grab it.

As the door swung open, I could see that Ed looked over and saw that I was walking down the hallway. After sleeping in the hospital all night, in a rock-stuffed chair, my light-blue linen shirt was more than just wrinkled, my hair went in several different and opposing directions, and my cranky attitude was the icing on it all. I felt and looked as though I had been stuck in a yoga pose and hadn't quite untangled from it.

Kravitz's chair landed with a sudden bang as he got up and stood next to me in a few steps.

I began to babble. "Ed, well, this is a bit uncomfortable for me to discuss with others. Not that you are others, I mean to say that I am still not easy talking about my different abilities with anyone other than Libby, and the only others are usually select FBI people. Sorry."

Ed decided that it was kind of cute that I called the agents, FBI people, it made them a bit more human he thought.

"Would you prefer to talk outside?" he asked.

"Yes," I was relieved to be out of earshot but unable to get myself moving, lost in a whirl of mental confusion.

He took my elbow and turned me to the door. "Right here," he said while motioning me out to a small patch of grass. I looked up, the sky's cloudy somber hues seemed to match my mood.

"It is about Libby's SUV. I need to touch it. Specifically, I must examine the tire that blew. I can find evidence on it that only I can find." I looked at him and took my eyes from the clouds.

"O-kay," he hesitantly said.

I heard the pause and asked "Would this get you in trouble?"

"Not if I am with you. You don't mind, do you?"

I realized that he was wondering if his presence would interfere with what he thought of as my psychic tricks. "No, I would like you to be there," I reassured him.

"Good, we have to go to the impound lot and it's a bit of a drive, but it won't take too long. Let me just clue Princey in." He went back in and grabbed his jacket off the back of his chair and got the keys. He pointed to the big tag that said Impound

Lot. Princey gave him a thumb's up and went back to his phone call.

Detective Kravitz unlocked the rusty metal gate to the lot. Libby's SUV was tucked away in a far back corner. The crime scene investigators had already done their work, but because of a small bit of police forms left undone, they still were not willing to let Libby have her car back.

"Are you sure that this isn't going to get you in some kind of trouble?" I couldn't help but feel Ed's nervousness. I attributed it to doing something that he was a bit uncomfortable doing but he didn't seem to me to at all be a rule following type to me.

"Nah, don't worry about it. Nobody could give a flying leap what happens out here. I mean, I'm here with you so what could happen?" His genial smile was beguiling.

Detective Kravitz seemed quite certain about his answer so there was nothing new to concern me except for the story in Libby's SUV.

I walked over to the blown tire. It rested on the cracked asphalt. Thankfully no one had repaired it yet. Before touching the tire, I circled around the entire car to get a sense of the accident. I needed to perceive those images that still clung to the car without my memories of the event getting in the way. It wasn't easy to do.

I put my attention where I first saw Libby and so was drawn to my own horrible emotions that emanated from the driver's side window. I pushed past my own fright. Like a spider's web, Libby's unconsciousness covered the driver's space. Thick mounds of her comatose psychic smoke stained the interior windshield surface and the tan colored driver's seat. I took it all in, and then crouched next to the car and ran my hands along the outside of the driver's door. Libby had left a sizable psychic wave that pierced the inside and went through to the outside of the door. It mentally pricked me as I passed over the energy. I could sense her attempting to prevent the vehicle from spinning out of control. She must have been very angry. Libby was what mother would say, "was angry with a wild purpose." I could feel that she gritted her teeth hard while trying to brake. My knees grew a bit shaky as I stood up to catch my breath. The memories that had been glued to door, I found splattered on my shirt, I shook them off.

Walking over to the tire, I hesitated for just a moment wondering if I had missed anything and then deciding that I hadn't, I sat down. Ed was fairly bursting with curiosity, but he was doing his best not to interfere by asking what I had observed. I was grateful not to be distracted. It allowed me to keep my attention focused.

Warily, I placed my index finger on the tire and felt a disconnection with the world around me. The pull of a small hole opened up. The hole was dusty and the sides of it were jagged. It had flattened out with the car's weight resting on it. As I fully opened up my senses , I got an electric kickback from the inky space. "Ow!"

"Are you okay?" Ed's curiosity had now turned into concern.

I nodded yes. "It hurt me mentally to touch it so I pulled away from it, like I would if I had touched a hot burner."

"Right," Ed agreed as though he really didn't need my explanation. He was maintaining what he felt was a steadying influence for me.

I soldiered on, but as each second passed by, my resolve to perceive it melted away almost as quickly. The sinister feeling invaded me to the core; I didn't want to feel it again, ever. Sweat beaded on my forehead, and it made a path downwards, obscuring my vision with salty water. My heartbeat intensified as I told myself to force my finger back to the hole once again and feel his evil.

With a shaky hand I reached out and placed my finger on it. I closed my eyes and perceived that the jagged little hole was covered in a mental black veil to prevent awareness of its existence. "Hiding the clue?" I remarked.

"Hide the what?" Ed squatted down next to me.

All I could do was shake my head, no. I didn't want to engage with him. I needed to stay with this. Ed stood up and took a step away from me realizing that he might disturb what he thought of as my mojo or magic thing that was happening near him.

I bolstered my determination and centered my thoughts on the hole. I felt the rips of the rubber and then felt his desire towards Libby. Finally the vision was forming. He took out the dart and was gleefully happy to *Get her*. His intention was quite clear.

Excitedly, I broke free from my self-induced psychic state. "The tire blew out because someone blew it out intentionally Ed."

Ed nodded. "Just what I thought, I knew that she wouldn't run off the road. Can you see who it was?"

"Not yet but maybe...maybe I can." I put my finger back on the hole. This time the prick I felt as I touched the hole wasn't that bad. As I had faced the worst of it, I could then see that the hole was made by a steel dart. The person had fired a dart gun to stop my sister. "He had a dart gun, it was well planned." I pushed myself off the asphalt and walked around to the other side of the car and felt wobbly again. I grabbed the driver's door handle to steady myself.

"Tess are all right?" Ed asked.

I opened my mouth to answer but a flood of memories came at me. They popped and snapped out in a trail of blurred paintings that swirled about, and then stopped abruptly as I was gripped by the feel of expensive gloves. They were the large, stylishly cut and new. He had a passing thought about keeping them clean as he touched her door handle. I could feel him smugly thinking about how easy it was to grab her, and then there was nothing. He must have let go of the handle. I wanted more but it all vanished; all but the feel of those gloves. It was as though I could feel them reaching out towards me.

Ed's intense gaze pulled me from the void. I looked for the stability that emanated from Ed to hold onto. I gathered my thoughts and told him what I could, as unemotionally as I could with a wobbly voice.

"I can say that it was definitely a man that did this. I felt him. I felt his large gloves on her door handle and before that, I could perceive that the dart made the hole and that the hole was covered in a thick blanket of blackness. And I know that he wanted to take Libby. Why Libby? Could it be someone that she arrested?"

"Not sure, maybe. But it sounds like you've got something that you can use to lasso him with, huh? And don't be worrying about Libby, she can take care of herself better than any other officer that I know, except maybe me, or Princey. And we'll take care of her, promise." Ed gave me a sly smile to reassure me.

I looked into his eyes. I wasn't so sure. "Guess so Ed. I wish that I had gotten more."

He nodded. I stood.

We left as the late-afternoon sun nudged its way through the clouds. I allowed myself to wander in the patches of darker blue that were spreading over the horizon, pushing the grayness away. I walked steady, grateful to have inspected, and now, be done with her car. As I eased into my relief, Ed eased away from his.

Chapter Eleven

Louis sat down on his rumpled bed. He gazed adoringly at his prize that was huddled on the green mangy chair. The ripped dish towel that was sloppily placed on her, was now stretched to cover most of her. The balled-up, tiny body was trying to hide but it wouldn't work. Not with him. Louis kicked his shoes off. They flew from his feet like rockets exploding on the fourth of July. He looked at her, drooled a bit, and pondered great pain and joy. Energy surged through his evil desire.

"Life is just a bowl of cherries," he sang out as he walked towards her. A corner of the towel moved where her right toe should have been. Louis watched like a cat seeing a bird at a feeder. He thought of his magnificent appetite. It was easy to be hungry with his doll so close by. A blast of wind buffeted the large oak next to the window and made it howl. He smiled.

Jennifer had always been a good girl. She had never run away, she never hid a report card from her parents like her friend Beth did. And there was only one food that she would secretly knock into her napkin to throw away later, and that was peas, no one could blame her for that, she reasoned. Presently, these were all her sins that she could commit to and list. They raced through her mind as she weighed possible retributions and the reason why she was there. Scared witless by this unknown man, whose intentions pushed relentlessly towards her, she recalled being hit hard by a crashing wave while looking for seashells on the beach. She tumbled into the sand as the wave rolled over her, pulling her out to the deep blue. Until this monster, that had been her most frightening memory.

Louis ripped off her covering. He waited for her shock to give him new pleasure when instead, she began to sing one of her favorite songs. Jennifer reached down into the recesses of her determination and fought back like a tigress. She sang as loudly as she could and made herself think of a chocolate milkshake. She felt the ice cold chocolate move slowly down her throat.

"Hey, hey, this won't work with me doll!" He took her shoulders and shook her as hard as he could. Jennifer continued to ignore him. She was gripping tightly to her world of chocolate filled with sunshine, as she mentally shoved his world away. Never before had she used her abilities to this extent. It was much easier than she expected and allowed her to escape from the horror. Jennifer continued to taste her favorite flavor and gently moved herself out and slightly away, from her body. She was amazed that it could be so easy! But was that what was happening? Could she really just fly like a bird? Jennifer dreamed of circling higher, feeling a wind carry her away, beyond the mad man's grip.

Her delight turned Louis's rage into a cold, frozen dagger. He stopped shaking her and picked up his favorite little knife from the kitchen table, and without hesitation, slashed diagonally across her chest. The pain slammed her back into her body. Her eyes opened, filled with tears as she realized that he would never stop. He would always be able to get to her or inside of her. She screamed for someone to rescue her. The sound slammed against the grimy walls unanswered.

Louis's nostrils flared as he mentally sucked in her pain; it took the edge off his rage and brought him into his pleasure zone. He looked at the knife and was happy. The blood was only on the tip. Satisfied that she would not die, that his toy would last longer, Louis walked to the sink. He placed the blade down on the same spot that he had always did. A deep, brown stain was now covered with the bright red of fresh blood. He tauntingly spoke, "Yeah baby doll, remember my kiss is just for you." Louis Lanzac turned around and blew her a kiss.

Jennifer's chest bled slowly, forming a red heart shape on her cold, small lap. She wanted to close her eyes again but kept her wary eyes on him. She had to know where he was at all times. Her gaze stayed on the large hands to make sure that no knife was nearby. The madman took a piece of paper towel off of a roll and ran it under hot water. He grabbed a bar of Ivory soap and approached her again. This time she did not try to move away, fear held her still. Louis put his hand on her waist, and began to clean up his bloody mess.

"Soap and water will make it all better, won't it doll?" He asked, as he mocked her tears.

Jennifer began crying uncontrollably. Each stroke of his soapy fingers was like an echo of the sharp knife slashing across her.

"Yeah baby, let me get you all cleaned up" he hissed at her. Louis ran his soapy fingers over her cut. The blood and soap formed a small pool on the edge of the dirty green velvet chair. He wiped off the last of the foam, and taped a clean white bandage over the cut.

"Now you look like my little Miss American Doll contestant. Say, you look like you won, baby girl, with that banner down your pretty little chest." Louis was on a roll now and felt like his old self, invincible.

He plopped her down on the worn plaid sofa and sauntered toward his camera. Time for another photo of his beauty queen. He thought about tearing off the bandage so that the wound would bleed again. His fans would love the blood. He turned towards her but stopped himself mid-stride with the thought that the bandage might actually work better. They could see that he had done something to her, but no one would know how bad it was. He could them keep them all hanging on for more gore later, even his one friend, Julio would be left guessing.

"Yeah, they can make it up for themselves. That will be better and we're not done yet." He happily exclaimed to her.

Louis grinned as he took the photo of Jennifer spread out on the sofa wearing only her banner. He was still smirking when he logged on to torture.com and uploaded his little queen. "Oh my fabulous fan-boys, just look what I've given you all to dream about!" Absolutely delighted, Louis couldn't stop his wretched smile from eating up his bogeyman face.

And as Louis sat with his idiotic grin frozen on his lips, staring at the digital reflection of what lay just before him in the flesh, another person began smiling but for another reason. A German computer genius had been patiently waiting for the demon to log on. He was waiting in the depths of torture.com perversity, waiting like a fox for a rabbit to come out of his hole. He did, and now the chase was on.

Josef's fingers flew across the keyboard as the image downloaded. A twisted hell formed on his screen. He looked past the image and kept focused on the data trail. At this moment the trail was alive, and she was alive. He made himself not think of his daughter, Ute, bleeding and naked with this freak. He thought only of computer patterns and methods to unravel the location the fastest way possible. No one was better at this chess game than him. There was not a digital backdoor that didn't have a key, as far as Josef was concerned. Soon he found the country. And while Louis smirked into the night about his superiority and about his prize, that would soon be dead, Josef nailed down the state of Virginia. It was definitely Virginia, in the good old USA that housed this freak. The numbers continued to fly as his mind put the pieces together. The knowledge shook him. Josef's eyes popped wide, it led to central Virginia, to Charlottesville!

His wrists ached as he pushed himself to move as fast as he could down the digital highway. Josef was like an expertly trained state trooper on the tail of a cop killer with the fastest car that Bavaria could manufacture. HTML was the road that he skillfully cruised. The lights flashed, uncomfortable sirens pierced eardrums. He was hot on it when the trail went dead. "Shit" he muttered in his best put on Brooklyn accent. His wrists went limp and he let out a deep sigh. The bastard got off line. Game ended.

Josef got on Skype and woke up Eddie. A tired voice greeted an excited one. Now there were two people who knew a bit more about where Louis hung his hat.

The SIOC room in Quantico, Virginia, had just gone electric. The FBI's cyber cops were also on full alert. Several teams of two worked on the various grabber sections of the downloading image. Sam, the youngest cyber cop at the FBI, noticed that the idiot had a clock that was just barely visible in the right hand corner of his image. He blew up the corner of the photo - it was 2:38, the same as their time! "Look," he was pointing at the large screen, "It is the same time as us, 2:38."

"I just got confirmation that the feed is from the East Coast."Another voice called out in the room.

These cyber cops were experts at monitoring online activities to control criminal occurrences. They had entered a new sphere of law enforcement with this case though because of the high stakes involved. This wasn't what any of them had experience in doing. Hours whooshed by while they hunted for the number one of the FBI'S Most Wanted List. But the top criminal was elusive and evaded detection again.

Sam, the junior agent Hannigan had put in charge of the graveyard shift, wondered if he should call Special Agent Hannigan and tell him that the perp was back on line and that he had newly developed information - he was on the East Coast. But he thought possibly his boss wouldn't appreciate a middle-of-the-night wake-up call from him that could lead not to a specific location - just to the entire east coast. Sam's jumble of thoughts of Hannigan's assorted moods convinced him that it was better not to call. Instead, he hunkered down and worked as fast as he could to make those thoughts dissolve.

Louis closed the heavy doors, jumped into his car and let the gravel fly as he made his way down the rutted driveway. Delighted that he decided to savor Jennifer's death for a while longer, he was off to finally meet his true love, Julio. Julio's praise over his most recent doll photo, along with pleading for Louis to, "eat him up," stirred his addiction for pain deeply. He had to go, there was no other choice.

Far away from Quantico, as the twittering morning birds woke up. Jennifer felt the pain that lingered in her festering cut, but that did not trouble her anymore. She was centered, perceiving all around her. Her new vision scanned miles away. She perceived the center of Charlottesville, the tops of trees, the heat that emanated from the power station. Closing her eyes she reached out and felt people, and let their life energy connect with her's. She soared high above, feeling much bigger than her tiny body.

Chapter Twelve

George, the hotel manager, saw Frances over by one of the shrubs next to Room 8. It looked like she was picking up something right next to the door, or maybe, she was coughing a bunch? George couldn't decide what was happening. He moved a bit closer to the window. It was vomit; she was vomiting all over the shrub. "Jesus Leo! What do you think is wrong with her?" George was talking to his parrot, Leo. Sometimes, Leo talked back. He was about ready to take his eyes off of Frances's breasts and start looking at the bank statement again when he heard her scream. She was now running and shrieking her way across the driveway to him. George got up, hoping that she wouldn't puke on him.

"Frances, what in the Sam Jones is it?" He hollered.

"George, George, he's ah, there's ah, oh my God!" Frances began to shake as she pointed back to Room 8.

He focused on the room and saw the door was open, her upright vacuum cleaner was knocked over on its side. He didn't wait for Frances to collect herself and tell him what was wrong. He clearly saw that something was very wrong. George trotted out of his office and got as far as the open door and then lost his nerve to go one inch further. He thought of Frances watching him and so made himself step inside his cheap motel room. George looked for the television first, Good that's there, he thought. This made him relax, realizing that this hadn't been a robbery. The no-name brand television, with a remote that never seemed to work, was still intact and he wouldn't have to shell out another $69.00 for a new one. He thought that maybe the room had just been trashed until from the corner of his eyes he noticed a flash of burgundy. A thick pool of blood covered a quarter of the cream-colored sheet and had soaked through to the flattened mattress. His eyes were riveted, fixed solidly on the naked dead guy that lay butt up on the bed. George froze, unable to digest the reality of the situation. Frances's screams in the background snapped him out of his self-induced stupidity. He prayed that he could back his way out of the room and make it to his own bathroom before he got sick.

It took the Goochland County Sheriffs Department all of 15 minutes to get there. Both members never had a murder to investigate before. Officer Perry, the dumber of the two, kind of got the feeling that he was going to the prom. It was a special occasion for him. He wondered if he should wear anything special to it. He decided to get the big gun; that was what he needed to wear.

George had cleaned himself up and had Frances seated in the office. She was pale and shaky.

Officer Perry and the Sheriff, Matt Hodgkins, pulled up to the seedy entrance. The neon light was missing some letters, so that the sign hanging in the window just said, "Ope."

"See it's gonna be okay now, the sheriff's here." George patted Frances cold hand.

Without knocking, they came in. "Hey George," Sheriff Hodgkins said. He then looked at Frances, she was still wheezing and tearing up.

Officer Perry, was bored with the preliminaries. He saw Leo and made his way over to the cage and stuck his index finger in the cage.

"If you want to keep that finger you better take it out of Leo's cage!" George had given this warning countless times to children.

"It's just a dumb bird, aw, he can't hurt me." Officer Perry put his finger back in and this time Leo didn't hesitate, he jumped off the perch and just missed digging into the finger that kept being offered to him. Perry decided to quit playing with the bird.

The sheriff cleared his throat; he often did that when Officer Perry's behavior was embarrassing to him. "George, tell me what happened. Who saw the body first?" He asked calmly.

"Frances. She went over to clean the room. The room was paid for and their car was gone, so she thought to go on over, get it done as early as possible, go see the grandkids, something like that. Isn't that right, Frances?" George asked her.

Frances nodded her head and kept the Kleenex stuck to her nose.

"So, she saw him first." George was interrupted by the sound of barking dogs. They were very loud and quite excited about something. George turned up his volume and continued, "So, I looked over and saw that she was sick, throwing up, and I was gonna go over to her when she started to high-tail it back here. She was running like her pants were on fire, screaming the whole time. She was too shook up to tell me what the hell was going on so I went over and saw it, uh, saw him. Then I came back here and called you." George left out the part about him getting sick too. He tugged on his toupee to make sure that it hadn't moved out of place as he had bent over the bowl.

"Sheriff, should we call the State Police?" Officer Perry was ready to let go of this one. He had never seen anyone dead and changed his mind, he didn't want to see it, not now. This time the sheriff cleared his throat twice. Perry turned and looked outside with a fixed gaze on Room 8 and tried to imagine someone dead.

"I think that we better go take a look." The Sheriff wanted to see the crime scene, mark it off and then find out the particulars about who stayed there and what they looked like; what kind of car they drove.

"Sheriff, a dog just ran out of one of those rooms I think. Look! He's going back in now. Wonder why?" Officer Perry kept his hand on the door knob.

Sheriff Hodgkins was the first one outside. He ran as fast as his bad leg would allow him to go and made it there before Perry or George. "God damn it! Get the hell outta here," he yelled at the two flea-bitten dogs that had begun feasting on Julio's rear end. They had pulled him half way off of the bed. One of the mutts had already peed on the mattress to mark his territory.

The crime scene had now become the feast scene. Sheriff Hodgkins was so angry that all he could do was yell and shake his fists at the dogs. Officer Perry arrived, out of breath, but with his own laser-sharp assessment of the scene he knew exactly what to do. He got out his big fancy gun and aimed it at one of the dogs. He missed and hit the corpse, splattering blood and skin on the dogs and the sheriff's pants legs. Just as Sheriff Hodgkins was turning around to stop his idiot deputy, Perry got off one more shot and killed one of the dogs. The other mutt decided that he knew what to do also, and with his deductive reasoning and lightning quick responses he made a leap for Officer Perry's neck.

Good move you stinking mutt, the sheriff thought as he pulled out his revolver and shot the dog dead.

. . .

Julio's body would have made a great photo Louis thought as he drove away on a beautiful Monday. He enjoyed motoring in the white Caddy and had a fine day for it, leaving in the early morning, he was enjoying every mile. Louis hummed down Interstate Route 64 on his way back home. Pushing the pedal hard, he watched the mountains come closer. This was a four-lane highway which went through mostly rural countryside that was picture-perfect. Louis felt indigestion burn a new hole in his chest and this interfered with his put-on enjoyment of the mountains. He always had a checklist handy as to what should make others envious about him or his life, and he derived fulfillment from checking things off on that list. He knew that his luxury Cadillac outdid most of the other cars that he passed, check. He knew that most people would pull out their eye teeth to be able to drive with such a magnificent mountain view, check. All in all, this made him quite satisfied and gave him a creepy clown smile that he painted on, sans colors, quite adeptly.

After an hour of his put-on bliss, the city was almost upon him. He went in the direction of Route 250 bypass, towards Charlottesville. Louis hummed an Elvis tune and stepped a little harder on the gas.

Jennifer's childhood would soon be at an end. Louis decided it an hour ago. He believed that she would be the pivotal point of his wonderful life and bring him fame on torture.com. "Too bad that Julio would miss this! But, oh well," his words were swallowed by the wind as he pushed the gas pedal even harder, accelerating his way back home. Shoulders relaxed and hair tousled by the wind, he felt Elvis's crooning pulsing in his blood.

Carl Brown, a fairly new officer with the Charlottesville Police Department, was feeling bored as he went down the interstate. So far, nothing and no one had done anything wrong for hours, nothing was out of order. He thought about turning off Route 64 and going the back way into town. He knew that he could probably catch some college kids doing something that he could write a ticket for, but then it would take him so much longer at the station and then more time to get home. Carl looked at his watch, he never trusted the clock in the car, and decided to stay with the interstate for two more exits. It was shortly after that decision that Louis blew by him.

Louis was singing along with Elvis on the oldie station and enjoying the power of his engine. Louis didn't notice the Charlottesville cop until Carl had his siren blaring, and the flashing blue lights glowing in his mirrors. This was ending his joy and Louis couldn't tolerate that. Nope, this was something or someone now, that had to be dealt with. He put on his best smile and slowed his monster engine down. Carl motioned for him to pull over. Louis saw a forlorn exit ahead. He pulled off and went down a weed-carpeted ramp.

Carl's first thought upon seeing Louis was that he was a complete nerd, must be some kind of computer geek to afford that kind of car. There seemed to be a full-on invasion of these types from god-only-knows where, he thought. Ever since the state of Virginia had put this ugly, invasive, technology corridor near Charlottesville, there was a constant supply of needless techies - worthless sots that all felt very entitled. They brought with them a superficial valley cool, all the way from California. Carl thought of that far off land as though it were the Land of Oz, or as his mentor called it, 'The land of nuts and fruits.' He always laughed, it was a good joke and perfectly described the California-hipster- twat-knot guys to him. Yeah, this is going to be a quickie! Pull the idiot over, give him a ticket, and away I go. I'll be home with my baby! So what if this added some time, it will be worth it.

Louis complied like a scared rabbit, just as Carl thought he probably would. He considered what shows he would stream from Netflix that night as he slowed down and pulled a bit left and in back of the shiny white Cadillac. Carl was just reaching for his handset when he saw Louis madly waving for him to come forward. He wondered if this guy was going to pretend that something was terribly wrong and that's why he was speeding. One of his favorite stories, he briefly recalled, was pulling over a man that told him that he was waxing nostalgic while zipping down Route 29 South, twenty-five miles over the speed limit. Seems that he had gone to UVA and just being on that road gave him a mad rush of nostalgia, that in turn, created a lead foot. No, probably not going to be that good a lie, he thought.

The sight of this computer geek frantically swinging his arms threw him off kilter. He got out of his car and began to approach the vehicle, but his academy training took over before he took a full step. The geek could wait. Carl got back into his car, and punched in the license plate number. He thought that the geek could wave his underwear out the window for all he cared. The tag brought back nothing noteworthy, it was a rental. Carl opened his door and soon stood next to his newfound freak.

Carl was bored, and couldn't settle on what to order from Netflix. "Good Morning, can I see your license and the car's rental agreement?" he asked in a monotone voice, while deciding that he would get Die Hard With A Vengeance again. He loved that movie.

Louis took the rental agreement out of the glove compartment and timidly gave it to Carl. Next, he pulled his best, littlest gun from under his left butt check, and with a mock-nervous smile still glued to his face, he shot a neat hole in the center of Carl's forehead. Carl fell backwards. Louis's mask slid off his face revealing a wide smile. Carl's skull was fractured from the explosive fall on the blacktop making the crime scene a bloody mess. Louis gunned the motor and left without another thought. He was back in his groove, his heart beating smoothly.

The exit for Route 29 business was in a couple of miles. The white Caddy turned off Route 64 and soon was in downtown Charlottesville. Louis felt much more comfortable and thought about that dumb cop taking away his joy. He knew that the whole city would soon be alive, consumed with the talk of him. All of the cops would be looking for him. No thrill could top this, except one, and she was waiting at home for him to play with. He stepped on the gas, weaving around the slow, Sunday traffic and thought of his delicious girl.

Jennifer felt him coming closer. She recalled her sensation of flying, going far away where he couldn't go. She wondered if her parents could find her, or possibly the police.

She had resolved in a rather matter-of-fact way, that the nightmare of Louis' sick world would not consume her. She held on to that tightly, focusing all of her attention there. But possibly there was something else, or someone else, that now was pulling her attention. Jennifer felt a caring emotion aimed at her. She felt another presence whose thoughts called out. It was butting her expanding mind like a determined cat wanting dinner. She saw a faint image form of Tess. There was a face now to go with the feeling of her. *Maybe there was someone who understood? Maybe I am not alone?* she mused. But her impressions were elusive vapors that hung in the air held only for a few seconds. The heady scent of Tess and rescue were soon gone, but the impact of her enlivened world stayed, giving her strength and new determination.

Chapter Thirteen

Libby didn't mind being around Stefan Hannigan. He was much better looking than any other federal agent that she could remember meeting before. And his scent melted her down to the core. Libby breathed deeply, filling her nose of him. An exotic mixture of cedar, cardamom and freshly split cherry wood make her nostrils flair and her eyelids flutter. His looks, his scent, it all was an intoxicating brew. Slowly, she was inching her way closer to him as Angeline looked on, smiling. "Didn't take you too long to recover, huh?" She whispered to her partner with a knowing look about her being on the prowl.

Hannigan was at the station looking for Kravitz when the heart-wrenching call came in about Officer Carl Brown. At first, the dispatcher thought that the officer calling in, meant that Carl had shot someone. "No, Carl got hit, right in the face! Put a rush on the bus! Jesus!" Officer Kitlowski's anguish was present in each syllable.

Louise's shaky hands found the phone. Bitter tears formed; *God, it doesn't get any worse than this*, she thought. She called for the ambulance but Louise knew that Carl Brown was dead. "You don't get shot in the face and live to tell about it," she muttered to herself as she braced for the long walk down to the Chief's office. It was a matter of protocol that he would be told first. She glanced down at his secretary, the woman looked up and before a question could be formed, Louise moved straight ahead and knocked on the Chief's door.

"Come in." The Chief said, with a higher pitch than his regular low register. He was in a cheery mood. "Hello Louise, I hope that you are here for a donation to our Little League?"

He looked up into her eyes and saw that she was not there for that purpose. He believed that the eyes say it all, and Louise's were swollen and rimmed in red. She gave him the body blow message and then scurried away before releasing an avalanche of tears. The Chief felt old as he contemplated picking up the phone and telling Carl's parents that their 23 year-old son was dead. "Damn, damn." The secretary could hear him exclaim through the closed door. The official wheels were now set in motion.

Of all the different types of homicides; homicide per infortunium (accidental), homicide de defendendo (self-defense), justifiable, negligent, reckless, vehicular, manslaughter and homicide in the first degree, there was one category that had not been legally codified out loud - cop killer. But this was by far the most deadly of the murder categories. It was the one sure way to go straight on the hell list at a station. The covert hell list was the unwritten record of all the criminals that would go straight to hell with a cop's helping and unseen hand. No one spoke about it. Carl Brown's murderer, or murderers, would soon top that list.

Hannigan had become tired of waiting, his calls, emails and texts had gone nowhere but into empty space as he tried reaching out to the irritating and obtuse, Detective Kravitz. He decided to come to the station to find out if any new information had come in on the kidnapping from the Charlottesville Police. Hannigan clenched his fists after seeing the time. He had been waiting for a long ten minutes. He put on his best smile for Libby and began to move away from her admiration, towards Kravitz's door. The door sprang open and out strode a very angry Detective Kravitz. He was consumed by a rage that was palpable to everyone nearby. He blew by Hannigan, and stopped squarely in front of Libby.

"Its a shit storm! Officer Carl, Carl Brown, was hit. A bullet straight through his forehead. I want you to come to the scene with me. The Chief okayed it." Ed barked out his order to Libby.

Ed was marching in a justice parade, with Libby bringing up the rear, as others in his swirling sphere seemed to roll off into their own grief and anger. The hell list just rolled out. Over his shoulder he called out, "So Angie, now that I've got your partner, you get to stay here and jump on the computer for me and get all the info that you can on that white Cadillac."

"Got it," Angie replied. She watched as Libby gave an over-the-shoulder look at Stefan Hannigan. Angeline turned back to her computer and began her hunt for blood.

Hannigan's ears almost bent backwards listening to the white Cadillac comment. He sat down. Stefan was trying to be unobtrusive while he waited for Angeline to give him all the information on the white Cadillac. His uncanny ability to read others had not failed him yet. He was quite confident that he could get something out of her. For some reason, Hannigan believed that this had something to do with Jennifer Starke. He really could not make a logical connection as it was derived from intuition and not from facts. He relaxed his large, panther-like frame into the chair and watched her closely.

Thanks to Carl's call she had the license of the white Cadillac. This was the first path to follow. She contacted the National Crime Information Center to determine if the rental car was stolen. There seemed to be a hiccup with the site and then she realized that it was because the car was just now being reported as stolen. She clicked on the link and saw the car was taken from a specialty rental company. It wasn't brought back when it was due. She knew that when the expensive cars don't come back the hour that they are due, they get called in. This was required by most insurance agencies. They don't like it when the pricey vehicles go missing.

Angeline had the company name and soon, the phone number. She dialed and reached a rental agent.

"Hello, this is Bryan with Highpoint Luxury Autos, how can I help you?" Bryan looked back down at his Twitter feed, detached and bored as usual. He started to stuff another Cheeto in his mouth when she broke through his mental haze.

"Bryan, this is Officer Jefferson from the Charlottesville, PD. I am calling in regards to a stolen rental vehicle reported by your office. It was used in the commission of a felony. I need all the particulars of that rental, the name used, the driver's license used, phone number, credit card and..."

He cut her off. "Officer, ah, I need to get you the owner, Mr Owen, just a minute please." Cops always made him nervous and scared.

Bryan put Angeline on hold, brushed the orange crumbs from the front of his stained shirt and walked over to the boss's door, leaned heavily on it, and said through it, "Mr Owen, the police are on the phone for you."

"Its about time that someone got back to me about that Caddy. Did he say if was stripped or not? God, I can't believe how the day is going. Okay Bryan, I'll pick it up." Bryan had already gone back to his desk and jumped back into his Twitter melee, while stuffing himself with enough sticky, orange tubes to give him chipmunk cheeks.

"Yeah this is Frank Owen." He placed his hand in the center of his chest putting pressure on the pain, as his unrelenting heartburn started again.

Angeline could hear the stress in his voice. "Yes, Mr Owen, I am Officer Jefferson from the Charlottesville Police Department. I understand that your vehicle was reported stolen this afternoon?"

Owen had already decided that reporting it as stolen might be an exaggeration so he backed that down and said, "Just missing probably. That guy, he was a nice guy, don't think that he has actually stolen it. Good looking and seemed to have a wad of cash too." He was afraid that if he was premature in reporting, although he knew it was time for him to report it, that he'd lose money on the contract. He argued with himself the next scenario that his doubt ridden thoughts screamed - what if the car came back? He'd look like a fool. Mental images of the police pulling over his customer, and then a lawsuit, and a certain loss of a wealthy customer; a customer who wanted only the most expensive car on the lot! He took his hand off his chest, burped up a bitter concoction, and now was unconsciously rubbing his forehead.

Angie sat up a bit straighter and told him, "Well, Mr Owen, that vehicle was used in a very serious felony this afternoon and I need all the details of the rental transaction."

"A felony? Wow, did something happen to the guy who rented it? I mean, this just doesn't seem right. He had a black VISA, a black one! Lordy, lordy!" Frank exclaimed as he gathered up the papers and relayed the information to Officer Jefferson. "But you know, I just briefly saw him, the kid, Bryan actually dealt with him. I can tell you some about him but I didn't look at him as much as that black VISA, I've only seen one other of those!" He was getting excited just thinking about having such a large credit limit on a card that made you spend it only on luxury items. He stopped blabbering with a new realization forming. "He didn't steal that card, Jesus, did he? Did that jerk steal the card and my car?" The truth was beginning to knock at his door.

Angeline spoke with Bryan again as he had the most exposure to the perpetrator and got what she could over the phone. She got his agreement to come into the station and have a sketch artist work with him. Bryan was excited to leave work early. He wondered if he could land on some cop re-enactment show, if the crime was big enough. He got in his Kia, planning what he would wear on TV, and what girls he could hook up with now that he was going to be a reality TV star. He brushed off the remaining orange crumbs from his goatee and sped away.

Stefan was done. He had carefully documented all that he could. As he stood up, Angeline became aware of his impending escape.

"Excuse me, excuse me," she pointedly said to him. "I know that you have been waiting a long time. Can I take a message for you or help direct your inquiry?" Angeline paused hoping that she could get this handsome guy's name and number for Libby.

Stefan realized what she was up to. He smiled, an actual genuine smile, and said that he was Special Agent Stefan Hannigan and that he had wanted to see Detective Kravitz but he would try again later. He slipped his graceful, long hand into a cashmere suit coat pocket and gave her his card with the magic phone number that Angeline would make sure that Libby followed up on. As she eyed the card, he glanced at the computer screen. He knew that you could never have too much information. Being observant was drilled into all of the Special

Agents and since he considered himself one of the most special, he made sure that he noticed every detail that presented itself.

As he walked away, Angeline took one long look at his backside, just to ensure that Libby's big stud would measure up to hers. He would.

Chapter Fourteen

The Party Rats, as the five fierce girls called themselves, had decided to go out for a stroll. They had finished off all of the vodka, and since there was nothing left to suck down, snort, chew or hit, they went off for a bit of rolling "partaying."

Jinx decided to go up to the freak's house. She thought that he was the best show in town. She pulled up her thigh-high socks and pushed down the olive green cap and stood up. "So I wanna go and check him out, see what he's about now," she said to the other girls. Each of them knew who she meant. Jinx had this fascination for him. She often dragged them along on her discovery adventures through the dried-out grasses and crumbling walkways up to the woe-filled mansion.

Tish didn't want to get dragged along this time. "Yeah, we ain't doin' that. I'm sickah lookin for this mangy-assed dude, Can't you come up with somethin' bettah?" Is this really all you can fuckin' think of now? And what's with striped socks? You look like somethin' outta a kid's book."

Jinx rolled her eyes and spit on the floor right next to Tish.

"Shit, I'm not gonna watch you two go at it today." Marissa

was fed up with their constant belittling and the petty competitions that always seemed to blow up and get someone hurt. She looked back at the red and black striped socks and walked over to Jinx. "Okay lets go. Lets just go and do it now and then we'll find somethin' else doin' for later, right?" Marissa turned and looked at Tish, waiting for a compromise.

Tish nodded and stepped over the spit then took her rightful lead once again.

The Party Rats' parade made their way to Louis' love shack. All five of them had been there many times in the past. Tish pushed the rusted, cut, metal fence back to one side and one by one, they went through it and climbed the steep hill through the dense woods. Years ago it was deemed the perfect place to get high and not be seen by anyone. Even during the brightest days a murky dark hung back there. It swallowed giant patches of day, giving the knotted tree roots shadows to hide in. Jinx followed the trail back to her perfect hiding place that brought her to the delightful gloom that she secretly wished could be her home.

It was fortunate for the Party Rats that the ghoul had never seen them. He heard Jinx once, and thought that it was a squirrel. Louis was too fully engaged in his torture and porn sites to investigate squirrels.

Louis unlocked his gate as the girls scampered up the hill. He had ditched the white Caddy hours ago and was back in his own wheels. Slowly he took the car up the hill. He savored each second, dreaming of his future pleasure with Jennifer, listening to his powerful motor hum. He treasured this time as he crawled up the driveway like a snake moving through tall grass on a hot day.

The sound of the car door closing reverberated in Jennifer's mind. The mental chase would be on again and this time, she intended to win. She made herself look down to the bare floor and shoved all thoughts out of her mind as her eyelids closed tight. Louis whistled as he got out his heavy key chain. Listening in the tall grass, none of the Party Rats could recognize his tune as he unlocked the door and stepped inside.

"Hey baby, I've had a hard day and I want to relax with you." He gleefully calculated earlier that his greeting would shake her and make her cry.

Louis took off his sweater and then, as was his habit, he kicked off his shoes. He sat down inches away from her on the cold, bare floor, and reached out eagerly for his doll. Jennifer remained untouchable in her faraway world. Lost in passion, he licked his lips like a dog, reaching out for a a bare shoulder when a piercing bong blasted through the room. Louis jumped up in a panic. He knew that it was his computer with an alert message. "It never ends!" he sputtered at the wall.

He stared at the screen, "URGENT, URGENT, SECURITY BREECH!" The message flashed in large, red letters over and over again. He clicked on a symbol below the message and the rest of the email opened up. It was an encrypted message from torture.com. Louis fiddled with the mouse and unscrambled the rest of the message.

The girls had never been so close to the house. Jinx decided that she just had to peer in the window so that she could see the fabled ghoul up close. Tish was carefully stepping over a heap of poison ivy and going slower than Jinx. Jinx was impatient and was ready to push Tish out of her way when they all heard the alarm go off on the computer. At first the girls began to panic and bolt away, but without too much scuffling, Jinx got them all still again. Whispering, she said, "No, its not a house alarm, its a computer sound, I know it." Jinx kept her voice down and motioned with her finger over her mouth to keep quiet. She crept back closer to the window again to sneak a look inside.

Tish raised her right foot and expertly balanced her army boot over the poison ivy.

"Fuck! Fuck, I'll fucking kill them." Louis was off the deep end into a rage. His message warned him that this site was no longer safe and that possibly everyone's email addresses had been compromised. He picked up the closest object to him, a book, and hurled it across the room. It smashed into a picture, knocking it off the wall with a loud crash. Jennifer let out a scream and began to cry. Louis turned towards her. His hands were shaking and his temples bright red. That is when the migraine hit like a locomotive and stopped him dead in his rage. He wailed and moaned with pain. Jennifer had just regained her inner calm and strength that she had practiced all day.

Jinx bolted this time. Things had just gotten too weird even for her. Tish's shoe lace got caught on a bramble causing her to fall down into the big patch of poison ivy that a moment before she had safely navigated around. She shrieked and Louis heard them. Through the pounding of his migraine he heard someone was outside his castle. He took his rage away from Jennifer and aimed it towards the double doors.

Jinx got Tish up. Marissa and the other girls were a few steps ahead. They ran for the cover of the woods.

Louis, a step away from the door knob, realized that his shoes were off. "Fuck" he yelled. He went back to his shoes and shoved his feet in as quickly as he could. Bolstered by a new determination to kill whatever government spy was outside, he opened the door. Louis was positively demon-like now. His neck muscles were so tight that it made his jugular vein bulge out. He could see no one. Then he felt them. He felt their hearts pounding wildly; their breathing was loud and labored. There were so many of them!

The Party Rats ran as fast as they could. Instinctively they knew that they were now being hunted and each step forward took them closer to safety. Jinx was the first to lose her footing as the hill became steep. She tumbled down the embankment with the world spinning by her as if she was inside a dryer. The rest soon joined her. They leapt over the small stream and kept on flying down the incline until they burst out onto the street.

Louis walked further out into his yard, staring into the dark woods. His head felt like it was in a vice. The pain was so severe that it inhibited his ability to reach out and mentally grab them. Whoever they were, was still a mystery, but he was certain they were human. "Ow!" His screeching voice echoed in the forest. Holding his head with both hands, Louis turned around and started back towards his car. He thought that he could run them down but as he went for his keys, the pain got even worse. Louis fell to his knees, whimpering. He wrapped himself in self-pity and cried until exhaustion overtook him and he was no longer able to move.

The Party Rats stumbled back down to the safety of their neighborhood. They were bruised, a bit cut up, and altogether terrified. "See, did you see that?" Jinx was inches away from Tish's face. "Cos I didn't, I damn well didn't see a damn thing and it's all cos of you!."

"Get the fuck away from me. It's your fault, all this shit is your fault! You just had to go there!" Tish shoved Jinx with both hands and then waited for her response. She held her stomach, tight, waiting for a blow, hoping for a bad punch so that she could let the rage burn into Jinx.

Marissa, stepped in between them. It was a dangerous move that she felt she might regret. "I wanna get lit now, can't y'all find us some dang juice? Ain't got time for this." She tugged on Tish, as her eyes looked up the darkening road. "We should be feeling it. Now. And what the sweet Jesus will we do if he comes down here? Could be coming now!"

"Yeah, so what." Tish glared at Marissa.

"Cracka will shoot you dead. And nobody will give a damn 'bout you, nobody." Her pupils widened as the truth registered with her. Nobody would care if she, or any of them, was dead. Just another gangbanger, can't stand up on their own, that's all that would be said about them.

Tish shoved Marissa down hard onto the black top. "Get out of my way bitch. Get the fuck outta my way." She muttered. "And I think he's a pussy, heard him screamin' like a girl."

As they sullenly strode down the middle of the street there was much debate between them about the screams that they heard coming from the ghoul mansion. Jinx was certain that she heard a girl's scream; the others weren't certain and thought that the ghoul was alone.

"I was the closest... so I heard the best," Jinx asserted to the wary bunch.

And as their bickering faded into the distance, Jennifer tried to mentally call out to them. She tugged at the space near them. No one could hear. She tried to tell them that she was there, that she needed them to save her. And that is when she got the idea to place a kind of a picture of her in the house, all tied up, in Jinx's mind. She placed the picture right in the middle of her head and hoped that it would impact. It did. Jinx was now totally certain the it was a girl's voice and that she had to go back and help her get away from the ghoul. But first, she decided, she needed a drink, maybe, lots of drinks.

Chapter Fifteen

All of the people that should have been at the crime scene were there. Nothing would bring a bigger crowd of police than this type of crime. Yellow crime scene tape marked off Officer Brown's car, and the litter strewn, weed-covered pull-off of the isolated ramp. It was difficult to move and not bump into another cop who was trying to keep the scene undamaged for the forensic team that had sped their way from Richmond.

Officer Kitlowski had arrived first. He established the obvious fact that his best friend, Officer Carl Brown, was dead. A short time later, the coroner agreed.

Fingerprints were being hunted as the dust flew and photographs popped. Carl's hands were covered with plastic bags to protect any evidence that might be under his nails. Ceremoniously, the coroner went through her checklist to determine the time of death. First she checked for livor mortis, the marbleized discoloration of the pools of blood and how it settled in the body, and then rigor mortis, which parts were turning stiff. It was obvious that Carl had been popped in the head and died four hours ago.

The scene was being turned inside out looking for any speck of a clue - only one piece was easy to see - a car's tire tracks that took off at a rather high speed. Whatever else that may be there was keeping itself hidden. This was not going to be easily solved like a television mystery show. The position of the body was noted, the state of his clothes, the litter that had been nearby was collected. A diagram of the scene was being drawn up when Detective Kravitz and Officer MacGregor pulled up. Kravitz bulled his way past the other officers and headed straight for Officer Kitlowski. Libby was not too far behind. Ed stopped as Kitlowski was carefully measuring the distance of a blood splatter.

Kravitz turned to Libby. "Let me know what you find out Officer." He said rather matter-of-factly to her.

"Yes, sir. What is it you want me to do?" Libby saw that the crime was already being dissected by every flavor of police that the station could offer up. She wrinkled her nose, squinting into the setting sun and waited for his response.

Ed tried to mentally push his request to her. Nothing happened. He brought his voice down low, and sounded almost menacing without meaning to do so. "I want you to go and figure out something out that I can't do by myself. Okay?"

"Go collect something that you don't know about?" She really was attempting to be polite with the awkward situation but even her whispered response sounded a bit snarky. "What do you mean?"

Ed lowered his forehead and rolled his eyes. "You know."

She got his meaning clear enough, go divine something. Tess must have blabbed something, she realized.

The ambulance arrived on the scene. It was waiting to take Carl for one of his final rides. The last photo of his fatal wound needed to be taken. That being done, the ambulance sped away with Carl secured in the back. The rest of the police force had enough left to do without the body being present.

The investigators were busily collecting clues that would lead to nowhere. There was no physical evidence other than the car's tire tracks. The type of car, and even the license plate, was already known. There was no DNA, no fingerprints, no helpful pieces of trash. Carl's car would be taken back to the station to check for latent prints but none would be found. The only clue Carl had gotten when he called in for a tag check sometime before he was killed. It wasn't much, but that is all that they had. Except for the one ace up Kravitz's sleeve, Libby. They really all had Libby, but no one knew that, and this was something that could never be discussed. So as the Forensic Unit collected clues, and officers kept the scene clean, Kravitz ran his thumb up and down over a beloved cigar, while he paced back and forth, watching his last hope psychically sniff out the area. Stopping, he made detective small talk with another detective, Detective Howes, from the Albemarle County PD, his eyes circling back to Libby.

Libby began in the brush, back where the perpetrator's vehicle would have been parked. She wanted to stand there with her eyes closed, but not wanting to seem odd to the others, she got down on her haunches and pretended as if she was looking on the ground for clues while she put on a pair of gloves. Libby focused her awareness on the surrounding ground and got not one psychic bread crumb. Libby stood up and crossed by the side of the car where Carl was shot. She noticed a strange tingling sensation in her left foot. She stopped and looked around at the others. Some were wrapping up their tasks, all seemed to be involved with their own activities and no one cared about what she was doing other than Kravitz. She could feel Ed's apprehension. While scanning her attention, Libby mentally heard from the two seasoned officers directly behind

Kravitz. Carl was the topic of conversation, as they both were weighing the odds of ending up like Carl. This was the dreaded scenario that many of them had played late at night in their own beds, after a threatening day at work. One second you are thinking about picking up your dry cleaning and the next, poof, you're history. The sea of unspoken emotion at this crime scene was almost overwhelming to her.

For Officer Abigail Lucy MacGregor, standing there, attempting to be at her most perceptive level, was difficult. Libby could only be a warrior. She refused to understand death in a personal way. As an officer who only had a few years in with the force, the thought of dying on duty was not that real to her, none of her peers had even been shot. She stood there, with her glistening shield of youthful immortality hanging over her heart and a desire to save the world unspoken.

The sensation happened again as she stood in front of where the freak's car had been parked only a few hours ago. The tingle followed up her left leg and raced to her forehead. The throbbing pain burst its way from a black screen that seemed to act like a trap door on the ground. She pushed the metaphysical door with more energy and out popped a migraine. "Yep, that's it." She said to herself and then slightly rocked over the hot spot and each time she would receive the same sensation. Carefully avoiding the last awareness of shock and death that spilled and flowed from Carl's energy in the same area, she looked over again. She focused on the pool of blood that hours ago had gushed from him and thought that she saw a faint impression of another blood pool underneath. She stared deep into it and watched as a vision of Jennifer's face formed in the blood.

"Detective Kravitz, I think that I've got something," she quietly said as he stood next to her.

"I've got all that I need here so let's go." Kravitz let the officers know that they were heading out, got back in on the driver's side and away they went. "So whatcha got for me?" Ed asked her before the crime scene was out of sight.

Libby seemed hesitant at first. She went over the vision another time in her mind while Kravitz shoved his impatience back down and drove. "He killed someone else first, probably today. I saw two pools of blood. Two. I am not completely convinced but I believe that I saw Jennifer's face in the second pool of blood. The perp must have known about her, he was thinking about her?" Libby stopped and stared down at her hand, yes, she decided, it was Jennifer. "All right, I'm certain, it was Jennifer." She failed to mention her fear: Jennifer most likely was dead if she was seeing her in a blood pool. Being a warrior, she would not speak about her unsubstantiated fears. She took a shallow breath and continued, "And he has a migraine, could be a problem that he deals with all of the time, I am not sure on that one. I am sure that the the perp doesn't emote much, there was not a bit of sorrow or any kind of justification - there was nothing, zip! He doesn't read like 98% of the population. It felt like he had nothing to do with pulling the trigger. He thought his hands did it, not him. Weird, huh?"

" Just like a text book psycho." Detective Kravitz said as he pushed the car to go even faster.

Libby subconsciously massaged her forehead trying to push off a headache that wasn't hers to have, mourning in silence her new fear that Jennifer was probably dead.

Chapter Sixteen

Louis, having returned from his unsuccessful outing to find the Party Rats, got tired of being a puddle on the front lawn and decided that he could cry just as easily in his own house. He pulled himself off of the grass and stumbled back to the front door. Placing his long hand on the front door he turned the knob and gave a slight push to open it. This time something pushed back. He couldn't go in, not with this amount of effort. Louis knotted his eyebrows together and raged. The door owed it to him. He pressed his entire weight into the wood and the door remained still. Nothing budged at all except for his right shoulder. His world seemed to be going in reverse. The door seemed to be pushing back towards him. The hinges creaked and the bricks that held the frame, moaned. Louis spread his hands wide across his head as the migraine came back in full force.

The chill of the cold spring crept down the back of his neck. Louis was convinced that this must be a dream or some kind of cyber curse since his home had been violated. Surely this had to be linked to torture. com's extinction, he reasoned. His muddled mind got lost amongst the pain and the symbols that flitted by. "What does it all mean?" The monster cried to no one.

The walls inside the grimy carriage house had now become familiar to Jennifer. She felt that she knew each crack. She did not differentiate from where her body ended and the floor and walls began. Like a blossom unfolding, her awareness kept expanding.

Louis was beating on the window near her. Jennifer, knew that she may only have one chance to reach someone and tell them that she needed help. She thought of her mother and then, her new friend - the lady that cared, who lived far away. The sensation of wind blew around her small body. The spiritual breezes blew her far away from her prison, high and up above. She would find this friend and tell her. Louis's pounding was left far behind.

I was watching a small chickadee doing a side-step; it reminded me of a boxer getting ready to throw a punch. The chickadee was small but intense, and he intimidated the larger titmouse so much that he left the feeder. Life can often be like that, it's the attitude that makes a winner, I thought as I watched the seeds greedily disappear.

My right ear heated up, the blood flow rushed to it and that is when I realized that it was Jennifer. "Sweetie, I am here. Can you feel me near?" I telepathically sent her.

I wasn't prepared for what happened next. I felt a small hand on my right shoulder and I could hear her little voice say, "Yes." I was so startled by the volume of her presence that I took a physical step backwards and turned around half expecting to see Jennifer there. I needed to keep myself calm.

Jennifer thoughts came rapid fire. "He has me in a dirty

house in Charlottesville. I'm on a hill, I think. I don't know the road, but some girls were outside here and I told one of them about me. I mean, I tried, but all she wanted to do was drink. I think she and the other girls were rats, oh, I don't know! I don't know exactly where I am!" I could feel her begin to fade from me a bit as sorrow filled her heart.

"Okay, that's okay. Can you look and see anything in that room with an address?" I asked.

She snapped back in control again with a new purpose guiding her. "He has an old phone, it's like one my grandma has. Maybe it's got a number?" Jennifer was a smart girl.

"Yes, see if you can get a number! I can find you with that, all right?"

She put her attention on the old burgundy phone that was hanging on the wall. It took more of her attention to try to read the numbers. She kept a tight grip on her line to Tess so she stopped beaming Louis in the forehead a bit. That was a mistake.

Louis snapped his head back as some of the force was taken off the center of his forehead. He believed that Jennifer was creating his headache. "You little bitch! You are boring a hole right inside of my head!" He let go of the bars that he had been shaking and took a step back from the window. He frantically searched the bushes and found a large rock. "I am gonna smash your head in, bitch!" He proudly announced as he hurled the rock through the window.

The glass shattered easily and the shards landed near Jennifer's legs. That made her angry. Never before had Jennifer felt as much antagonism towards a living creature that she now felt towards her ghoul. Jennifer had earlier gotten Jinx's sentiments towards him and was in complete agreement with her. He was a horrid, ugly, monster that had to die. She could see it now, he had to die. With her new certainty about life, Jennifer had more self-confidence. She was resolved that she would ignore the horrid ghoul and concentrate on her mission to get the phone number.

Jennifer put her attention back on the phone. Her awareness pervaded the cold, burgundy colored plastic but nothing was there. She could only perceive an old cigarette burn that marked a corner of the phone. It had left a blackish center in a pool of melted plastic. The grotesqueness of it repelled her. She made herself stay with it and look closer. He had no written number on the phone.

"He doesn't have one!" She cried out to me. "There's nothing there, nothing!"

Panic crept in. Louis was now hurling himself against the door determined to break it down. He hoped that it would break his head out of her grip as well. The pounding grew deafening. It filled up Jennifer's mind so loudly that I began to hear it too.

"What's he doing?"I asked.

"I hope that he splits his head in two! He is throwing himself at the door."

Bang! bang! bang! The sound reverberated in our shared mental space.

The hinges began to give way. Jennifer opened her eyes and looked at the door. The frame was shaking with each hit. She tried to scoot her body away from the impending tornado.

"Jennifer, Jennifer!" I could feel her attention beginning to slip, and then it snapped back to me.

"The ghoul is shaking the door down," she calmly replied. "I think that I will let him in now and get him to tell me where we are." Her voice seemed determined and it sounded an octave lower.

"No, no, that isn't a good idea. Just keep him out, can you do that? Can you please do that for me?"

As I pleaded with her, she thought of her options. She really wanted to have him in the house so that she could hurt him head-on.

"Honey, you don't know him the way that I do. I know him, did I tell you that?" I had more of her attention now.

"No...you didn't tell me." Her voice seemed to trail off into deeper thoughts about it. She almost didn't believe me. Almost.

"Okay, I can keep the monster on the other side of the door. I am sure I can." I felt her relax a bit. She was growing comfortable with her new position of power. I didn't want her to get too comfortable. Louis was a real monster and the evil that was inside him existed as an unknown quantity for me. No one could predict his insanity and how he would behave.

"Do you see any mail around, maybe a magazine? Anything that would have his address on it?" My mind was spinning. I was groping to think of some way that she could get his address.

"I'll just read the number on the door!" Jennifer felt a bit brighter as she moved away from her darker intentions with her realization of how easy it would be to get the first part of his address.

Gleefully, Louis got her thought also. He ripped off the old, worn numbers that had barely hung on next to the door and then fell down laughing. "Hey you little bitch, you'll never leave. Never!" Louis was now in on the psychic party line. This was not a good turn of events. He got up and pranced around his front lawn, taunting us both with his presence.

There was a slight rumbling, I could hear a low, deep moan; then the earth started to shake. Jennifer thought that it was Louis. Louis thought that it was her.

I ran for a doorway and held my body within the frame. I could feel my apartment building sway.

An eerie confusion settled on everyone in hip C'ville. Earthquakes were not supposed to happen in central Virginia. This unholy phenomena would surely make rowdy California slip off into the Pacific Ocean, but it was nothing that us, on the well-heeled East Coast would ever have to worry about.

Nature had the last laugh while our ivy covered walls shook and the psychic party line was disconnected.

Chapter Seventeen

Everything hung on a delicate balance. Josef had pinpointed the creep and he was not far away from his dear friend, Eddie. He was having a difficult time believing his own information, so he checked it three times, fearful of making a tragic error. The answer was always the same, the madman lived in Charlottesville, VA. He might even go food shopping, or possibly would eat at the same pancake house that was popular with Ed, and with many of the Charlottesville police. He knew that Kravitz put away a lot of pancakes.

Josef called with the news of where their psychopath lived. Ed seemed to take forever to pick up.

"Hey Josef! You ain't gonna believe what just happened here, my friend. We just had a 4.7 earthquake! Yep, we certainly did! And let me tell you, nobody here has a rat's ass clue on what to do! Nobody. Not even the mayor knows what to say yet. I think that they're waiting for FEMA but FEMA ain't gonna come down as this is nothing as disaster scenes go. This ain't no Katrina! What are they gonna do anyways? Send hundreds of federal workers to come and hold everyone's hands and tell them that its gonna be okay? Phah!" Kravitz was deep into it.

Josef finally heard Ed stop to take a breath so he jumped in, "Eddie, I know where he is."

"So I'm figuring that they'll wait for the Govenor to get on their news station and" Ed coughed.

Josef tried again, "Ed, I found him. He sleeps where you do. Got it? Verstehen?"

"Ah...did you just say he sleeps where I sleep?" Finally the detective got the clue that Josef was hitting him over the head with. "He's here?" Kravitz sat silently as it sank in. The dead-man-walking, as that is what Ed now called him, lived here. That explained a lot to him. Kravitz thought of all the events surrounding his life in the last week and they seemed to snap together like a neat puzzle with this news. He got out one of his Stim-u-dents from its cardboard container and began to clean his gums. If he couldn't smoke in the crowded station, and he certainly wanted at least two cigars now, he could pick at his gums and suck the mint flavor as a distraction. "Are you one-hundred percent sure about this?" His excitement was impossible to hide in his voice. Ed was practically bouncing with joy.

"Ja, it has got to be there, I am sure. And I know that he has got a 434 area code. So it is one of the Charlottesville numbers, richtig?"

"Yep, that would nail it to central Virginia. But how did you get it to Charlottesville?"

"Sorry, I've got the first three numbers of the exchange too. So, not bad, eh? Faster than the FBI, faster than a speeding bullet, right?" Josef Dornbach was satisfied as he knew he was the fastest tracker on the planet still.

"That bastard lives in my town. That means that I will get the pleasure of getting him. I think that he killed one of our very own today, Officer Brown, and I think he killed someone else this morning too. So the guy who did this also probably took the daughter of the head of the fucking FBI. He is the top on multiple Hell Lists now. The feds can taste his blood too. But you did great! You always were the best and you still are, my friend. Let me have the first three numbers of the local exchange." Eddie was sitting straight up in his chair, holding a silver pen that a very old girlfriend of his had given him many years ago.

"Ja, it is 979. So, that is about all from me now. I won't have anything else until he gets back online. When he does I'll catch him, right? I'll let you know and you tell me you got him, ja?" Josef sat smiling as he held his daughter's photograph in one hand.

"Thanks buddy, you just helped make the world a helluva lot safer. I will call you with the good news." And with that promise they were both off the phone.

The Party Rats had found a new supply of vodka. It seemed that Gloria's mother was so upset about the earthquake that she wobbled out of her house, leaving the front door wide open and the open Vodka bottle on the floor, next to her sofa. Gloria's mom, Helen, was a lush and always had a good supply of booze. Her father's pension kept the bar well stocked. She might need a new roof, but she never lacked for a pretty good selection of hooch. Besides getting the vodka, they also took an unopened bottle of gin. Now, they really could party into their next collective state of oblivion with lots of fuel.

The five girls went back to their usual place, avoiding the ghoul's haunt. They entered the abandoned mill, stepping over several mud puddles from the last rain fall. The mill had been built in the late 1800's and had sat abandoned for the last ninety years or so. It had been a long ten years since anyone was foolish enough to try to renovate the rotting wooden structure. The tin roof had been replaced but the stone foundation was only partially done and then stopped, for lack of funds. So here it sat, with a relatively shiny roof on a decaying frame that lay on a foundation that was more unstable than it was before the partial renovation. Walking on the second story floor with your eyes closed was the girls version of Russian roulette. The ground floor was just about as rotten, but the group opinion was that you had better odds of dying if you fell from the second story. If you fell from the ground floor into the basement, you'd probably would only break some bones. And all of the girls had broken at least one bone in their rough-and-tumble life.

Tish and Marissa entered first. Tish grabbed Marissa by the ass and whispered, "Hey, you wanna come in the basement with me? Come on. I know you want to little girl." They both laughed. Neither one of them felt like little girls anymore.

As they disappeared together, Jinx looked at Gloria. She held the mostly drunken bottle of Vodka in the air and smiling, announced, "It's just us and Sophie left to drink this and that superfine gin down. Let's go over to the hole. I am freezin'. Got any matches?"

Jinx made a small leap over a rotten floor board. She looked down and watched Tish pin the other girl down in the wet dirt and then push her blouse up. Just as the bra was coming loose, Jinx yelled down, "You sluts are gnarly!" She tried to think of something else more descriptive to call them but they ignored her slurs as they ripped off each others clothes. Jinx was too drunk to think of anything else to say so she tumbled her way back to the hole and sat down.

The hole was their fire pit. Near the north corner of the mill, a stone chimney of sorts rose up from the basement. Many years ago, in another failed renovation project, someone turned it into a grill. Now it served as their fireplace and conversation pit, as Marissa had dubbed it one day. She had seen that word used to describe a lavish, inside fireplace in "O" magazine, and since Oprah was her hero, she attempted to pressure everyone to call it their conversation pit, but to the others, it remained 'the hole'.

Sophie pulled up a rotten floor board and brought it over. It broke easily into manageable pieces. She tossed the pieces in the pit. Jinx gave her the vodka to use as their fire starter. As the flames shot up, Sophie sat down next to Jinx and rubbed her chilly palms together to get warm.

"I am sure, sure that I heard a young girl screaming her head off in the ghoul's mansion. I bet he has her tied up too! How bout we go back when we're done with this?" Jinx took a swig of the vodka and waited for Sophie and Gloria to agree with her. Time to have even more fun was how Jinx looked at it.

"Nah, I dunno. 'Cept for all the noise, maybe we'd go." Gloria motioned outside towards the road.

All sorts of sirens had been going off the last twenty minutes since the earthquake. It seemed that most car alarms felt that the shake of the earth was an alarming event as well. The entire fire department roared around town. Herds of ambulances were dispatched with their accompanying sirens. It sounded like a pack of elephants were crashing through the city. Charlottesville was not having a good evening. The event was as perplexing as a blizzard to this southern town.

Gloria rose up, hollering over the din."We need some more fire." She could see some pieces of wood that were small enough for her to carry back were halfway down the mill, next to the king post. As carefully as she could totter, Gloria made her way to the wood.

Sophie and Jinx decided that they needed gin. "I'll get the cups and some water," Sophie said to her as she made her way to their hidden cooler. It was a thrown-away styrofoam cooler with rat bites on one side and a thick dirt blanket over it all. The building creaked. Sophie froze. Jinx kept drinking the last of the vodka, as Gloria bent over to grab at a piece of wood that had started to swing within arm reach. The wood was hanging on harder than she expected. She tugged and felt it give way. The building moaned and creaked, as the aftershock shook it hard. Dirt pushed through the unstable foundation. The lower half of the building struggled for a new foothold while the center of the building made a ghost-like wail. A handful of seconds passed when the king post let out a sharp, painful lament which was deadened by the a thunderous crack that ran the entire length of the post. The death throes of the old mill began as a nocturne and finished with the gusto of an unleashed orchestra gone wild. The girls realized that they were part of its ending. Dust clouds covered Tish's and Marissa's nakedness. A rock bolted out from the foundation, opening a large hole in Tish's neck. Marissa tried to shove her off her torso. Her mouth and nose became filled with a wave of dirt as it burst through the foundation. The walls tumbled down. Jinx dove for the north window but she stumbled on the vodka bottle and fell halfway through the floor. Sophie almost made it out. Gloria felt a searing pain in her left shoulder as the mill gracefully danced to its demise. Like a grotesque ballet, the overhead joists and posts pirouetted in mid-air, rotating in flight until they smashed into the first floor; most then making their way to the basement. And then the roof started its suicidal march. Nails popped like an Irish drum setting the rhythm to a jig. The building exploded, and the ground heaved the old surrounding sycamore trees into their graves. The girls never thought that they would hear anything more dismal until the silence set in, taking all reason from those left alive.

Chapter Eighteen

Special Agent Hannigan was taking a chance but it was a delicious chance well-calculated. So maybe it wasn't such a chancy thing to do after all. He picked up his cell phone from the ground and selected her number. The phone rang four times before she could find her phone.

"Hello" Libby had been sound asleep.

"Oh, I am sorry. Did I wake you?" This is Stefan Hannigan, he seemed to almost sizzle his words as he purposefully left off Special Agent. He paused.

"Yes, I remember you." Libby pulled herself straight up from under her mustard-colored linen sheets in an alert sitting position, mimicking a puppy waiting for a treat. She vividly recalled seeing him in the station a scant few hours ago.

He could feel her delight. "I am happy that you do, it makes it much easier for me as I certainly noticed you." He now put a full-on sizzle to his bacon. Stefan's smile was almost audible to Libby. "First, are you okay?"

"Yeah, I am fine." Libby thought that question was a bit of a let down from where she hoped the conversation would go to, she continued as she stretched her stiff legs. "I was just a little tired earlier but I feel much better now. How are you?" She asked as she rubbed the sleep out of the corner of one eye.

"Fine, and if I am lucky, the house came through it all right as well. But I may have lost one of my oak trees." Hannigan could feel that she was confused. "Libby, you do know about the earthquake, don't you?"

"Huh?" She thought that he must be teasing her. He seemed to be capable of being a good jokester.

"The earthquake, it happened about 30 minutes ago." His words hung in the air.

"Oh my god, I was asleep then. Was it bad?" She asked as she threw her legs over the side of the bed. "How could I sleep through an earthquake? Libby was fully awake now.

"Don't worry, other than ridiculous mass hysteria over what really is a non-event, nothing much really happened. At least nothing that should worry anyone as beautiful as you. Actually, my real motive in calling you was to ask you to go to lunch, maybe dinner. I would love to see you smile again. You have such a warm smile you know." The bacon was done frying now.

Libby involuntarily flexed her toes, anticipating his future touch. "Well, let me see. Not sure if I can fit that into my extremely jammed schedule. What do you have in mind for my warm smile?" She began to giggle and just as Hannigan was going in for the close, the earth began to shake again.

Libby clutched on to the side of her iron bed as it shook its way across her bedroom on the bare wooden floor. Hannigan had been perched on the edge of his car and now found himself sitting on the ground with his cell phone lost to parts unknown. Their connection was unexpectedly severed.

Libby remained in bed until she was certain that the quake was over. The bed had almost made it to her bathroom door. She looked around and saw that a few books had fallen to the floor, some of the pictures hung crookedly on the wall but other than that, everything seemed to be in order. "Tess!" she called out. Libby located her cell phone, punched in her sister's numbers but the only signal she could get was a busy signal. She tried to call the station, busy. She tried Tess again, busy. The lines must be down, she fretted. She next noticed that the digital clock was dark, that meant no electricity. She knew that she needed to get down to the station fast as it would be jammed with people needing help or at least an explanation of what had just occurred. Libby was mentally muttering about the phone lines and cell towers were being overloaded with calls and cursed that her most enjoyable conversation with the most handsome Stefan, had been cut short. Thinking of him, she pictured his broad chest naked and could almost taste his luscious, kissable lips. An ambulance siren's blast brought her out of her carnal desires. She called out to Tess telepathically.

I stood in the doorway feeling my building sway. A deer skull crashed down from the top of a display case as I heard books dive off my shelf. The world then went silent. I heard no birds, no sirens, no music from the downstairs studio that always had some kind of music playing. But the lack of these sounds was not as terrifying as the low rumble that sounded like a train's engine with the first sway. I will never forget that sound as it made me let go of Jennifer. She was lost to me, like a small wave becoming part of a tumultuous vortex. My emotional whirlpool drew my thoughts further inside and then I felt Libby as the aftershock hit. She was reaching out to me in on our invisible line.

"Tess, is anything okay?" Libby and I used this punchline when we were checking up on each other.

"I am fine, fine. You? Oh, okay, but Jennifer isn't. Pick me up on your way to the station." And with that, our special connection ended.

The upended city acted like a petulant child. The inhabitants of Charlottesville were dangerously and recklessly moving downed electric wires with no help; gunning their engines and roaring off to get through some of the larger intersections that no longer had traffic lights. The usual southern charm had turned into a full-out, moonshine crazy. The main power plant was sitting like a huge, dead, uncharged Tesla and no one had found out exactly how to get it up and running. This perhaps, was the most dangerous thing that had actually occurred, except for the mass panic that was running through the town. Gossip travels fast and panic travels at light speed.

There were mostly fender bender accidents scattered about. A few serious accidents clogged ramps to the major highways that then created back-ups on the major roads throughout. Dozens of trees had toppled down, some blocking roads, some taking down the power lines. All of this added confusion made the traffic snarl even more. Chaos ruled the night.

Detective Kravitz was still at the station and on his computer when the ground began to shake again. He opted to ignore it this time. Ed had just printed out the location of the first three numbers and was contemplating a cigar when the aftershock hit. All the lights sputtered out and then the generator kicked in; most everything had power once more.

"Yo, Princey, you okay?" Ed called out. Princey had been sitting at his desk but now Kravitz couldn't see him. He heard a loud thud as all of Princey ungracefully was thrown off his chair.

"Yeah, yeah I think that I'm all right. Ow!," Princey moaned as he tried to stand back up again. "I think that I might have twisted my ankle. How about you?" He asked Ed while inspecting his ankle a bit closer and deciding that it was just a bad bump, there would be a bruise and nothing else.

"I'm good, still sitting here thinking that I could probably enjoy one of my fine Dominican friends while everyone is consumed with this new emergency." Kravitz pulled out his cigar and happily lit it. He was excited with his progress. He got up and gave Princey a hand.

"So, why don't you offer me one too? Seems like this is the best way to keep a cool head under emergency conditions. Let's sit down and think what should be done first." Princey held out his hand like a child waiting for his present. Ed complied. Now they both felt as though there were back in high school, smoking in the boys room. But this time they knew that even if the teacher came in, there was so much panic that their indiscretion would go unnoticed.

"I've got the location of where the top A-List creep lives! At least, the general area. And I figure that since this stain probably killed our Officer Carl Brown, we should have the first shot at him. The feds can wait a little longer. Besides, there's something about Hannigan that I don't like. I don't know what it is but something isn't kosher there, know what I mean?"

"Well, anybody that you don't like Ed, I don't like either." They both took a big hit on their cigars and exhaled at the same time. This was real bonding going on.

"I've got a great lead for us. The perp lives in Charlottesville. He's got a 979 exchange. Take a look at my print out. See how most of this is a subdivision built by, who are they? Ah..."

"Yeah Ed, that is the Rivanna subdivision." Princey filled in the blank for him.

"Righto. There's this little section there that is still a bit rural. Some low-rent type places there, some old places as well - homes that rich people used to live in, correct?"

"Correct." Princey nodded in agreement. "They still dust off some of those old places for Virginia Garden Week each

April." His wife loved Garden Week, so Princey had attended some flowery event every year that Rosslyn did, carting her car-full bundle of plants to their large SUV and then driving them home. She had not missed a year yet.

Ed's quizzical expression showed that he wasn't married to a Southern lady, and had not a clue what Garden Week was. Ed decided to keep Garden Week a mystery and turned back to the matter at hand. "Okay, so now I'm thinking that he'd hang his hat either with the local trash or maybe up in one of those old rich homes. Are you game?"

"Let's go. I'll grab the ..." Princey was unceremoniously cut off by the Chief.

"Okay detectives, do you think that you can put the brakes on this chit-chat. I've got a near-hysterical mayor screaming for policemen out on the street, not sitting in their offices." Chief Townsend was on a roll, rolling all over them. Without waiting for an answer, he moved on.

"We were just on our way out. Weren't we? Detective Kravitz." Princey said to the Chief's backside.

Chief Townsend snarled at the next group sitting behind their desks as he moved on down the hall.

"Yep, we sure were." Kravitz grabbed his jacket. They both maneuvered their Dominican buddies around to their backs. It made it a bit difficult to walk out of the area, but walking side-ways, like a crab, seemed to fit in with the pandemonium.

"So how about we take my buggy?" Kravitz loved to show off his big muscle car.

"Yeah, now I really can relive my high school days!" Princey shoved all six foot, six inches with ease into the big orange beast. They drove away with cigar smoke trailing out from both windows.

Darkness now ruled the city. The only lights they saw were from other cars' headlights. Princey reached over and turned on the radio to get a take on what had happened and what was happening now. Ed drove with no concern. His mood matched his car's looks, tough and powerful. He was basking in the certainty that they would find Jennifer. He and his good buddy, Princey, would solve the case, save the girl, and get the stain. It was as easy as one, two, three for him. At least it should have been that easy.

Libby picked me up 45 minutes later. Most days, it would have only taken ten minutes. But the streets were clogged with downed trees, power lines and abandoned cars. I heard her at my door. I embraced her without even saying hello. My nerves were stretched thin and my disappointment in not finding Jennifer clouded my thoughts and ruled my emotions. I had too many thoughts weighing me down, so much so that it was making me tired.

"Are you okay?" Libby seemed to look through me.

"Sure. You?" I avoided telling her how confused I felt.

"Almost as good as new!" She touched the small bandage that was still on her forehead and smiled.

Then I saw it, Libby was high on a conversation that she must have had with a man, as the smell of female pheromones filled my room.

"I just need to get my purse and then I am all set." I walked back to the sofa, shining the light to find it when I noticed a strange wire sticking out from my favorite lamp that had taken a tumble during the earthquake. "Hey Libby, look at this. What is that?" I cocked my head and bent closer to get a better look.

Libby got out her huge flashlight that hung down from her belt and squatted down next to it. She eyed the wire coming from a bug that had come loose when it fell. She motioned for me to be quiet, as she pulled the bug out. She told me telepathically, "You are buggy sister dear. This probably isn't the only one."

I nodded my head in agreement and motioned for us to leave. My artist's loft was no longer a private place for me to be. I felt violated as though I was a skeleton in an anatomy class waiting to be picked apart. I wondered if there were any statutes that would have made these bugs permissible, maybe the Patriot Act? But no, I was not a terrorist in anyone's imagination, so I decided that this was not legal. But why? Who would it be? It had to be someone with ambition, good contacts, expensive equipment and what? Oh, it surely could be Special Agent Hannigan. That thought pleased me the most as he was the slickest of the slick, from what I observed of him at Quantico. He certainly would have the wherewithal to make this happen. Maybe he did this as part of my security check; unlikely, I decided. We closed my door and went out to the gloomy hallway.

I heard a door whoosh open, candlelight spilled out into the darkness. It was my neighbor, Sam, a very talented artist that had acclaim, and a bevy of rich ladies that seemed to follow him about like a puppies looking for a scratch behind their ears. "Hey Tess, everything okay?" He stood partially outside his doorway.

"Yes, I am fine, the apartment is intact. How about you? Your paintings are still hanging, no damage?"

Sam's eyes found Libby. She stood just behind me. "They sure are. I wish, though, the quake had shaken up some more buyers for me. How about you?" He asked as he pointed to Libby. Sam turned back to me. His red hair was glistening in the candle light. I wondered if Libby could make out his blue eyes. I was sure that she saw he had one of what I called a yoga body. Those were the mythical creatures that had supple muscles, not one ounce of fat, flexibility that was impossible for me to conceive of, and perfect posture. "Are you bringing protection where you go now, or possibly a buyer for me?" He noticed her uniform. Libby gave him a big smile. Sam felt encouraged. "I know what, she's really a mail-order-bride for my birthday present. Right, Tess?" He winked.

I looked at his big nose and decided again that without that nose he would be just another pretty boy. "Sam, this is my baby sister, Libby. She doesn't collect art, she works for the city's protection, not mine, but I think that you are on to something with the mail-order bride. I would trade her for that mermaid and koi painting of yours. I love that one! What do you say? Sounds good to you?"

Sam nodded and made a move towards Libby. Even in the dark, I could feel her blush.

"Here she is then," I pronounced, "she won't eat leftovers and she snores. Other than that, she is a lot of trouble. Oops, I mean fun. Happy Birthday!" We all stood laughing in the shadowy hallway.

Handsome Sam opened his door wider. I could see the soft glow of many candles lighting his loft. "Would you two like to come in for a visit? I could show you the mermaid painting Libby, let you see what Tess is trading you for."

I could feel her reaction towards Sam was hesitant. She was not flirting as much as she usually would have with such a handsome man. I sighed. She really did like this new guy, whoever he was.

"Thanks Sam. I would love to see the mermaid, but another time? I can feel my boss fuming over not having everyone at the station right now. I gotta go there." She gave him a half smile.

"Rain check?" I offered.

"No doubt. I look forward to it, ladies." He replied.

Libby shone her flashlight back into the dark hall, as Sam closed his door. He changed his mind and swung it wide open to give one last message. "Tess, I almost forgot. What is the name of that electrician that you had over last week? I desperately need a good electrician to help me with an installation."

An electrician? I didn't have an electrician over. Libby heard my thoughts and injected hers. Sam must have seen the man that bugged my apartment. I fumbled, not sure what to say.

"Wasn't that one of your students?" Libby was thinking like a detective. Now I could get a description out of Sam without telling him about the intruder.

"Yes, let me see, I can't quite remember. Do you recall what he looked like?" I asked him as I tilted my head to one side.

"He was a brunette, average height and weight, that probably sounds like all of your male students!" He chuckled at himself and continued, "Ah, he wore a light blue jacket and a red baseball cap. I recall thinking that the jacket and the cap didn't look good together, Funny how I can pick up on that memory but not much else. Oh wait, he had on a wedding ring. That should help, not too many of your students are married, are they? The guy was in his early thirties. That's about it."

"Oh yes," I lied, "I remember now, that was Paul Keith. And actually, I wouldn't recommend him. He left one thing undone and didn't tell me about it. His bill was a bit high too." I hoped that this would end Sam's desire. "See you later Sam."

"Till then." Sam closed his door as we went down the dark stairway alone.

Libby was quick to comment, "Before you go back to your little nest you need to make a plan about your bugs. We can either exterminate the bugs or trap them. I think that we should check with Detective Kravitz on what to do."

"Do you really think that we need to?" I didn't want to be a bother to Ed.

"Or, we could check with my new friend whom I just had a

nice little connection with. This would give me the perfect reason to call him back."

I could feel Libby blushing again in the dark. "Know what I mean? Anyway, he is a federal agent who might be more qualified about bugs than Detective Kravitz. It's Special Agent Stefan Hannigan. I've got his number and I could call him right now?" Her contentment was now bordering on elation. She seemed to swell up and rise like a helium ballon at a kid's birthday party.

Before I could stop myself, I blurted out, "Libby you might have his phone number but I don't think that you have his number at all."

"What do you mean? He probably knows all about these kind of things. I would have to guess at the equipment, who might have access to it, just about all of it. I am sure that Stefan has studied this. He could really help and I know that he would be happy to help me." She said the last quite confidently.

I was at a loss for words. I knew that this would be a hard-won argument that would be taking place in the dark, during a panicked time. This would only exacerbate both our opposite views on Hannigan. We'd pull at them like taffy and when it split, tears would be inevitable.

"You have been fooled by a very smart guy. I know that you won't believe me now or even want to hear any of this, but I am going to tell you."

"Listen," Libby pulled on the sleeve of my brown tweed jacket and spoke through gritted teeth. "I know that he is okay. I have no doubts. Come on, this guy is sending me off into another world and I am enjoying it very much. I know that you can feel that. What, are you jealous because you don't have anyone?" She was glaring and fuming like a storybook dragon.

Standing in an unlit hall, a dark shadow was my only visible vestige but I stretched myself as tall as I could be, cleared my throat and then took one deep breath. "I do not know precisely what it is with Special Agent Hannigan, but I am certain that something is wrong, probably very wrong. He may have had my apartment bugged. I don't think it would be appropriate to ask him for help. I don't want him around us at all. And I don't want you around him either."

I started for the car while Libby put her sparring gloves on. "You're kidding, right?"

I repeated my stance. "I do not want you anywhere near him. He is dangerous and dark inside. Even I have an almost impossible time reading him. He is very adept at putting out his intention so that you just see what he wants you to see as he hides the rest."

Libby cut in, "You are just getting paranoid. I understand, you having to relive your childhood monster would wake up all of your nightmares, but you're wrong about him. You are making him sound like some kind of mythical Svengali. I promise that I will look up both sleeves." Libby hung her stupid smile across her face again.

I erupted, "You must be sexually starved! You are not willing to listen to me at all, are you?" Both of my gloves were off now.

"I am sure that he is fine. Really." Then Libby gave me one of those looks like I was one of the stupidest people on earth.

"Okay little sister, I was going to be a bit nicer when I told you this but you have boxed me into a corner." I paused to see if she would listen. Libby put her car keys back into her pocket and turned to face me. "Special Agent Hannigan blew out your tire with a dart. I know that it was him because he left the same arrogance and calculating self-righteousness all over your tire that he spews about everywhere, and then he hides his identity and intentions with this blank screen thing of his. He is damn good at it too. It's his signature."

"Get in." Libby growled before turning on the engine and jumping into the fray. We drove through the crowded streets until Libby lost it. She pulled her newly returned Toyota 4 Runner up on the sidewalk and took off like it was a median strip. Her headlights bounced erratically on downed bicycles and cracked sidewalks. Libby was unwilling to be Hannigan's next patsy, victim, or anything that wasn't fitting with the idea of girlfriend. She cursed me with enthusiasm all the way. I mentally cursed him. Somehow we made it to the station in one piece. She would definitely need a front-end alignment, and possibly, no, most definitely, a good guzzling from a bottle of tequila. But she was on duty, so she got out sober, slammed the door, still throwing insults my way, left me shaken in a car that had been turned into a war horse by my very angry baby sister.

Chapter Nineteen

"Why? Why must you do this to me?" Louis began to cry again as he shoved his now mud-covered cell phone in his pocket. He was so exhausted. He was not satisfied with his life. Louis looked around and squinted hard. He saw that the neighbor's lights were out as well as his own. He rubbed his eyes and looked again. He was nervously picking at the bottom edge of his shirt. He would roll it in a tight circle for a few inches and then he'd let it go. Up and down, tight and then loose. He used this as a meditation to calm his mind. Once he felt stable he stopped and confronted his problem. The bitch was more powerful than he imagined. He saw now that the little bitch put out his lights, the neighbors lights, all the lights around. He stood on his own lawn and was afraid to touch his own door. Louis rubbed his head, thinking of the pain that he had endured from her. It hurt him to look at his house. He could not believe that the bitch had him outside! He furrowed his brow and gazed at the half moon.

Louis was indecisive. He was left without his normal toys as they were inside his forbidden castle. He had no gun, no knife, only sharp rocks that he threw at his own fortress. And now that he had tasted his Julio, he had no one left to talk to; he was not even able to reach his fan club at torture. com. Disgusted, he howled and swore.

Louis ripped up clumps of the cool grass and touched them to his temple. The dirt felt good. It helped ease his mounting frustration. He lectured himself that he just needed to come up with a new plan, that should be easy, he reasoned. After all, he was a very smart man, a genius actually. He thought of all his toys locked away and then thought of his doll. A calm settled over him. He realized that he always got to play with his dolls. He had a delicious one inside. She was new and unused. He would be able to amuse himself with her again. Louis held onto that thought and gleefully plotted into the night.

Chapter Twenty

"No, turn there, right there by the mail box." Princey was getting tired of giving directions to someone who wasn't willing to take them. "Would you just put me out of my misery and turn right!"

"Okay, okay but I think that it would be quicker for me to go down to Chestnut and turn there," Kravitz was pushy but Princey could push back.

"I have lived here all of my life, each damn minute of it, and I tell you that if you turn on Chestnut we'll end up in a dead end. That street don't go through." Princey was now tapping his cigar on his knee. "Ed, I will get us there."

Kravitz relented and took a right at the mail box. The Trans Am crawled its way up the hill.

"You know, this used to be quite a wealthy part of the city a very long time ago. You had the university president, a gaggle of lawyers, a handful of the finer merchants, and of course, the politicians had their homes here. There are some beautiful examples of Federal style homes. I think that two of the plantation owners had their city homes on the hill too. Quite a nice view of the river from up here. Don't you think so?" Princey asked a very bored Ed.

"Yeah, not bad." Kravitz wished that he could turn off Princey's unasked-for tour of Charlottesville. He popped in a CD, arming himself with the magic of Motown. When Marvin Gaye began singing "I Heard It Through The Grapevine," they were both keeping time to the music. The high from the hunt made every sensation burn bright.

"So what do you think, should we just drive around and look first up here, or do we go down to Carlton and start there?" Kravitz was now in a much better mood.

"We're already up here so let's start here. It is pretty much a big circle with a couple of streets off the main road. I think that I see Steep Hill Street coming up." Princey motioned toward the first spoke of their wheel. There was an old greenhouse on the left side of the road and on the right, a bit further up stood a dilapidated mansion. It could have been a Hollywood set as it looked perfectly spooky in the moonlight.

Both men got out of the safety of the Trans Am. Marvin Gaye seemed a universe away now. "Hey Eddie, you got a flash-light that works?"

"Let me check." He turned the light on and the beam was steady. "Yep, we gotta torch. How about we go to that Herman Munster type place first?"

They walked over to the old building and poked around the bushes and then shone the light inside. Kravitz opened the front door. Nothing in there or in the greenhouse. They went back to the car and made their way to another creepy, unlit street.

"So Eddie, how's your mom doing these days? Has she settled in yet?" Princey had a strong urge to make some small talk and get his mind out of the Stephen King novel scenarios that were now playing non-stop in high-def.

"She's okay. She's visiting her sister in Queens right now. I'm glad that she wasn't here for the big shake up."

"Yeah, I know what you mean. It's hard to get these women to calm down after experiencing something like that. My grandpa used to say that women suffered from 'an attack of the vapors.' I never really understood what he meant at first, but after being married for twenty-three years, I believe that I know exactly what he meant."

"I bet you do! How is Rosslyn doing? Is she keeping busy with the boys?" Ed politely inquired, attempting to avoid saying anything adverse about his partner's wife.

Princey was happy for the inane banter. He was just about to answer when he noticed a commotion a bit further up the street. It was a downed power line. A group of people had gathered and were putting up some kind of barrier so that no one would touch the downed line. Ed and Princey headed directly for it. Kravitz kept the headlights on as they stopped the car and got out.

"Charlottesville PD," Kravitz informed the crowd.

"What's going on here?" Princey asked a man that seemed to be the head of the group.

The helpful citizen seemed on edge. He had an aggressive stance that Kravitz noticed as soon as he was standing on the cooling asphalt. "The power line is down and we can't reach anybody to let them know. So no electricity, no help, no phone line and the cell phone only gets a busy signal. Can you help us or are you too damn busy with something else? Someone could die if they touched this. But our deaths don't seem to matter up here cause no one will come up here to do anything!" The resident was getting too surly for Kravitz's liking.

"Yes. You are right to be worried about that line. Thanks for keeping everyone far away from it." Princey was always the diplomat. "We will let the power company know that you need someone up here right away." His tones were even and pleasant. It had the desired soothing effect that Kravitz wished he could possess.

Ed decided to take advantage of the group of people and bellowed out, "Does anyone know of anyone that doesn't seem right up here on the hill? Maybe some guy that lives alone and seems standoffish, kind of like he hasn't anything to do with you or the neighborhood?" Ed held his breath while this idea circulated amongst the group. Lots of muttering, but no one had anyone to give him.

Ed felt that he knew it would be a waste of time to ask, people are too afraid of others in a situation like that to be open with an authority figure. He was mentally slapping himself for being stupid when an elderly woman approached him. She had on a flowery print dress that she probably made herself and shoes that only an orthopedic surgeon would love. With a soft accent that placed her from central Virginia, she commanded Princey's attention and left Ed feeling that he had just possibly met the oldest living member of the Charlottesville Garden Week Committee.

"Mister policeman, I have a cousin that lives on Riverside Avenue, Mrs. Antoinette Timon, and she has a very odd man that lives there. He sells used cars, and you know what type of riff-raff does that. All the used cars aren't really right, are they? So if one does that for his livelihood, well I declare! Almost no saying what else the likes of him might do. I am Laurabell Custis and I know from what I speak!" Laurabell then snorted a tiny snort and huffed away with her chin held high. No good-byes were given.

"She sure has gumption! Got to hand it to her." Princey said to Kravitz as they got back into the Trans Am.

"So was that what you'd call a Southern Storm Trooper?"

Ed cracked a grin. He knew how to yank Princey's chains and took pleasure in this pull.

"I wouldn't write her off so easily. The way things go down in a southern town, which Charlottesville is really just a small town that got a bit too big, the gray-haired ladies know it all. They have their powdered noses in everyone's affairs. God bless her, she might have given us a real clue." Princey's conviction was built on being raised by, and married to, strong-willed Southern women that had hot tabasco sauce coursing through their veins.

"Yeah, could be. I know my ma would definitely agree with that!"

They went on to the next street, talking about the old lady and wishing that life could be that simple. Just pick the rotten profession and you could find the rotten apple. Sure would make detecting criminals a snap.

Often the truth *was* that simple.

Libby was not willing to let go of Hannigan yet. I believed that he was rotten to the core and she did not. Presently, we were at a stalemate. I sat in her SUV waiting for clarity, or at least a sense of emotional control. Things would not go well between us until I could find my sense of calm. I pensively sat and got lost in the dull twinkle of the generator-powered lights. I was comforted seeing the illumination as it cut through the dark, beckoning me to go inside. I grabbed the bit of peace that I had formed and wrapped it around me and stepped out into the night.

The station was filled to the brim with questioning and demanding citizenry. The cacophony was deafening. I looked for Libby, soon forgetting our differences now that the hysteria was palpable. I saw her golden blond head in the sea of neutral colors.

"Ah, huh. " Libby said to John Brown dismissively and then moved on.

John Brown was a regular. He had come in hoping to get the skinny on what was happening. John liked to come in every few weeks and confess to whatever alarming crime had occurred in the city or anywhere nearby. He enticed the officers by bringing chocolate, glazed, and jam-filled donuts, along with a hefty jug of fresh-brewed coffee. Sometimes he brought the more expensive caramel-covered coffee cakes. Spudnuts, the local coffee shop and meeting place for much of the neighborhood gossip, appreciated John Brown's civic- mindedness in keeping the local constabulary well fed. The detectives schedules, his favorite ones, determined the timing of his stops. The detectives put up with his stories, as long as they were brief. John always felt so much better after confessing. But today, Libby had no news to give him nor time to waste.

Chief Townsend was calling out for the Head of Operations. It seemed that all the officers, detectives and support staff were there. The Department Communications Center was overwhelmed with calls from the folk that were lucky enough to still have a connection. The Desk Sergeant had been pulled in to help with the bombardment of calls. The Watch Commander motioned Libby over, away from John. A group of officers were heading towards the Patrol Officer Roll Call and Briefing Room. He wanted her to be included. She reluctantly grabbed my arm and pulled me into the room with her. No one seemed to care that I stood next to her.

All eyes were on the Commander of Operations. A flow chart had quickly been made and was hanging in the front of the room, covering up the photos of the top ten most wanted list. The thin blue line had a new priority now. The room became hushed as the Commander raised his hand. "I am glad to see all of you present. Shortly we will be going over the emergency assignments but first Officer Landis will be briefing you on the earthquake so that you can correctly inform the public when they question today's event. Officer Landis." The Commander moved to the side.

Joe Landis had been in charge of Community Relations for the last twelve years. He was well known by the press and was liked by just about everyone that he met. As he briefed the room, I noticed that his right elbow seemed stiff and then I picked up from him that the had slammed into his stone fireplace and whacked his elbow during the quake. As my attention wandered around the room I could feel that several others were a bit bruised and many of them were shaken up. I noticed that Detective Kravitz and his partner were absent.

"Hey Libby, I don't see Detective Kravitz, do you?"

She said nothing back to my telepathic message. This was one of the most infuriating aspects of our relationship. Whenever Libby had the slightest upset with me, she would mentally cut me off. The door closed. I nudged her and she barely looked over at me. "I don't see Kravitz, do you?" I asked her with my voice.

Libby slowly looked at all of the faces crowding the room. "Nope, not here. He might be at home or..." she paused and then looked around the room another time. "I don't see Princey, Detective Noble, anywhere either and those two are always together. So they must be out and about. They probably cut loose before we were rounded up."

I nodded in agreement. I knew that Detective Kravitz was a bit of a rogue. I knew that he wasn't above lying to get what he wanted, as he sent away the helicopter pilot so that he would be the one to drive me home from Quantico. He didn't know that I knew that fact. And I knew that he really had not one iota of an idea of what being around me was like. But I had gotten a few of his thoughts in pictures, so I saw how he did see me. I am quite certain that if he knew that, he would run the other way. No man wants to know that a woman that he is sexually interested in has that ability. Actually I concluded years ago that it was a decided liability. But I liked him and I trusted him, sensual pictures and all.

Only a handful of officers had been left with their usual assignments. The basic structure of headquarters had to remain in place but many were shuttled to traffic control, communications, general patrol and the new special category, Quake Command Support. The new group would be stationed in the Watch Commander's room and was the Chiefs and the Commander of Operations most critical team. At long last, Libby's name was called.

"Officer MacGregor, you are to stay with the investigation into Carl Brown's murder, along with Detective Kravitz. Detective Noble will head up that team. And as long as I am on that subject, Officer Jefferson you will continue to be the admin support for them."

So, the hell list would continue, earthquake or not, I thought. Now it was decided that we would continue to work together, at least I hoped that Libby would let me stay. I had to get her to drop the wall that was between us. Angeline came over to where we were. She seemed brighter than most of the other officers. "Well, did he call you?" She asked as she raised her thick eyebrow. It was a very small gesture that was packed with a tacit understanding between them. Angeline noticed that I was standing behind Libby. "Sorry Tess, I didn't see you there. Glad to see that you're okay."

I smiled in response and concluded that Hannigan must have called the station and gotten Libby's number from Angeline.

"He called me but I am thinking now that maybe Special Agent Hannigan isn't as good as he looks." Libby continued unfurling her new thoughts, "I mean, what would a guy like that want with a lowly officer like me. He has professional altitude, I am sure some fancy degrees, and it would appear, he must be independently wealthy. I don't think we'd mix well." I could feel the wall melting away.

"I can think of several reasons why he's interested in you. None of them have anything to do with what school you went to, or how much cash you have in your bank account." Angeline 's broad smile and sparkling eyes-of-mischief were infectious most of the time. But this time I looked at the floor and not into her beaming chestnut-colored face. She inched closer to me, "Did you get a look at that man? Now that is a fine specimen of masculinity. He looks like a Greek statue, dresses fine and he smells so good. And we all have to come from something. So he's from money, did you see the car that he drives? It's a new Corvette! Lord help me, I am married." She laughed. It seemed to stir up the depression that penetrated Libby's countenance.

"Yeah, that may all be true but it still stands that he is a federal agent and I am a lowly police officer. We don't mix! We don't hang out together, we don't even go to the same dry cleaners. So what does that guy want with me?" I could tell that she was sincere by this observation, it was no longer something that I had to make her agree with, she saw the contrariness of it herself. "Guys like him date prosecutors, models, or better yet, judges. He goes after well-educated women that support themselves in high cotton. Not someone like me that has a reckless side and whose biggest monthly expense is a mid-priced SUV." Libby dropped her shoulders and that told me that she was resigned to this reality.

Angeline decided that her best friend had made up her mind about the catch of the year and she was determined to trash this guy, just like all the others. "Okay girl, I don't know if you ought to throw this one overboard quite so fast, but I can see that you are." Angeline was perturbed and felt that she had hit her own brick wall with Libby once again. It was time to let it go. Anger would not change a thing.

The room cleared out. We made our way back to the hallway. I thought about Jennifer. The melee affected my connection to her and I was desperate to reconnect. "I need to collect my thoughts. Is there a room that I can go to and be alone?" I asked.

"Usually I would say yes but it seems pretty packed in here now." Libby replied as she looked around.

"Tess," Angeline pointed over towards a closed door. "You could use Detective Kravitz's desk. Both he and Detective Noble are out, so their office is empty."

"Thank you Angeline." I was relieved to find a spot.

As we passed the Information Desk I heard a smallish man excitedly say that the mill had fallen down on the party rats, or at least that is what I thought he said. It seemed odd to me that the Desk Sergeant wasn't too excited over the man's news. He seemed bored to me. The sergeant looked away, over the little man's balding head. "Okay John, I'll pass it on to Detective Howes. But you can surely see that we have our hands full." He motioned him away. John Brown dejectedly trudged through the crowd, reached the door, and left without another word.

"That's odd." I said aloud.

"What's odd Tess?" Angeline asked.

"A man just told the Desk Sergeant that an old mill fell on some group of people, or maybe he meant a person, and the Sergeant did not seem to believe him. What is even stranger is the man seemed as though he was accustomed to not being believed. How odd!"

"Was he a short man, receding hair line?" Angeline asked. By this time Libby was listening to our conversation.

"Yes, he was. Seemed lonely too and a bit lost, "I added.

"Oh" Libby exclaimed. She knew exactly why he was treated like that and who he was."You've now seen our semi-weekly confessor, Mr John Brown. Most often he comes with treats for the officers who listen to his bogus confessions."

I like his coffee cakes the best." Angeline was most certain about the cake.

"I love the jam donuts!" Libby countered. "I wish that he would pick me to confess to and then I could be assured of getting a donut each time and I wouldn't have to root through the leftovers. But I guess that it's better for your hips that he doesn't?" Libby poked her left hip and Angeline laughed.

Libby rolled on, "I dunno partner, looks like its too late for you to be worrying about the size of your hips. I'd throw caution to the wind cos what do you have to lose, huh? Chow down one or maybe all of the donuts he brings." Libby snorted and smirked, being in a somewhat jovial mood again.

"Now you are just being nasty. Where did you get such a mean sister? She's gettin' on my last nerve!"

They were still enjoying their conversation as I opened the door and went into the quiet office.

Far away and under a massive amount of debris, the girls struggled for each breath. Tish and Marissa were dead and Gloria was near to it. The gash in Gloria's shoulder and in her back were bleeding out fast. Jinx could feel that at least one leg was broken. Once she felt that pain, she began to sweat and noticed that she couldn't feel the other leg at all. Jinx was precariously wedged between the first floor and the basement. If the building shifted anymore she would fall through to her doom. It took all of her strength to hang onto the floorboards. Quietly, Jinx called out to the others. There was no response at first. Then the eerie silence was broken by Sophie. She heard Sophie moaning about ten feet ahead of her. Sophie had been the closest to freedom when the mill came tumbling down. In her last attempt to make it outside, she lunged for the window. Part of her right arm and hand made it to freedom through the small opening. That was as far as she got. A large beam had landed partially on top of her. She was resolved not to die and held on.

John Brown decided to go back to the mill. Everyone at the station was so busy. He walked all the way to the mill to hold Sophie's hand again and tell her that he was sorry. He was sorry that no one believed him. He was sorry that he had cried wolf so many times. He knew that he would never be believed again. But this time there was a real wolf and this time he really saw it.

Chapter Twenty-One

"You know, there is no smoking in here," the tall lanky man said to the woman standing next to him. That is when he noticed that he was looking at her eye to eye and that bothered him. Agent Sexton gave him one of her extraordinarily cute smiles and said, "Ralph, you know that I do not smoke. If anyone smokes in the agency anymore it is the old guard, haven't you noticed that?"

He was a member of the old guard - meaning he was over 50 years old, he grew up on classic rock, and didn't consider it oldie music, just the only rock and roll there ever was, and at one point, most of the old guards smoked back in the day, and at least half of them still did, including him. "This is very expensive equipment that I am in charge of." Ralph was now pointing at the wall of technology to make his point, "It is vital that this not be exposed to smoke. It is my responsibility to inform anyone that enters this room of that fact and not prejudge whether they smoke or not." He turned away and stood in front of the optic scanner. The door whooshed open.

Rows of confidential digital information was stored there. The lights were bright but not harsh. True sunlight bulbs had been used to lessen the glare on the computer screens. Although there was a row of computers set up, there was no internet access. Among other secrets, this room contained the personal information of all of the FBI agents and employees, including the director himself. It was a pristine room with whirring machines, and the meanest old guard dog, Ralph.

He was quite proud that there was not a speck of dust in the room and eyed Agent Sexton's red high heels as she entered his domain, afraid that they would mark up the shiny white floor. Colleen Sexton walked over to the terminal. He shook his head slightly in dismay as she passed by him. Ralph was 58 years old and still could not accept the fact that women were agents.

Colleen found what she was looking for. She had searched the files for C.A.R.D. Agents whose surname began with H. There he was, Stefan Hannigan. Special Agent Hannigan, she read, must have made one of his superiors a bit anxious about his job as there was a review about him that read like a dressing down. Seems that he probably made the guy feel as though Hannigan was after his job. This may not be so unusual in the corporate world - the fact that you had to be looking over your shoulder to see who was coming up behind you and see if they could step into your shoes - but the agency worked differently. At least on the surface it did. Agents were expected to walk the agreed upon path, with no pushing or shoving allowed.

Hannigan was known to be brilliant early on, but recently, he had said some things that went beyond ordinary brilliance. He seemed to know a bit more about certain cases than his security clearance gave him access to and his boss noticed. This meant that we was solving more cases than what was expected with knowledge that was not his to have. Af first, his Supervisory Special Agent, enjoyed taking the credit for the excellent handling of the cases that were also done so expediently. Then the tide turned, and he heard that his wonder boy was now bragging about himself to his peers. He should have been bragging about his boss, thought Colleen. Now Stefan's boss had pulled a few strings to get Hannigan's ass thoroughly examined for a potential security outness. Either way this would go, guilty or not, his meteoric rise was over.

Agent Sexton sat on the cold metal stool and read his dossier. Let's see, Stefan Hannigan, born in Connecticut, he's now 42 years old, she calculated, unmarried, odd for someone with his looks and ambition. His parents are Polly and James Hannigan. He went to Princeton University, graduated with honors. Oh, he played lacrosse - a rich boy sport she noted. She continued to read his file, noting all the trappings of a stereotypical, entitled, shamefully wealthy child's lifestyle. His father was a successful entertainment lawyer for a mammoth recording company in L.A. but he managed to stay in the city, New York, to do most of his work. His mother, Polly, was a socialite that contributed her time to various charities, mostly ones that got money for the MOMA and the MET. They had a girl too, Penelope. Stefan went to boarding school when he was eleven years old. It seemed that his sister stayed at home. She thought that was a bit unusual, younger boy out, older girl stays. She wondered if he had done something that got him shoved out of the nest. Reading further, she realized that he never lived at home again. The rest of that report read like he was an Eagle Scout. She looked at another section to see what his neighbors and friends had to say about him. The neighbors had nothing bad to say about Polly and James's boy. That was to be expected, she thought. Then she scanned down to see about his friends. As she read their remarks, although they were positive, something seemed off with all three statements. "Wow, all of these friends used the same adjectives to describe him."

"Huh?" Ralph said. "Are you talking to me Agent Sexton?" He had a very perplexed look.

"No, sorry, I didn't realize that I had said something aloud." She came out of her detective world for a second.

"Right." Ralph was content that he did not have to make conversation with this woman.

Colleen stuck her nose back into the report, focusing on a select group of adjectives. No one uses the exact same adjectives to describe a person. They were all interviewed separately, not together. This was done so that one person would not just go along with what the more dominant personality would have used as a description. Although they were scattered in the statements from his friends, she noted the adjectives were all alike - they were parroting each other. Colleen paused and began to play with the gold cross that hung on her necklace. The words seemed to now float a bit off the screen. She mentally saw the FBI shield and wreath with their motto below - Fidelity, Bravery, Integrity. Damn him, he must have been laughing all the way to the academy at Quantico! No one picked up on this? She knew that these supposed friends must have been coached by Stefan. The reports from the three young men all used the words fidelity, bravery and integrity to describe Stefan Hannigan, certainly the most cunning and shrewd imposter that she had ever investigated. She took her eyes off of the screen, and looked over her shoulders, as she straightened her posture on the uncomfortable stool.

Agent Sexton began tapping her long, polished fingernail on her lower teeth. She wondered who he really was and what was he hiding. "Interesting. It would seem that the perfect Agent Hannigan might have a flaw after all," she announced to the clean white walls. Colleen then stood up and purposefully walked over to the steel door with her three-inch red heels clicking in the empty room. She did not make a single mark on the glistening white floor.

Chapter Twenty-Two

Libby sat down next to me. It was fairly quiet at Kravitz's desk. Angeline went back to her computer to see if there was any more information about the white Cadillac. I could see that we were now in agreement about the not-so-Special Agent Hannigan. I put my elbow on the messy desk and rested my chin in my hand and looked at Libby. She looked back and gave me half a smile.

"You must admit that he is pretty to look at." Libby crossed her legs and got more comfortable in Princey's chair.

I collected my thoughts. "He is handsome, educated, well-dressed, rich and possibly one of the most arrogant and vain men alive. At first I attributed that trait to living a life of privilege, but that wasn't the whole story. His arrogance is the mark that he leaves on every thought, every intention that he possess. It's his tell. At first I thought he was just being self-assured. But no, it went much deeper than that. He is certain that whatever decision he makes is completely the right one. If you don't agree, you are most certainly wrong. Most people like this I find boring but with him it acts like someone throwing a dagger at your back as you are walking away. Kind of hard to ignore that." I shrugged my shoulders and went on. "He ties each of his observations in a neat little bow, with that idea. Once I saw that, it was easier to spot his touch on objects, no matter how he tried to hide it. And I can see that he hides himself from others all of the time, it's like a game for him. Kind of like an adult hide and seek, except he is certain that you won't find him. Very manipulative."

"Bless my stars," Libby whispered as she touched her temple. "How stupid! How could I be that stupid."

My hand reached out to hers. "Don't be so hard on yourself. He is one of the most shrewd game players that I have ever met. When Detective Kravitz and I were in the impound lot I touched the hole in your tire and felt that a dart had made it. I could feel that there was a dark covering surrounding it. It was as though a cloak had mentally been thrown around the physical hole to hide it."

Libby nodded. Once the curtain was opened you couldn't help but see the truth.

"I have never perceived anything like that Libby. It shook me up. I didn't tell Kravitz that I was so upset. But I did tell him about the incident, that a man had removed the dart in your tire and was about to open your door, and then he took off. I am sure it is because he saw that I would pull up behind you. So now the question is, why did Hannigan shoot your tire out? And why did he bug my apartment? Do you think that he is trying to cook something up so he can pretend to solve it? Maybe he's going for a promotion? I know he's competitive, I saw that when I first met him." I let go of her hand and looked at the high-tech watch that I wore to keep notice of the minutes that flew by.

"Tessie, are you sure it was Hannigan with the bugs? Maybe it's the monster. Maybe he wants to know more about you now that he knows you are on the case." Libby's voice had gotten lower with the mention of the monster.

I never knew the monster's name so to us he would always

be the monster. Speaking about him with my little sister took me back to the time that it happened. I felt ten years old whenever I recalled it. It was like falling through a crack in time. Mysteriously, I would slide back to all of the ancient feelings, decisions and hopes that I had when I was with him. I tried not to slip, ever.

"Libby, if the monster wanted to know what I was doing, he could probably come and get me. That's the way he works, head on. I don't think it's him. Definitely not him. I would know. Wouldn't I?"

Her deep sigh filled the room.

I got off the mysterious speculations, and concerned myself again with the little girl. "I need to try to reconnect with Jennifer. I was in touch with her for quite a while. We were trying to find anything that could tell me where she is, then earthquake happened and I lost her. I have to find her as she is liable to do something she shouldn't. She has gotten in touch with so many of her abilities that she thinks she can outsmart him. Jennifer wanted to let him back in the house after being able to keep him outside. She decided that she could mentally best him and prevent him from physically hurting her. That she could will him into inaction. I know that is unrealistic. His pleasure includes controlling others by giving them false hopes and then stomping on them, but yet..." I hesitated to go on, maybe I was just putting my own failures on Jennifer. I reconsidered and looked at just the facts about it. "She was controlling him with pain I think, possibly a very bad migraine. I didn't even know that it was possible to do such a thing. Did you?"

"No Tess, no." She appeared to be as worried as I was now that Jennifer might let him inside.

I looked towards the door and heard footsteps coming fast and then veer away. "So the most evil monster of all is being controlled by a ten year old girl and I can't even find out where they are. I am afraid that I won't be able to stop this, that it is going to happen all over again. A dead child, a lost cause." I applied an old trick and pinched my nose to hold back tears.

My sister leaned closer. "No, you are not ten again, and we will find her. This is not then, and besides, the armor of guilt that you wear hurts no one but yourself, so drop the shield down, will you? I am here with you."

A small tear went down my check with her words.

I had determined after being kidnapped and made to tell the horrific story many times, that it was a natural reaction for the majority of people to recoil from evil. A few, I could tell, reveled in it. They disgusted me and it became easy for me to recognize them as his brethren. But most others wanted to get as far away from evil as possible. People might think that they wanted to know about the forced sex, the death threats he made daily to me, his tortures and my pain, but if I told them any true bit of it, they would emotionally shut down. I could feel it. And after too many years of berating myself about not finding the monster with my abilities, and not saving the other girls from him, and their early deaths, I faced my truth - I really didn't want to find him. I really didn't want to relive it again. And when I saw that, I was finally able to let go of most of the pain and guilt that went with it. It was permissible to not know something. Some things I just didn't want to know about, or see, or find, as they might be finding me back. But this evil that was staring now at me, I would face head on, no matter the consequences.

"The monster is with Jennifer and I must help her."

"What do you want me to do?" Libby asked.

"I am not sure, I was hoping that Detective Kravitz would be here. I know that he had requested one of his contacts to locate her with his digital skills and that he had given him some information that would help locate her. I thought that with my new knowledge of her being in a dirty, rundown house with tall oak trees and vines entwined on the shutters, he could use that information to find her. But he's not here, he is already on the chase. I am not sure what to do other than try to talk to Jennifer again."

Libby scooted closer to the desk. She began to collect and then stack Detective Kravitz's papers to one side. She moved in front of his computer and turned it on. "While you look for Jennifer your way, I am going to snoop my way."

I closed my eyes and tried to reorient myself to Jennifer's presence. I got a vague sensation of cold. I decided to go with that sensation and see if anything developed. The chill crept into the top of my thighs and seeped down my legs, turning my feet into ice cubes. I shivered. There was only blackness and cold. No thoughts or emotions were present, only emptiness. An involuntary shudder brought me back to Kravitz's desk. I looked over at Libby. She was pulling a paper from the printer and she looked quite pleased with herself.

"What did you get? Could you find her?" Libby asked.

Her words seared into me. "I only felt her coldness. She may be unconscious, possibly asleep?" In secret, I was praying that she wasn't dead.

"Tess, I saw her face, I'm sure it was Jennifer. Detective Kravitz had me go to Officer Carl Brown's crime scene. I saw her face in a pool of blood. I only got that about her, it was just a face. But I thought that she could be gone, dead. Just like you did now."

Her words sat heavy between us.

"I can't think with this." I was torn and pushed my fear away.

"You're right, Tessie. We have to go on as though we can save her. What if Detective Noble had given up on you? He would never have given up and neither will we." The warrior was back.

I nodded my head and brought my chin up, to follow through on whatever plan we would decide to do.

"I've got what Detective Kravitz last printed out and it shows a bunch of locations clustered around a phone exchange. Here, take a look." Libby handed me the papers.

"Do you know these streets? I don't think that I recognize them." I told her.

"Tess, I think that they might be located in an old section of Charlottesville. It's an area that was settled in the early 1800s, but let me get a map and verify it." She went down the hall and quickly returned. "Yep, look," Libby said while pointing at the far eastern edge of the city. "See, the streets are right there. Remember when all those new houses went up on the hill about two years ago? It is above them."

"Rivanna, I think that is what it's called." I gave her back the map. "Do you think that Detective Kravitz and Detective Noble would mind us going there?" I wasn't sure if I really would add to this mix. I had one too many differences of opinions when working on my last terrible murder case, and I did not want the trend to continue. I particularly wanted to keep open my good rapport with Detective Kravitz.

"I am part of their team, remember?" She chided me.

"Of course. But would they want me there?" I asked her.

Libby did not bother to answer. She walked to the door, opened it, and motioned for me to come. I got up with purpose. The noise from the station spilled onto our quiet. It clung thickly to the walls. "You are with me, and so he has got to take you." A twinkle in her eyes let me know that Libby felt something was afoot between the very New York Detective and her southern sister.

. . .

Special Agent Hannigan was having a bad day. He lost his chance with Libby and so he was unable to get the intel that he needed to catch the bad guy before everyone else. No one else was allowed to solve this. Stefan knew that his boss, SSA Ross, was looking to get rid of him. Only saving the Director's daughter would put him back on his expected and deserved, rocket-ride to fame and glory. It was owed to him.

After the quake, Hannigan contacted work and made a flimsy excuse about checking on an emergency gas leak at home. He had an uncomfortable feeling that the world was getting a bit too small for him; something was squeezing his style and he didn't like it.

The city was chaotic. Hannigan expected that chaos would blow through eventually, but now it was at a heightened level. He turned off his cell phone; he was not available.

Stefan concluded that Detective Ed Kravitz could be the stumbling block to reaching his goal. By all rights, he should not even rate a second thought from him, but something just stayed stuck in his mind about the city cop's scuffed shoes, cheap suits and lack of cologne; lack of anything worthwhile. Yet, the continuous apprehension that he felt thinking of Kravitz could not be denied. Stefan decided that Kravitz must be a worthy opponent, or why else would the thought of this man be consuming him?

Stefan, satisfied that his observation was correct, pulled out his comb and made himself look as fabulous as a Versace model. Reaching deep in the front pants pocket he found a small bottle of his favorite Italian cologne, splashing it on either side of his neck made him feel more in control. He made sure that the diamond in his family ring was perfectly centered on his long, muscular hand. And with a trail of smugness oozing from all of his pores he was ready for the next challenge.

Chapter Twenty-Three

"So, Princey, this seems like the last side street we got, don't it?" Kravitz was getting stiff sitting in the car. He was anxious to get out and walk Riverside Avenue, not just park there. The street was one of the oldest in the city. According to historical accounts it had originally been an Indian burial spot and was considered a sacred site by them. The developers did not see it the same way as the Monacan tribe did. Money talked, and so the tribe was reduced to half of an acre with a small monument to acknowledge their claim and history.

The gnarled white oak trees stood silent in rows lining the avenue. They were ancient and hung over like tired soldiers leaning on their rifles. Clouded moonlight was the only illumination in the neighborhood.

Several houses could be seen from the Trans Am. The closest, were the more modest homes that were similar to those they had seen at the beginning of the spook tour. Ed slowed the large engine and crept deeper down the street. "Ed, what do you bet that the old lady's cousin lives in one of these places?" Princey shone his flashlight out the car window motioning to the closest house on the left. It was two stories high and had long, rectangular windows. The front door was framed by narrow sidelights. "Now that," Princey continued, "is a fine example of Federal architecture. It may be a bit run down, but the bones of it are strong and I admire it for not having the fussy Victorian bric-a-brac hanging on it. Those Victorian houses always remind me of a pieces of over-frosted cake!"

"It looks like a big brick box to me, old man." Kravitz was not willing to get on the tour bus again. He pulled the car over and they both got out and approached the house. "Wonder if the two old broads, Laurabell and her cousin, dress alike? Laurabell sure made my mom look like she's got style," he said, nodding his head from side to side.

The house had once been painted cream, but after years of rain, the occasional snow and much neglect, most of the paint was gone; it left the red brick exposed. A pair of thirty foot magnolia trees flanked the front entrance. The brick walk up to the house was lined with bird feathers. Kravitz squatted down to get a better look at them.

"What do you think? I think that this bird, whoever it might have been, lost that encounter. How about you detective, can you detect anything else relevant in this now active crime scene?" He smirked a bit as he stood up.

Princey shone his flashlight on the feathers. "You know that I do consider myself an amateur naturalist and I would say the these are the tail feathers, and oh, I think that these are the wing feathers also, of a Carolina wren. It's a bit hard to see in this light but I do believe that is who lost the fight. Now what type of accipiter would most likely strike is the question." Princey rested his left thumb on his belt as he pondered which type of hawk had made a meal of the wren.

"Okay Mr. Natural," Ed couldn't help but take at least one jab, "Lets keep moving. I can tell you which bird it was, it was the bird that is not hungry tonight." Kravitz was on the move again. He walked up to the door and started to knock on it when he thought that he heard someone moving around upstairs. He looked up to the second-story window and saw something move quickly by. While he was still staring up at the window, the front door creaked open slightly.

Kravitz bent his head towards his partner and whispered, "Hey, hey, over here." He pointed to the door, motioning that it was now open. "I didn't do that," he breathlessly told him. Then Ed pointed upstairs and made a sign with two bent fingers, of someone walking, and pointed upwards.

Princey got it. He nodded at his partner and then quietly walked up the three stairs to the door that was ajar.

"So," he said in a voice just barely audible, "why don't we see if anyone is home or not." Princey's large hand landed and the door swung wide open. The sound of the creaky hinges echoed within the sullied walls. They both peered inside, their flashlights glinting on complex spider webs. The house appeared to be deserted.

"I am thinking that somebody in here might be in need of assistance after the quake. Wouldn't you agree Detective Noble?" Ed's voice brimmed with false sincerity. He knew that judges liked to have search warrants before police enter someone's castle uninvited. They were not invited.

"Yes, in my opinion Detective Kravitz, it is our sworn duty to protect the good citizenry of Charlottesville. After you." Princey bantered, as he made a grand gesture that was just as graceful as a gameshow hostess pointing to prizes that one could win.

The house greeted them with billows of dust. Ed parted the cobwebs, holding his gun next to his body. Princey was as close as a shadow. The old oaken stairway was about eight feet from the foyer. The house was split, two rooms on either side of the staircase. Princey went to the right and Ed took the left two rooms. The old lonely house now seemed to be content to have their company. As they walked on the wide floorboards more dust swirled with each step. The sound of a faraway siren broke the silence. No one was on the first floor. They met again at the foot of the stairs.

"Are you ready for some fun now?" Ed barely whispered.

"I want to go first this time. Last time you got to go first, and you got to go first the time before that, remember?"Princey whined.

Ed rolled his eyes and motioned with his free hand for Princey to lead their expedition up the stairs. As Princey passed in front of him, Ed touched his arm and whispered, "These old stairs have got to be as creaky as Bela Lugosi's coffin."

"Ed, could we just cut the horror references for tonight? You're probably right so I'll be extra careful going up. I'll hang to the side next to the wall and avoid the center part of the steps. You too, right?"

Kravitz nodded and Princey started up, hanging on to the grimy wall. They both made it up the stairs without so much as a single creak. Princey shone his flashlight towards the room on the right and as he began to creep down towards that room, he accidentally stepped on the tail of a fleeing mouse. The mouse complained loudly and the two detectives froze in unison. Neither one said a word or made a motion. Ed was desperately attempting to suppress a sneeze as the throughly dusty house was irritating his sinuses. He made motions as if he was going to loose his battle with the sneeze.

Detective Noble looked over at him and said with his eyes, "Please don't do that."

"Screeeech!" The harsh sound rattled the old walls as a barn owl flew out of the room on the left. With two strong wing beats the owl was over their heads. It swooped down the staircase and left through the open door to freedom.

"What was that?!" Ed yelled as he bent down to get out of the bird's path.

"That was an owl. I think it was a Barn Owl. They love old deserted structures. They also love mice. I guess I ruined his dinner selection for the evening." Princey was referring to the mouse that got away.

"Great, now you gotta be a natural, uh, what did ya call yourself earlier?" Ed wrinkled his nose and finally let go of his sneeze.

"I said I was an amateur naturalist - someone whose hobby is nature. I like to know about the natural world around me."

"And I need to be a naturalist detective now, is that what it's come to?" Kravitz enjoyed his joke. "Maybe I should get a pair of binoculars, and what do you call that thing that Rosslyn showed me that last time I was over? It was something that she's put her posies in?"

"It is called a flower press."

"Right, so I get my binoculars and my flower press and then," Kravitz started a belly laugh.

"Hello? Hello... Detectives? It is Mrs. Timon." They both shone their lights down the stairs. In the doorway stood a lady with the same type of old-fashioned flowered dress that they had just seen earlier that evening.

"Yes, ma'am. What can we do for you?" Princey made his way down the stairs. Kravitz impatiently remained in place.

"Well, sir, I was just visiting with my cousin, Laurabell, the lady whom you spoke with on Riverview Avenue," her voice lilted upwards at the end of most sentences with a soft Virginia accent. Princey had already decided that she must be a local or possibly she could be from Lynchburg, but not from anywhere further south than that. "She told me that you requested knowledge of anyone in the neighborhood that is a tad odd, perhaps dotty? There is someone that did come to mind and I feel that it is my civic duty to let you know about him." She crossed her arms. "If I had my druthers, well, it's not for me to say, now is it?" Her arms stayed tightly shut. She was editing herself Princey noted to himself.

"All right ma'am. How about if we step outside on the stoop where there is a little more light." Princey waited for the elderly woman to turn away from him to go outside. He motioned to Kravitz to stay put. He knew that Ed was anxious to check out the other rooms upstairs and he did not want him to do it alone and especially not with Mrs. Timon present.

Ed gave Princey the thumbs up.

"We could take a walk over to my house if you would like to talk in more comfort. I could make a cup of tea, I have a gas stove so the power outage isn't a bother." Mrs. Timon was very gracious and quite happy to engage in her favorite sport, gossip.

"Thank you so much ma'am. You are too kind, but my partner, Detective Kravitz, and I are on duty."

Mrs. Timon let out a sigh as loud as a bicycle tire being deflated by an errant nail.

"Now if you could tell me who seems unusual to you, ma'am," Princey prompted her to tell her tale.

"Why yes, I most certainly will. He lives right across the street from this very house!" And then she pointed across the street to another Federal style building, and then tightly crossed her arms once more. "Mr. Charles Noth is the man's name. I have been waiting a blue moon's month for him to respond to a polite request that I made. You see, I have been having a bit of a problem with some of those children from the Carlton area. You are familiar with the Carlton area, aren't you?" Princey started to respond but Mrs. Timon kept on going without taking more than half a breath. "Mr. Noth, actually I do call him Charles," she uncrossed her arms and put them on her hips. "Well, Charles and I were to have afternoon tea and discuss what course of action to take in regard to this wanton vandalism that has become so prevalent in our neighborhood. Everywhere one goes now, you see this sloppy writing, goodness knows what is says! Charles says that they are symbols that these children scrawl on every imaginable surface. They are an eyesore! He, of course, agrees with me. He told me that he was committed to helping me solve this horrid situation but Charles has not answered my telephone calls, he has not responded to my letters, nor will he even answer his door these days. It is the most rude behavior, don't you agree, detective? And now, now I suspect that he may be sharing company with Miss Pricewater. My cousin, Laurabell, you remember her?" This time Princey didn't even attempt to respond. He dutifully nodded. "She told me that Miss Pricewater has been purchasing tea like a bloated tick sucking on a hound dog's neck, I declare that this is very suspicious. Miss Pricewater has been going to the Woolen Mills Market quite frequently to do her shopping and Laurabell works at that market each Thursday and Friday afternoon. Oh, she also bought several new outfits lately and has changed the style of her hair! After forty years wearing her hair in the same fashion! And to top it off," although the edge of dark had passed, leaving inky black skies, Princey could see that Mrs. Timon's eyes were narrowing, "I saw her in front of Charles's house two weeks ago Saturday." Mrs. Timon seemed to have wound down. She pulled out a used tissue from the sleeve of her dress and mopped up a tear that began to fall.

"Would you like us to make sure that Mr. Noth is all right?" Princey asked, trying to ease her upset and hoping that she would then go home.

"Oh no, I am sure that he is fine. I just think that it is rude of him to have neglected my inquiry for this length of time! And anyone who is this rude must be considered odd." She stuffed her tissue back into her blue flowered sleeve and said no more.

"Thank you for your information Mrs. Timon. I will finish inspecting this building for safety reasons and then we will visit Mr. Noth and speak with him. I will let you know if there is anything else odd." His voice was soothing and earnest. He nodded his head several times, hoping that this would subconsciously make her nod her head in agreement and go.

"Bless your heart Detective Noble," Mrs. Timon pronounced as she turned away to go back home. Her heart was lighter and she filled it with hope.

It was then that Princey recalled what her cousin had said about the used car salesman. "Excuse me, ma'am but Laurabell mentioned another odd character, a used-car salesman that lives on this street?"

"Oh, that must be my tenant, Mr. Louis Lanzac. I don't know why she dislikes him so. He has always been so kind to me. He pays his rent on time, I could set my watch by that! And he keeps the yard as pretty as all get out. He is quite handsome, I might add. Unlike my last tenant who was a ne'er-do-well. He had long hair and wore an earring. An earring! And that noisy hound of his; awful! My, the stories that I could tell you about him!"

Princey did not want to hear those stories. He decided that Mrs Timon must have legs made of steel and that she might stand there indefinitely caterwauling into the next day. "Thank you again for all of your help." His volume was up a notch now in growing frustration. "Can you please point to your house."

Mrs. Timon seemed to take offense, at what, Princey had no idea. "Oh, did you not know that I may be a Timon by marriage but I am a Custis by birth and my family home, Brightly Manor, is at the end of this very street. I am surprised that you, a detective, would not have known to whom you were speaking, humph!" And having announced what was the most important thing in the world to her, Mrs. Antoinette Custis

Timon turned on her heels and began the march to her ancestral home.

"Thank you very much ma'am." He called after her.

He went back into the house. Kravitz was not waiting at the top of the stairs. He bolted up the stairs two at a time. There, in the back of the hallway leaning on the window sill and smoking one of his Domincan's, was Ed.

"So did the old bird finally finish her song and fly on home, Mr. Natural Detective?" He nonchalantly asked.

"She did indeed. Seems as though Mr. Noth, who lives across the street, hasn't been as attentive to her as she would like, and seems that he might be taking up with a rival, Miss Pricewater. So she is mad as a hornet about it and has decided that the good Charles Noth is a suspicious character. He should be investigated by yours truly. We must interrogate him to get into this lady's good graces. I did ask her about the used car salesman that her cousin had told us about and she had nothing but praise for him. Maybe we can skip him then; take him off our list."

Ed took a long pull on his cigar and let the smoke roll out over his tongue unhurriedly. "I have always hated used car salesmen. I vote that we keep him on the list and that I am the one to harass, oh, I mean, talk to him. Nothing is doing here."

"I see your point. The clock just keeps ticking. Let us go and see about the much maligned Mr. Noth first. There might be a good reason why he is unavailable. Could be that our man might be hiding there. Could have spotted an empty place. Who knows?"

Kravitz pulled the door tight and was happy to end his tour of a Federal home.

Antoinette turned her doorhandle and entered the exquisite Classical Revival style mansion. She was still miffed that the detective had not heard of her. She was elated, though, that he would be investigating Mr. Noth's very odd and rude behavior. She was also satisfied with herself for helping out the Charlottesville Police Department in making the neighborhood safer. Antoinette strode into the large parlor, crossing her eloquent burgundy Oriental rug, heading straight for the crystal decanter filled with fine Portuguese port. As she poured a glass, of what would be the first of several celebratory glasses of port for the evening, she thought again of the nice, handsome tenant she had, Louis, and it made her smile. What Antoinette had neglected to mention about Mr. Lanzac to the detective was that he had gifted her with a fine car. It practically had no miles on it at all. Her smile grew as the port flowed.

Louis was good about giving treats. "Treats to keep them sweet." It was a motto that he lived by. It was the way he trained his people.

Chapter Twenty-Four

Kravitz and Princey were debating whether or not to visit Mr. Noth. Ed pushed to go and meet the illustrious used car salesman. Princey was determined to keep his word, he made the point that it would not take a great deal of time as there was most certainly nothing wrong with Mr. Noth, and that the man lived only a few steps away. He also reasoned that Mr Noth must have found a new friend and moved on. And what if he was on vacation and the perp was using his house? The phone number was from somewhere up here. They agreed to walk across the street first. Kravitz was happy to end their banter as his neck hurt from having to look up at Princey for an extended period of time. He moved his head from side to side and then began to rub the back of his now stiff neck with gusto."Well Princey, I can honestly say that you are a pain in my neck! Uncle! I give up, let's go to the old guy's house."

They walked lockstep across the street and stood in front of another Federal style house. This one was in much better condition and much larger than the other, Princey noted. The walkway was lined by old dark-green boxwoods that had been expertly pruned into shape, standing seven feet tall. Their fresh green smell mingled with the heavenly scent of a jasmine vine that grew nearby. The brass door handle shone as if it had just been polished, and the narrow windows that were on either side of door, were clean enough to look through. Shining their lights inside showed a home that was well loved. A rich cobalt blue carpet, with thick pile, wound its way up the curved stairway. Oil portraits of the long-dead hung on the walls. A small, oval table with graceful curved legs stood near the bottom of the impressive staircase. A large blood-red Chinese vase rested in the center, a few letters were tossed to one side.

"My good God, who would have known that something this grand was still on the hill?" Princey marveled.

"So I guess that with all this grandeur we ain't gonna stand here and discuss who gets to go in first this time, are we?" Kravitz was still a bit cranky over their last debate.

"You can knock, but this time we are following procedure to a T." Princey wasn't joking. He knew that the wealthier citizens seemed to have the most knowledgeable lawyers on speed dial.

There was no response to the knock. He knocked again. Again, it went unanswered.

Turning to step down for another vantage point, Kravitz saw a glint of white under one of the sprigs of the boxwood. Ed stooped to find a pile of newspapers. "Either this guy is fed up with The Daily Progress's editorial view on something, or he hasn't been around to pick up his papers in a very long time."

Princey eyed the stack. "We may have a very good reason to assume that something may be amiss with Mr. Noth. If someone as particular as his house would make him out to be was going out of town, I am sure that he would have made arrangements for his newspaper to suspend delivery. Don't you agree?"

Kravitz's knees popped as he stood up. "Yes, and it's my turn." Ed turned the doorknob. It opened easily, as it wasn't locked. They both looked knowingly at each other. This was another bad sign. Kravitz entered first. His footsteps were muffled by the rug in the entrance hall. On the left was the living room. Ed stayed to the left and Princey turned right towards the formal dining room.

His flashlight lit up the crystal chandelier. Nothing was out of place amongst the splendor. Princey pushed open the double swinging doors that led into the kitchen. He began coughing as soon as he stepped into the room. Princey involuntarily put his sleeve up to his nose and made himself go closer to what he knew was the unmistakable smell of death. There, next to the open antique-brick fireplace, lay the remains of what he presumed must be the much maligned Mr. Noth.

"I found him Ed."

"I am just detecting that myself."

Ed shone his flashlight on Mr. Noth's face. A bug squirmed out of a hole in his cheek, making the yellow adipose ooze as it travelled down on to what once was the southern gentleman's face. "Look at those bugs! I have never seen the kind that is crawling out of his face before."

"For God's sake Ed! You know that I hate body bugs!" Princey's stomach was in knots but he made himself bend down and take a closer look.

"So how do these bugs fit into the amateur naturalist zen type of thing that you've got going on?" Kravitz asked his partner, attempting to pull him out of his horror bug zone. Just as Ed was highlighting the characteristics of one the largest glop-covered insects, all of the lights unexpectedly came on. A classical recording began playing somewhere upstairs, and the sound of a printer whirled on in the background.

"Thank you Rappahannock Power Co-op! It wasn't bad enough that I had you shining your bug light, now I get the whole insect experience brightly lit up!" Princey threw up his hands and almost toppled over onto Mr Noth.

Ed grabbed his shoulder, pulled hard to stop Princey's large frame from going forward, and stopped the impending disaster. His partner regained his composure, and stood up.

Princey pointed upstairs and Kravitz moved towards the basement door. In a few minutes they both returned with not a sight of anything else amiss in the house.

"Let's see if the phone company is as quick as the electrical." Princey walked over the what he thought must be one of the last remaining rotary phones in the state of Virginia and was greeted with silence. "Nope, not working. I am going out to the car. I'll bring back some sweet stuff for you." Sweet stuff was their slang term for the salve that the medical examiner gave them to suppress the smell of a decaying body.

"Yep, that sure would be great, almost as good as a pizza would be right now." Ed's appetite was famous. He ate more than most and by rights he should have tipped the scales at 350 pounds plus. Mother Nature smiled on him, so his miracle metabolism handled every calorie that was thrown at it so far. Ed was a fit man.

"I'll see if you stuffed any of your old pizzas in the pizza box for a rainy day." Princey smiled remembering a time that Ed and him had been eating pizza at an endurance-style stake out. The perpetrator that they were assigned to follow, popped his head out of his seedy apartment and then blew away like a dandelion seeds being scattered by the wind. Ed was forced to abandon his specialty pizza from one of the hippest pizza restaurants in town, Fellini's. Princey had forgotten about it until a few days later when he was back in Kravitz's Trans Am again looking for a tire gauge. He opened the glove box and found the pizza, cold and folded in half and stuffed into the back, wrapped in what were then greased-soaked paper napkins. He mentioned his find to Kravitz, only to be told that the pizza would be fine there for a few days. Upon closer inspection, he noticed that a couple of pieces had been eaten. Princey would never let Kravitz forget it, so now the glove compartment was referred to as the "pizza box."

Princey, was in a much better mood as he walked towards the front door and stepped out into the fully lit- up neighborhood far away from the bug scene.

I was relieved to see that the lights were on again. Green Valley was not on any tourist route that I knew about and driving around in the dark there, made me wonder if my will was up-to-date. Libby finally ceased shining her huge torch type light out of the window at all the rundown houses that we passed, so I didn't feel quite as much like an intruder anymore. I tried to reach Jennifer but nothing was there. She was either asleep, gone or I was too exhausted. When I reached that state of what Libby called, "the walking dead exhaustion" could take me down two different paths. One, I would not be able to divine my own name, the other, an opposite state that allowed me to see the world as a much more alive place, colors would be brighter, sounds clearer, emotions light and airy and easy to read. This time, I just felt dead in the head. I was aware of every little ache and pain that my body felt. I tried to stretch out my legs and shake off the stiffness as we trolled down another sorry street. Libby, as usual, had a classic rock station cranked up loudly. She hoped that having music that shook the eardrums, might help us blend into our current environment.

"Tess, do you think she's still alive? I know that you've been wondering, so tell me, what do you think?" Libby was as direct as ever.

"I don't know. Truly, I have not got a clue except I do have hope, or it might even be a perception that she is asleep. I think that she is deeply asleep. But I am not sure if it is a wish or a perception. I am dead tired, fuzzy around the edges." I knew that Libby would understand.

An oak forest was just a few blocks away. Libby thought that no one lived down there but we decided to drive down and look. The road had the right telephone exchange, according to Detective Kravitz's printout, so we cruised down the lonely street with our windows still open and the music now off. The temperature was unusually warm, about 65 degrees. Libby was looking out the window more than paying attention to the road.

"Tess, do you see that guy by the...oh my, that used to be the old mill! She stopped in the center of the street and shone her torch light out of the window on to the collapsed mill. An eerie feeling settled in our SUV. Her keen eyes latched onto the male form. "Tess, I think that is John Brown over there."

"Help, help us!" The man pitifully cried out.

I could feel that it was spiritually broken and chaotic at the mill. Dark emotions hung with the downed beams and shards of tin. I did not look forward to being in it. The energy emitted from the mill began to suck me in. I fought my fears and cautiously opened the car door. Libby did not have to contend with these perceptions or feelings. Libby threw the printout on the dashboard as she leapt out of the SUV and ran towards John Brown.

"I recognize you, you're, you belong to the Charlottesville P.D.!" John was elated now that his eyes were on Libby. He was proud to finally have a real wolf for an officer to see.

Chapter Twenty-Five

John was so excited that he momentarily forgot about Sophie's hand and let go. "I can't believe that you found me! That you wanted to find me, that you're here!" He was dancing for joy.

"Mr. Brown take a deep breath. It will be alright now, okay?" She said to the man who was bawling like a wet baby. Libby had no skill-sets developed on handling citizens that were acting, as our father called it, like a hobo jumping up and down in front of a pay toilet. The situation with Mr. Brown most certainly fit into this category for her. She nervously looked over her shoulder to see where her big sister was.

I had no option but to leave the SUV and venture out into my future of gruesome realities. Shutting the door I began the long walk to them. Although the lights had come up in the city, there were no lights on or around the caved-in mill. The quarter moon was a small consolation. With each step I felt dread. I smelled the old wood and I became more certain of the terror that awaited me.

Libby approached the squad rooms biggest joke, not believing her own eyes. She balanced on her heels next to him.

"Sheesh!" Libby squealed as John placed Sophie's hand in hers without notice. It startled her, and I jumped out of my skin on hearing Libby's cry. I felt goosebumps form and then race down both arms. A foreshadowing of things to come, I fretted.

"Who is this?" She asked John. Without waiting for a reply, Libby scooted down even closer and felt the arm that the hand belonged to, inspecting it then to see that it was not crushed. She looked for and found a weak pulse. "Tess, Tess, down here!" She excitedly yelled.

The scream brought me running hard, jumping over debris in the gloom. I flew, relying on my instincts as I could not see the ground below my feet. At last I made it to her side; my legs like quivering jello. Libby shone her light on the girl's arm and hand. My cell phone was soon with Libby as she dialed the station. But there was no connection, all we got was a message that the call should be placed later, the lines were still overloaded.

"Damnation!" Libby thrust the phone back to me and stood up. The police radio in her car would work. She turned to run back to her SUV.

"Libby, I can feel that there are more people inside. So ask for more than one ambulance." She nodded and then ran up the mucky hill. I had almost forgotten about Mr. John Brown, the confessor, until he spoke up.

"Yes, yes, officer, I told you earlier that the mill came down on the Party Rats, at least I think she's one of them. There's about four or five girls here." John was still aglow, he was going to be vindicated and believed for the first time.

It took many tries until the dispatcher responded to Libby. "Yes this is Officer MacGregor. I am in Carlton, where the old mill is, I mean, was. It is at the corner of Pireus Row and Market Street." She went on giving the particulars as fast and as accurately as she could. She was lucky to have Louise answer. Louise always had a clear head and a calming influence.

"You are certain that one of the victims has a pulse?" Louise needed to make sure that it just was not a meat wagon pickup.

"Affirmative. And we have more than one victim, send another ambulance. We'll need a crew to move the debris too."

"Ten-four, I will have a rescue squad up there as quickly as possible Officer MacGregor." There was no promise of how long that would be. Libby cast her eyes back to the architectural nightmare scene.

John held Sophie's hand once more. "It will be okay, help is coming," he gently told her. The girl was silent.

I hoped that it would end well. As my eyes adjusted to the dark I could see that the mill had fallen in on one end and that the side nearest to the girl, was precariously propped up by the debris of the old tin roof. The heavy timbers were stacked up like a giant's game of pick-up-sticks. I walked the perimeter, stopping every few yards and listening, stretching all of my senses as far as they would go. My personal space seemed to expand far above my body, encompassing the mill. With each small step I became part of the horror inside. Most of the girls were unconscious, although I wasn't quite sure, they may all be dead. It made me sleepy, perceiving them. I felt myself falter on the spongy ground. My feet slipped on the damp leaves; arms and legs went in opposite directions as I tumbled into a large maple tree that had toppled over during the quake. My hip and elbow took the brunt of the fall. The soft earth cushioned my clumsiness as I lay face up, staring at the partial moon. It was so quiet during that brief moment. Nothing made a sound, and then, somewhere in a timeless place, I felt someone shivering in the mill. It was such a deep shiver, all the way down to the bones. She couldn't open her eyes and her extremities were cold. They were dead cold. Then I sensed her very real confusion. She thought that she may be asleep but then wondered why she would have such clear thoughts. She pondered that it could all be a dream, a nightmare that she would soon wake up from, and be out of its grip. The looming reality became clear to me - her body was dead and her spirit did not know this, not yet. Tears washed down my cheeks. The young were never ready to go. Their lives had just started and their dreams were alive and big. I tried to communicate to her, but I failed. Tish was enveloped in her own confusion and not ready to face the truth. It was all too soon.

I pulled myself up, and using the old tree to lean on, I brushed off the dirt and leaves. Nothing, I felt, was going to be easy tonight.

"Tess, where are you?" Libby was excited, I could hear it in her voice.

"I'm coming." I picked up my pace, this time being careful of the unstable ground. We stood next to each other. Libby had rigged up a spot light so that Sophie's arm was visible for the EMTs. John seemed to be more calm with his attention focused on the girl's welfare and less on his momentary victory of being right.

Her eyes glistened with mischief. "While I was on the radio reporting our incident, Detective Noble was standing by a car radio and heard me call in. He and Detective Kravitz are up on the hill, just a few blocks away. They found a body in one of the old houses there, deceased from natural causes he is guessing. They will be right down here to collect us as soon as someone is able to relieve them. It looks like we found the detectives after all!" Libby grinned and knelt down next to Sophie and John Brown.

I sat next to her. The early April wind picked up. Thankfully it came in from the south, allowing the girls that were still alive to be wrapped in a warm breeze. I put my attention inside the mill. It was like a fishing game, throw the line out, pull it back in again and see if you caught anything. If not, throw it back out to a different location. I stretched and pulled my awareness to it's limits, and this time, I found a real fighter tugging on the line. She was on the edge of unconsciousness. Her arms were numbed by pain, and her erratic heart beat and shallow breaths caused her head to spin as if dizzy from a merry-go-round. I could feel one leg dangling in space, the dust in her lungs. But what I felt most strongly was her determination to live, to make it out of there. I tried to rouse her, to get her to notice me, but it was no use, I couldn't do it. Then I realized that she was drunk, very drunk, but that might work to her advantage, as her pain threshold would be greater and this could prevent her from going into shock.

The evening dew had settled on the top of my uncovered head as the moisture from the torn up sod soaked into my clothes. I rubbed my eyes, in an attempt to shake off my exhaustion. I was torn between the dead and dying girls at the mill, and Jennifer. I must find her. I could feel the world closing in on her. I wanted, no needed, the monster to die this time.

Libby could feel my lack of energy."Tess, you look wiped."

There was no arguing with that observation. I felt that there was almost nothing left of me. My worries I held over my head and seemed to wear them like a crown of thorns; I dreaded that I would never get the monster; I was terrified that I would not be able to find Jennifer alive; I was overwrought that I would be left finding a corpse. These thoughts circled without end. Not again. I just could not have that happen again. The thought of Jennifer dead, ricocheted back to the dead girls in the Party Rats, and that is when I finally put the puzzle together. The Party Rats! "Libby, he said the Party Rats, right?" I sat up straighter, getting a second wind with my realization.

Her reply was measured. "Yes, I think so. Okay now I am

sure, John did say Party Rats. They are a local girl gang from Carlton. Why?" She could tell that something just fell into place for me.

"The last time that I made contact with Jennifer she told me that there were some girls outside the house. She said that she tried hard to reach one of them but all the girls wanted do was get drunk. And she called them 'Rats.' The bunch of girls around the house could have been the Party Rats! Isn't Carlton nearby to the hill?"

"That is a brilliant deduction! I hope that some of these girls remain alive and that they are the Party Rats. If so, we can get her exact location." Then under her breath she said, "Unfortunately, all we have is John Brown's word that it is them, I mean, he is not known for his truthfulness."

"Maybe this time he is telling the truth, that is how it reads to me. Look at the way he is showing true concern for that girl." I motioned towards her hand.

Libby turned her head, there was no denying it, looking at John Brown and the little hand that he refused to let go of again. She nodded her head yes. This was the first time that she had ever considered John Brown a truthful witness.

After what seemed like a month of Sundays, our help came. We had two ambulances, a fire truck, and a police cruiser with two officers present. The EMTs took over John Brown's place. The rest of the crew left their vehicles. I heard their dumbfounded reactions, shocked over the collapse of the old mill.

One of the firemen walked back to the ladder truck and got on his radio. "This is Engine #3, yeah, it's Pete. This is a whole lot worse than we expected. We need more of a presence here, oh hell, we need a construction company contacted that would have a large crane and heavy moving equipment. I don't know how effective a fire truck is going to be here. The structure is mostly collapsed. I can see one victim has her arm partially out of the debris and she has a pulse. Yeah. Ernie, she's got a pulse, right?" He bellowed to the EMT. Ernie nodded. "So send somebody here, we need help. I am not even sure if its safe to move any of the debris without causing the beams to collapse further. Hell, I just don't know how to do it safely. Okay? So you just let me know when you have someone. If you need the Engine for a fire, call us, otherwise we are staying here and I will try to think of some way how to help these people." Pete got off the radio just as Princey and Kravitz joined the melee.

"When it rains, it pours, huh." Detective Noble said to the first officer that he saw. He went to Pete and got his view on the scene. They both agreed that the earthquake and then the aftershocks had left the city a mess, and it was not coping well with this new type of disaster. It could take hours before anyone would be able to get here and help.

Kravitz found Libby and me, next to John Brown. We were all looking at the girls and the EMT, wondering what could be done to help save her. Frustration made the atmosphere electric.

Ed turned to Libby, tapping her forearm and then motioned for me to join them as they stepped away from the crowd. "Pretty smart, Officer MacGregor, I see that my last print-out is on the dashboard of your car."

I felt Libby tense, she didn't know if Detective Kravitz would find her intrusion amusing or not. I could sense that he was happy with her deduction and the solution was a good one.

"Don't worry, you did the right thing. This further proves that I like the way you think." Kravitz said proudly.

Libby smiled.

"Detective Kravitz, I spoke with Jennifer, telepathically that is," I felt that it was necessary to keep explaining this to him, why, I am not sure. "She told me that she was in a house, a dirty house that was up on a hill. She thought that she was in Charlottesville. She heard a bunch of girls around that house and that they intended to get drunk." I paused, trying to form the rest in a coherent fashion, but this was still a jumble in my mind as I had a suppressed feeling of inadequacy from my past failure that overshadowed my certainty. Detective Kravitz held his words and let me settle in with my conclusion. I could feel my own fear of my monster have less of a grip as I continued on, "Mr. Brown," I pointed towards him, "he said that these girls here were the Party Rats. Libby says they are a girl gang from Carlton."

"Yep, that's right Tess." Kravitz had heard of them as well.

"So you see, I believe that they were the ones around the house where Jennifer is being held. She referred to them rats. One of them should be able to tell us where the run-down house is that had a screaming girl inside. One of them, she tried her best to contact, so I am sure that girl will know, she'll know."

Ed turned and looked back with more urgency at the EMTs now that he saw the wisdom in Tess's conclusion. "Princey and I checked out most of the houses up on the hill but there were just a couple that are left. I think just one with a tenant house. It's the biggest damn house up there. We had the pleasure of meeting the lady of the manor, Mrs. Timon. She's got what looks like, a palace."

"Hey," one of the uniformed officers yelled, "they're here! I don't believe it!"

We all turned our heads. Coming down Market Street was a large flatbed truck with an even larger crane resting on it. Behind that, moving down the hill was another truck with a tractor sitting on top. They were followed by a parade of three smaller construction trucks, all filled with work crews. Our cavalry had arrived.

Chapter Twenty-Six

My chill grew deeper, I was grateful to get back in the warm and dry SUV. The construction crew asked that we all, except the EMTs, politely get out of their way. There wasn't much left for us to do here except to wait to see if the girl became conscious and could tell us where Jennifer was being held. I wanted to stay with her. My wishes were now being bandied about like a ping pong ball. Detective Kravitz and Libby were debating, their hand gestures resembling a boxing match, over which one of us should stay should one of the girls became conscious.

Libby her checks flushed scarlet, kept her mouth tight and hissed, "I am the one that's got a gun and I am authorized to use it. I think that beats a civilian that has no gun and would be a walking target." The air vibrated with her resolution.

Ed dug his virtual heels and spat "She's got the strong connection with her, not you, so you are staying here Officer MacGregor."

Just as their expressions and intentions were beginning to form into unwavering opposing viewpoints, John Brown piped up, "Detective, Detective!" Kravitz looked over to his right to see who was bugging him now only to see it was Mr. Brown. This was not what he expected or wanted.

"Mr. Brown, I really don't want any coffee or cake right now, so why don't you make yourself scarce, as this isn't a safe place to be at the moment. Look at all this heavy equipment. And you don't have a hard hat, do you?" Ed did not wait for a response. "Not a good idea, now is it?" Kravitz was still hot from the disagreement with Libby so he was spreading his anger about. "So why don't you skedaddle." His angry eyes cut from John Brown onto Libby.

John Brown's remorseful expression, topped with a healthy dose of self-loathing for his years of lying, hung around his head like cigar smoke hung around Kravitz. Pleading, his shaky voice barely audible,"Detective, I'm the one that told you about these girls. I went down there, walked all the way down there, and I told the desk sergeant about the mill, and the girls being trapped here. So when no one would help me, I'm the one that came back, I'm the one." John's eyes were beginning to tear up. Ed was not prepared for this, he thought to his horror that the man might cry. "And I sat here and held her hand and told her that it would all work out. I promised her," he was pleading for understanding. John could not say any more words. For the first time, he really did not care that he had been right all along. He only cared for the girl that was attached to the small hand. The hand that had chipped blue sparkle polish on it.

Ed stood for a moment and gathered his raging feelings and swirling thoughts. He perfected a plan. "Mr. Brown I would like to deputize you during this time of disaster to the Charlottesville, PD and ask that you continue to stay with this girl. We need your help." There it was.

John Brown's eyes became clear and he stopped sniveling. "I am most honored that you have requested my help. I feel that it is my duty to stay with these girls. You can count on me. I..."

John was overwhelmed but he at last had a worthwhile purpose for his life. " I will watch carefully for any signs that they have regained consciousness and then I will let the uniformed officers know. It was very wise of you to pick me. They won't be afraid of me." John felt more alive in that moment than all of his other moments of his life added together. He pulled his brown woolen overcoat tight together at the neck and strode over to happily assume his new post.

My cell phone rang. My first thought was one of surprise as I thought that all of the lines were not working. I then went down my list of who it could be and came up with mother in crisis.

"Hello," the dread was apparent in my voice as I was anticipating that mother would find a way to blame me for the earthquake and accompanying damage; it might have been a bit overblown sentiment, but at that moment, I whole-heartedly believed it possible.

"Professor MacGregor?" The female voice asked.

I stood in a bit of a stupor and didn't fill the void quick enough, so she continued.

"Professor MacGregor are you there? Can you hear me?"

I knew who it was now. It was the giant fed who treated me like a DVD player. "Yes. What do you want?" My surly attitude slipped out, she was one of the last people that I expected would call.

Agent Sexton could see that her handiwork still stung. "I am sorry about that trick. Really, I am. I see that it was not a professional thing for me to do but I had a difficult time comprehending, no, appreciating, your special talents. Surely, you must understand that?" She paused, waiting for an answer.

I let her hang for a few seconds. "You are not the first person to treat me like a freak and you probably will not be the last. I expected more from you though, as you are a woman and you know that we both have it rough being in what are traditionally male fields. And yes, I know that I am called "Professor Freak." My cheeks flushed on recounting this truth.

"Maybe we can come to terms?" Her voice was sincere.

"That might be possible." I hoped for the best. "What can I do for you?"

Her intriguing story unfolded. "I know that this may be a bit odd, and to be honest, I have never gone outside of normal procedures before but this time I am compelled to. This concerns Special Agent Stefan Hannigan. What can you tell me about him?"

I became confused, I did not expect her to be investigating one of her own. Just as I was going to begin, Libby jumped into the car. Her sentences were coming out with machine gun speed.

"Libby, I am on the phone, give me a minute." I could feel that her high speed babble was getting to the explosive stage.

"Sorry! I didn't notice. But we have to get going. We are following Princey and Kravitz. Look, they're pulling out now!" And having said that, Libby didn't care if I was talking to God or the Director of the FBI. She revved the engine and raced behind them, attempting to keep up with Detective Kravitz who had an even heavier lead foot than she did.

I reached out for the overhead grip and clutched it tight as we skirted by stopped cars and downed trees.

"Agent Sexton, I will tell you what I know about him but you may not care for it. But you might. I sense that you are wanting to, let's say, nail him for something?" I didn't wait for her to agree with what I knew was the truth. "Hannigan is very devious, slick, I should say, the definition of slick. He had my apartment bugged, and I am certain that he blew out my sister's car tire with a dart, causing an accident. She was not injured badly; she could have been though. His actions make no earthly sense. And the part that I dislike the most is that Hannigan did manage to almost cover them up from my perceptions - he threw out a kind of blanket of darkness to hide the events with, sorry, but it's hard for me to put this type of activity in words, I know this must sound strange, but I can sum it up by saying that he is devious, slick and charming. It seems to be very important to him to be charming. It is a way for him to manipulate others. You know, disarm them with your charm."

It was then that Libby decided to take a turn like an Indy 500 driver. The sidewalk disappeared and the houses seemed to blend into one pedantic suburban rambler caused by the tornado called Libby. We sped up a sharp incline, nearing the top of the hill.

"Is it legal? Do you know if he had permission to bug my apartment? Maybe a security check?" I tossed out different scenarios to Agent Sexton about Hannigan's behavior.

"It is illegal." That was all that she had to say. It was the truth, he was doing illegal activities while being a Special Agent of the FBI. "The CARD unit agents do not do illegal activities." She was almost reading my mind. "He has stepped on a few toes so his boss contacted my boss and I was told to thoroughly check him out. I did and he checked out very well. Actually, it was too good. All of the references that he listed as friends, each of the men described him using the same adjectives and phrases. This would only happen if they had been coached. That means that he lied, these are not friends, they are people that he has either paid, or blackmailed to say the exact good things about him and his past. He is too good to be true. I think that most people that have dealt with him have been taken in by his bespoke suits, impressive degrees and looks. So yes, he is a slick confidence man and he has taken on this demeanor for some nefarious purpose that I intend to discover."

"Do you know where he is?" I wanted to reassure myself

that he was not near me, not near Jennifer, not near Libby. Trepidation was becoming my new and unwanted, state of existence.

"He told his boss the he had to check for a possible gas leak at his house. But I went there, all the way to Alexandria, and he is nowhere around. He is not at Quantico either. I tried his cell phone and there is no answer. I can't find him."

"So the snake has slithered away. Well, wherever he is, I hope that you find him soon. I do not know what he is up to, but I have a strong urge to tell him that he will get his comeuppance." I slid into the door hard on the next turn, and lost my grip on the inside handle. Houses were still flying by.

"Thank you. I will take it from here." Then I heard her wonder, almost out loud, 'Do you think that I'll get him?' She wanted assurance so that she could save the world and make it a safer place.

"Yes," I said resolutely. "You will get him." I saw no reason to tell her that I could not see into the future.

Chapter Twenty-Seven

I wondered if Detective Noble was white-knuckling it the way I was. We turned onto Riverside Avenue and saw the mansion that ruled the hill. Mrs. Timon must have had every light on in the house. She probably went room to room to check to see if various bulbs had burned out and then inadvertently, turned on each one before she realized that there was a power outage. It made her house shine like a beacon in a storm. We turned into her long driveway which was flanked by a line of towering oak trees. I noticed a formal garden and possibly a pool. Her home was stately and charming. It looked like the type of place that Thomas Jefferson would have stopped by for supper and interesting conversation. The familiarity of it at first surprised me, but then I realized that this was the style prevalent at the University of Virginia.

We pulled up behind the detectives. "Do you think that Hannigan is around?" Libby had heard my conversation and absorbed the gist of it although she was flying at light speed.

"Nope, I think that the only one here is Mrs. Timon. And by the number of lights that are on, she must be still up, wouldn't you say?" Libby gave me a small, quick nod as she got out.

I reached out to see if Jennifer was nearby. I got nothing. My exhaustion, I knew, could hamper my abilities but I expected that our connection was so strong that I should be able to know if she was present. At least, I hoped so.

The front of the house had an elegant portico with three-part windows that I recalled were called Palladian windows. My eyes searched over the dignified architecture for Detective Kravitz and found him, with his hand already on the bell. The scent of hyacinth and lilacs were carried by the breeze that brushed my face. It filled my already overloaded senses as I walked up, and stood behind Detective Noble, the emissary for our party.

Three minutes went by before the grand lady came to the door, peering out into the darkness. "Yes, is that you detective? Sorry I have forgotten your name. Oh! Did you bring your wife?" She saw me and her mind then got cloudy.

"It's Detective Noble, ma'am. And this is my partner, Detective Kravitz, you met him on Riverside Avenue, and Officer Mac Gregor." He pointed to Libby; she could clearly see that she was wearing a uniform. "And this is our consultant on the case, on loan from the FBI, Ms. Tess MacGregor."

It felt awkward, I had never been given that title before. But thinking it through, it was an appropriate way to couch my credentials so that they would fit in with the others. It was true, that one law official could look at me on loan from another law organization. I preferred to think of myself as freelancing.

"Oh yes, Detective Noble." Her eyes now had a bit of shine in them as she could recall him now. "What can I do for you and your, ah, friends?" She still did not know what to really make of our odd coterie.

Princey collected his thoughts, but she changed her mind

and decided to have us all come in without any further explanations. Clearly, Mrs. Timon must see that we were not her peerage, so getting all the details about us did not concern her. "Please come in." She gave us a warm smile and a fully opened door.

The warm glow of antique lamps showed us the way as we followed her into the formal parlor. She sat down on a small, high-back crimson velvet chair. I looked at her formal sitting room, it reminded me of a classy funeral home that I had been to once. We all stood, not wanting to dirty or damage her fine furniture.

"May I serve you all a glass of port or would you care for water? Please, sit down." Her Southern hospitality would not to be forgotten.

"Thank you very much but we have to pass on that, it was kind of you to offer." Princey paused, he did not want to say the next sentence. He sat down close to her, placed his eyes on her gaze and imperceptibly to the others, relaxed his shoulders down. It was a subconscious move to make her feel a bit more at ease before he gave her the bad news. "We went to Mr. Noth's house and unfortunately, found him deceased." He paused to let the words make their way into her mind, and then continued. "He was unable to respond to your letters and calls as it appears that he passed away some time ago. I am very sorry for your loss Mrs. Timon."

Mr. Antoinette Custis Timon looked up with a helpless, glassy look and then howled. She sounded like a coyote that had been shot. I was unnerved by her response; the others did not seemed surprised. Princey got closer and took her hand in his. She turned her head, looked at him and began to sob in waves. I got up, and found a box of tissues in a hallway bathroom. Kravitz had stepped away from the grief and stood next to the fireplace pretending to watch it. I could see him mull over his own future, wondering if anyone would care enough to howl like a wounded animal when he was dead and gone.

Libby went over to Kravitz and whispered in his ear. He must have had a hard time hearing her over the howls as she leaned over again to speak. I gave the box to Princey, and he gave the tissues, one at a time, to Mrs. Timon. I looked over towards Libby, not caring to watch her heart be broken any longer. Libby motioned for me to join them.

"I think that we should check out her rental house. She said that it was on this piece of property."

Kravitz's suggestion was welcomed by us both. All three of us wanted to be out of this house.

"Is there someone that I can call for you Mrs. Timon? Perhaps your cousin Laurabell?" Princey was trying to unhook from her overflowing grief. We needed to continue with our hunt.

Her words, between big sighs mixed with sobs seemed to say, yes, she would like Laurabell here. I had passed the phone in the hallway and thought that someone of her generation probably still kept a physical address book and it would be handy by the phone. I motioned to Princey and then went down the hall. I soon found the number and happily had a dial tone. In less than ten minutes Laurabell was at the door and we were free to go.

Night time seems to make everything more frightful. The sculpted boxwoods in the formal garden looked like ominous silhouettes of Dr. Seuss characters waiting to wake-up my inner child with some horrible sound or motion. Everything is scarier when you are a child. I chided myself to enter. Some of the shapes were balls and cylinders; there were two on the far corners that I could now discern were shaped like huge swans. I remembered an old Irish legend, The Swans Of Lir, and how terrified it made me feel. The folk tale was about a group of children that were turned into swans and were cursed to stay on one lake, floating there for nine-hundred years. Mother had read it to me soon after my kidnapping. Her way to comfort me I suppose, but at the time I equated being held against my will to a very similar thing that happened to those children being turned into something that they were not and then being held captive on the lake. The thoughts from my past made me more on edge. I looked with a cautious eye at the swans and made sure that I stayed on the brick walkway as I passed by the unearthly creatures. There was a profusion of lavender up ahead, the scent of it enveloped me and took away a bit of the tension.

Libby was up ahead. She seemed to have stopped at the entrance of another formal garden. It was unlike her to hesitate. Putting each foot lightly down in front of the last step, I was doing what we called a 'fairy walk.' Soon I was next to her. I tapped lightly on her shoulder. Libby half turned towards me and gave me one of her special looks. It was the one that meant danger was near or was here. She didn't know which it was but something felt off to her. I felt her trepidation. I peered over her shoulder and saw a beautiful water nymph statue at the far end of the reflecting pool.

"Lets go in, you take the left side." She began to creep in without my agreement. Libby would always be the more bold one. I brushed another large clump of lavender, and threw my attention into the dark shadows, and waited for the weirdness to leap out.

Princey and Kravitz kept going down the garden path. They were not distracted by the scent of lavender or the feel of a warped space. Kravitz opened the iron gate, glad to leave the main part of the Timon estate.

"You're right. There is a, a garage? Or is it a house over there?" He asked Princey.

"I can't really tell but we'll see soon enough." Princey took the lead across a fallow field leaving the menacing topiaries behind.

The wind picked up as they approached the old carriage house. Not a light was on. The building seemed to crouch down, waiting for them to make their move and try to come in. A clump of ivy swung in the wind, beating out sounds that had no rhythm. The green tendrils, ripped from the oak tree during the quake danced like a hangman's noose.

"Hey Ed, do you think the Nationals are going to win again this season? I mean, they got a few more good guys so maybe they can keep winning."

"Huh, why are you talking about the Nationals?" Ed whispered to a now very tightly wound Princey.

Princey just sighed while he placed his right hand on his hip. The motion made his jacket move to reveal his holster. "Don't know exactly. It just seemed to be the only thing I could think to say that would be a distraction, you know. And don't forget, we are chasing a psychotic who is psychic. Maybe he knows were out here. Maybe he's reading our thoughts. And man-oh-man, just look at that weird place. Look, even the angles on that house seem crooked. Look at the doors, they are definitely not right."

Kravitz squinted and said, "Princey there is something wrong with those doors. It looks like the frame around those double doors is about busted off. And it looks like all of the windows have bars. Now that's a bit unusual, wouldn't you say so?"

"How about those woods over there. You don't see anybody over there do you?" Princey's stress, mixed with his imagination that was now entirely unleashed, created an emotional state that was explosive as a stick of dynamite. He pointed to the threatening gathering of old trees.

They both stood in the silence and listened. The wind took

hold of a wild grape vine and threw it against a shutter on the far side of the carriage house. Far away in the woods, a screech owl made a ghoulish cry. Both men became unnerved.

Kravitz calmed his reaction down and said, "You know, maybe with their new coach, they'll do something great this year. Should happen with all that money they throw at those players, huh?"

"Yeah, Ed, I think that you've got the right idea." Princey smiled at his buddy. That was as close as Ed Kravitz would ever get to saying that he was afraid.

They both walked near the house. "Hey Ed, what is that?" Princey shone his flashlight on a wooden number in the dirt. He kicked it with the toe of his shoe.

Kravitz bent down low and saw two more wooden numbers in the dirt. "They look like house numbers. Must be from over there," he said pointing to the two large double green doors. "But why would they be torn off and laying out here in the grass. Doesn't make much sense, does it?"

"I guess that he didn't want someone to know where he lived. Odd." Princey scratched the top of his head in bewilderment and they moved on.

Their steps fell heavy. Kravitz took one door and Princey the other. Each man had a hand on a doorknob and with their revolvers drawn, Princey made the sign and they pushed. Ed's door open first. He found no resistance and stumbled into the room, almost losing his footing. Noble was in, looking from side to side for a bad guy. No one was there to greet them. Their flashlights shone in every nook of each room and floor, as they split up, hunting for their prey. Kravitz heard no other breaths, Noble saw no bodies. They were alone, no bad guy, no little girl. Ed broke the haunted house feel with a flick of a switch. The downstairs lit up brightly causing both men to be blinded momentarily.

His eyes readjusted and Ed found a rock on the floor. He followed its trajectory to the closest window and saw broken glass on the floor. "So somebody threw a rock in here and maybe they tore down the house numbers too." He was ruminating that over, not able to fill in the picture of what had happened yet.

"Hmm, did you say something?" Princey had the refrigerator door open and was nosing about. His words went inside the refrigerator. He closed the door and asked again, "Did you say something Ed?"

"Just wondering to myself why would someone throw a rock inside here and why would they also rip off the door numbers. I was wondering if it could be some of those kids from Carlton that Mrs. Timon was talking about earlier. You know, just kids having fun being vandals."

"Maybe they don't like the guy that lives here." Princey offered.

"Yeah, they don't like him, so they fuck with him." Kravitz held his chin for a second. "No, gang kids don't do shit like this. They're more destructive. Where's the gang insignia, their marks?" Ed began to nod in agreement with his own logic.

Princey turned back to search the kitchen area again now that it was lit up. "Well, well, well, look at this! This is a mighty big knife sitting next to the sink here. And it sure looks like the counter is stained with blood. I am no forensic expert but it looks to my professional hawk eyes, that there is fresh blood on top of old stains of more blood."

"Let me see." Kravitz walked over closer and put on a pair of thin, latex gloves. He carefully held the long, thick blade and then evaluated the blood stain coloration on the counter. "Looks like some of this is definitely fresh. I think that we have found his lair."

"We're gonna need DNA evidence that it is Jennifer and

not some missing cat. You know that the D. A. will insist on infallible evidence." Princey was certain of that fact.

One of the dark green doors pushed open just a bit more. "Detective Kravitz? Detective Noble?" Libby called out before entering. She held her arm out to stop me from walking straight inside.

"Yes," Detective Noble was quick to respond.

We entered the carriage house. I could feel Jennifer everywhere in the room. My eyes grew wide. I thought of all of the terrible emotions that she experienced in this room as the images peeled off the objects that surrounded me. I walked through her memories; unsteady steps in a world of horror. I could almost see her little body sitting there, glass scattered about. Her rage grew and grew. I had to turn away from that spot. There was too much for me to handle. I saw images of him eating a rat, blood down her naked chest, Jennifer crying and the sounds of something, or someone, beating thunderously at the door. I could feel Libby watch me as I went from place to place. She knew what I was doing. She could feel bits of my life-force leaving me, draining into the dark evil hole that was never-ending. Kravitz started to say something to me and Libby motioned for him to be quiet. I continued to float through her horror. It was a ghoul's waltz, a dance with a heartless, evil man.

I walked to the back wall and saw it - the decrepit burgundy phone. I picked up the receiver with a tissue and saw the cigarette's burn mark on the princess phone base. How desperately Jennifer wanted there to be a number on that phone! A glimpse of a large hand slapping her head and then I saw her being dragged to an open door, screaming, screaming so loud, to no one. I choked on the vision. He had her again. At that precise point in time, I came face to face with Jennifer's abandoned hopes that were so familiar to me. The room lost it's edges and I felt dizzy, everything went swirling by. The images of her memories became so real, more solid than the objects that I saw in the room. My heightened perceptions went wild with her emotions, and her sensations, and the evil intent that wrapped itself around it all. My center was gone. Luckily for me, I passed out in Libby's arms.

Chapter Twenty-Eight

The audio was played over and over. Agent Sexton had run out of other leads. This audio tape had been possibly dropped in the wrong file, but since it was in Special Agent Hannigan's file, she felt obligated to investigate it. Colleen rubbed the back of her neck. This was a most frustrating experience for her. She was able to pluck more clues from Tess about Hannigan, but now, she had no one to bounce ideas off of except for a cyber cop that she had gotten permission to utilize. She quickly observed that Howard had to be one of the most personality challenged people on the planet. This guy, she reasoned, had no individuality that she could discern. As her friend Emma would say, He was from a 'personality-free zone.' Thinking of that made her smile, which made her Mr. Zero look over to her with anticipation. I guess that he's waiting for me to emote, she mused to herself. Mr. Zero reminded her of an old Star Trek episode where the aliens sucked the life force from the crew to use as their energy means. She could mentally hear him sucking now.

"Well, Howard, tell me," she paused and adjusted a bra strap. She saw that that made him uncomfortable and continued, "Can you take out any more of the top voice and have just the background sound?"

"Yes." Howard looked down at the keyboard and rapidly began typing. She slipped off one of her high heels and waited. "Okay." He looked back at her.

"Okay, what?" She asked.

"Yes, I have the background sound isolated. Would you like to listen?" His voice was monotone and he seemed to her to be bored with the task. But he was not bored at all, he was entranced with what he considered was the most luscious woman that had ever spoken to him, much less tugged at her bra strap in front of him. Now he could only picture her from the waist up wearing a lacy bra.

She started to say a smart remark but pulled back. "Yes, that would be helpful Howard." Colleen now mimicked his monotonous tone. She decided that the best way to approach him would be to treat him just in the same manner that he behaved towards her. Mimicking voice tone and attitude was easy enough to do. She briefly thought about her dream job in the Behavior Analysis Unit and that maybe if she could catch Hannigan in whatever he was up to, maybe she would get her wish.

In the background a whirring noise blocked out a voice. "Can you isolate the voice?" She calmly asked.

"Oh yes, it already has been." Howard seemed to almost be a little happy with that pronouncement. He played the voice.

"Play it again, will you?" She wasn't able to decipher what was said. The voice was very faint. "Again, and can you do it with more volume?"

"Sure." He was back to one word answers Colleen noted. And then, when she was getting comfortable in her assessment of Howard he asked, "Do you want to hear it with headphones?"

"Of course." She took the headphones, wondering why he did not give them to her in the beginning. Howard ran the audio again. This time Colleen heard a garbled voice of a woman in the background and a male voice ask for homes. The only word that she clearly could hear with the aid of the headphones was "homes." She tried to decipher the nonsensical words. It could be the man said "something on homes" or "izzy homes," maybe, "is it on homes?" None of it made sense. She could positively identify an electronic sound was present. Colleen decided to ask him to focus on that clearer noise and then go back to the voices.

"Howard, can you give me the electronic sound only?"

"I can do that Agent Sexton, but I could tell you what that sound is now." Howard had his poker face on again.

"Okay, why don't you do that." He had all of her attention, good and bad, now on him. Agent Sexton was running out of patience with the way he seemed to dole out vital information.

"It's a security door being opened with an electron tag for a retinal scan, you know, the new kind of ID cards. It is the sound of the Iris Acmes 2200 - Authenticam. Biometrics has gotten big." Howard seemed to be quite the expert as he sat, like a dog anticipating a bone, waiting for a pat on the head from the lovely Colleen.

She wasn't in the petting mood. She mulled over how she didn't have an ID card like that. Colleen knew that in very secure spots in the FBI, it was in use. She had heard about them being used in the private sector and surmised that the CIA and NSA would have them. Other than that, she knew nothing about them. "Oh I see." Colleen tapped her tooth with her fingernail. It was a nervous habit.

Howard felt that he had made some points with her so he continued, "I don't want to be presumptive, but would you like me to listen to the voice? I have extraordinary hearing. The audiologist compared me to a dog."

Colleen was dumbstruck. "Go right ahead."

He played the audio without headphones. "Oh, he said: 'is it on HOLMES?'"

"That doesn't make any sense to me. I understood that much but it makes no sense." Colleen was ready to brush him off as another bragging male FBI agent, this one disguised as a certified geek. Just another male agent determined to make her life at the FBI difficult. Colleen leaned down to grab her briefcase.

"Agent Sexton, he wasn't talking about homes, he was referring to HOLMES. " He pronounced it with a long o and an l sound rolling into the m's making his mouth looked like a fish sucking in water.

"What do you mean? The fictional character Sherlock Holmes?" She was miffed and tired of his triflings.

"In a roundabout way, why I do. They might of used that acronym as a joke, I mean the Brits have a very dry sense of humor. Okay, so it stands for Home Office Large Major Enquiry System - HOLMES!"

"And what is that exactly?" She asked, taking her hand off of the briefcase.

"It could be compared to our VICAP." Howard knew all about VICAP as he worked setting up the software for it. VICAP was the FBI's Violent Criminal Apprehension Program, part of the National Center for the Analysis of Violent Crime.

"Oh, I see. So this man is asking if it, whatever it is, is on HOLMES. That does make it interesting, doesn't it?"

She looked at Howard, waiting to see if he had any other revelations to make. He did.

"So do you know who has those new ID tags?" Howard was

in his element. This was another area that the cyber cops and geeks knew all about. "Large Fortune 500 companies use these now to help thwart industrial spying. We might be able to get a list of which companies have bought them from the Swiss, I believe it's Swiss made. Actually, I could check the Biometrics catalog online to get the exact manufacturer. And then there's the feds, of course, the CIA, NSA, DOD, and the Secret Service too, just last month. Those are the only agencies that have broad access to that kind security. It costs so much that not all of us have it yet. But there are always the elite of different groups, and they always get the good stuff. Several groups at the FBI, like CARD, oh, and there is the ATF and some IRS agents. Creepy that the Treasury Department has got it." Howard was in full blown geek mantra on his solid ground of not interesting info to anyone but him, and in this one case, Colleen. "Well, you were surprised huh? I mean, you don't have it, do you?" He was correct about that, Colleen did not have a retinal scanner tag yet. She choose to ignore Howard's assessment that she was not elite enough to have this ID.

Stefan Hannigan was a CARD agent, this might be relevant after all. The Child Abduction Rapid Deployment team was elite. With only 10 agents, a child abduction scene, no matter where it was, would have one of these agents there in one hour, two at the max. Colleen had a new thought that niggled at her. Any member of the CARD team would have to have a strong desire and dedication to protect children in order to go through the extra rigorous training that was required of this elite team. She thought of Special Agent Hannigan and wondered why in the world would he have trained to be a member of this group? She concluded again that he was after the prestige that being a CARD member brought. It fit with all of his professional moves, the guy just wanted glory, he had no strong desire to protect children.

"Does everyone in CARD have this?"

"Yes, they do. My roommate is a CARD agent in training so I know a few things that goes on there." He was trying to impress.

"Howard, I have only been to their headquarters a few times at most." She started to dismiss his bravado and then realized that this could be a new way to get information. "There is a CARD agent, Stefan Hannigan, that I am interested in. Have you heard anything about him? Or could you find out anything about him? Maybe from your roommate?" Colleen gave him a warm smile. This made him think of her lacy bra.

"Sure, I can ask him, but Josh, my roommate, doesn't involve himself in gossip." He scrunched the tip of his nose up at her remark.

She noticed the move and in a perfunctory, Bureau-approved tone, said, "Thanks. I appreciate all of your help. I'll be sure to let your boss know that you have aided in our investigation." Colleen picked up her briefcase and slipped her shoe back on. She was disappointed that the tape gave her nothing noteworthy and that Howard would not be dealing in gossip.

"Agent Sexton." Howard called out as she was heading for the door.

"Yes, Howard."

"There was the woman's voice on the tape. Do you want to help me identify it?" Howard pushed his glasses back up on the bridge of his nose. He liked Colleen and wanted her, and her lacy bra to stay.

"You could do that? You're hearing is that good?"

"No, not that good but I have another tool that I could try. It's a long-shot but it might rule out information, which in a way, gives you information. It is the Biometric Speaker Verification, the Voice Security System. Since this seems to be in a federal, top-security site, maybe whoever else is there could be ID'd with the voice system."

"Can we use this on the man's voice?"

"According to the report that was embedded on the file, it already has been identified. I thought that you needed to know who the female is. I mean, you did read the embedded file?" He gave her a look that made Colleen feel six years old with her hand in the cookie jar.

"No, I, I missed that." She quickly skipped over that mistake by asking another question. "Who is it then?"

"It's the agent you just asked me to check up on, Stefan Hannigan. Isn't that why you asked me about him? Don't you want to know who the woman is?" Howard was determined to use the next toy in his arsenal.

Colleen was gobsmacked. How could she have missed this! "Yeah, sure, of course I do." She stumbled with her words.

"Okay, well this should just take me about two minutes." Howard became lost in his equipment as Colleen tried make sense out of a jumble of misrelated facts.

"Agent Sexton it is *your* voice on the tape."

"Huh, it's me? How can it be me, are you sure?" Her perplexed look did not sway his certainty at all.

"The voice pattern is yours. It came up right away. Look here." Howard pointed to the screen so she could see the unique sound waves her voice made.

And then she remembered. She had been sent to find Special Agent Hannigan and reprimand him for leaving his prints on the chocolate wrapper. He had not followed protocol and this could prove to be messy in court so the evidence was tainted, not good. And since he was the senior CARD agent on the case, this very important case, the shit would be flung at him hard. She had brought the chocolate wrapper, put it down in front of him, and then stood her ground as to what he had incorrectly done, how precisely this was viewed, and then was surprised by a sheepish apology. Men who looked like him, in her experience, would have an attitude of self-aggrandizement that could bowl you over. A mealy-mouthed "so sorry," was not what she expected at all. She made it make more sense to herself by saying that since this was the FBI Director's daughter that was abducted, he must know that his rocket ride to the top stopped there. Or maybe he had plans to withhold information so that he would be sure to be the one to catch the perpetrator. Yes, that would most likely be why he acted that way towards her. His sheepish behavior was another cover-up to his true intent. He was going to get this guy and leave all other agents out of the flow of information. After all, he had left her out, Colleen reasoned. But something stayed stuck, why, exactly, were his prints on the wrapper? Could there be an even more nefarious reasons? She felt that more digging was in order.

"Thank you very much Howard. You have been a great help."

Agent Sexton shook Howard's hand firmly and walked away with the puzzle pieces clicking together the way her three inch red heels did on the well-polished floor.

Chapter Twenty-Nine

"Tessie, here drink some water." Libby cradled my head in her lap as she helped me drink.

I sat on the cold floor of the old carriage house. Princey and Ed were standing over us, both of them looked concerned. I felt embarrassed for getting lost in the imagery. "Sorry, I didn't realize that I would lose my legs."

"It's good to see that you are back in the world of the living young lady." Princey took away the sting from my embarrassment.

Ed squatted down to our level. "Got any other magic tricks up your sleeve? He asked. The corner of his eyes turned up as he gave me a smile.

"Nope, fresh out of tricks." I told him as I returned his smile. I noted that I was liking him more.

"Tess, what did you see?" Libby was back to business. She was right to get me back on track.

I shifted my position and sat up. I put my hand up to Ed, he took it and I was back on my feet. "She was held captive here. I can feel her all over this room. She described in detail the burgundy phone that's over there." I pointed to it. "Whoever rents this place, is the monster."

Libby heard the word monster and knew that I was facing my past as well as this horrid present. "Who is it?" Libby asked as she turned to face Princey. Libby couldn't contain herself one minute longer.

"His name is Louis Lanzac. At least that is the name that he has given Mrs. Timon. It might be an alias but we could get lucky and find his mug on a driver's license. If not, I'll get Mrs. Timon working with a sketch artist and we'll find him that way. Everyone has a face, and with a face we can get him." Detective Noble seemed to growl when he said the last."Libby, get Angeline on it."

I watched Ed as he snooped around. He walked over to a rickety desk and noticed that one of the drawers was partially open. I followed him to get a closer look. A manilla envelope's worn corner stuck out from the drawer. He pulled it out. On the front, I clearly read my name - scrawled with a wide black Sharpie. The first to come out of the folder was a large photo of me. It was a blown-up picture from my high school yearbook and I think that since I had bangs, that would mean I was in tenth grade. I was only five years away from the time when he grabbed me, but being a know-it-all fifteen, I was convinced that I had the entire incident under control, and that the nightmares were my only residue. All I had really done was just suppress the worst of my emotions and memories so that I could cope with adolescence. I pretended that sex was still unknown to me and probably would have passed a lie detector on that, as the rape had been shoved down into a very deep well that I never looked into.

Behind the photo was a slew of personal information that I found disturbing. He had written his own version of my biography in outline form. He knew where and when I was born, my parent's names, who my sister was, the names of all of my step-brothers and sisters, in fact it was my family tree for at least three generations. I wasn't even familiar with the names of one the great aunts that he had down. Next were copies of my school records, all of them; from kindergarten through the universities that I attended. The recommendations that were written for me to enter my master's program were there in black-and-white as well. That particular invasion of my privacy made me angrier than the rest. Ed passed back the next bunch of papers to me. The stack held all of the current stuff - my phone numbers, my email accounts and my personal address book. I realized that he pulled that from my phone, and the topper to all the information, as it was the key to all gateways of information on anyone, my social security number. I felt naked and defeated. I stopped peering over Ed's shoulder. I had had enough.

Ed felt a thickness in the bottom of the folder and shook out what remained. A disc fell on the stack of my unwanted biography. With the same wide, black Sharpie he had written "Lovely Tess" on it.

I became terrified. My name, and him using the word lovely, next to it, made me shudder. "Are you going to put it in?" My right hand began to shake with nervousness.

"I think that we have seen enough for now. I'll check this out later." Ed slipped the disc into his jacket pocket. I was grateful.

Staying close to Ed, and not disturbing my sister's phone call to her partner, I breathed-in the room and began to decipher any clue that I could find. I felt Ed's excitement to be on the trail of the monster, to be on the hunt. I concluded that the hunt held the largest shot of adrenaline rush for him; not the kill, or in his case, the capture. No, Detective Kravitz was at his best when he was chasing a clue. As I rambled through my evaluations of this man, Ed was doing what he does the best, finding more clues, evidence in this case that would make the crime indisputable in any court.

Ed had turned on the computer, easily hacking his way in without a password. There, in the center of the screen was the file "Doll." I looked on in horror as he double clicked and up popped pictures of a terrified and naked Jennifer Stark, including the famous one that an FBI agent had downloaded and put up on the room monitor at in the Strategic Information & Operations Center. "Bingo! Didn't have to be psychic to find this!"He motioned to Princey to come and take a look.

"I'd say that you one-hundred percent have this sick bastard." Princey was a man of few words when it came to this sadistic child murderer. This was the evidence that he needed, solid facts that made it so that not only could you throw away the key, you could take this one and parade it down to the prosecutor's office quite joyfully. He pulled out the newest iPhone, thanks to his wife's mound of inherited cash, and called the Chief. At last there was good news, and no body, which was the best news of all for him to relay. He knew the name of the kidnapper and they should be able to get Louis Lanzac's face out, one way or another. The mystery was unraveling. He gave the Chief Stefan Hannigan's name, as the contact for the FBI, and told him that there was a wealth of evidence at the carriage house.

The Chief told Princey that the Forensic Unit would be there in a matter of ten minutes or less. He said it loud enough so that his secretary heard it and got on her phone to make that happen. Chief Townsend knew that the feds would be contacted but he wanted his guys to get the first stab at it. After all, he reasoned, they're the ones that figured this whole thing out. So why not get all of the glory too, and with that much good press and goodwill earned from the Director of the FBI, maybe their budget would grow by leaps too. It was tantalizing. The Chief picked up his chin higher and smiled, quite satisfied with that future outcome.

The Charlottesville Police Department was progressive in its forensic investigations. They were the first and only ones for many years, to have a course for officers to become certified Forensic Technicians. Not even Richmond did that. But that accomplishment was overshadowed in one important area. They did not always have the latest technical capabilities when it came to their computer system, hardware or software. Being behind that ball made it impossible to hook up with the FBI's VICAP software. Even though it had been a freebie from the federal government, Charlottesville PD was out of synch. A matter of budget and the ego of a few of the old guard detectives, who hated computers, kept them off the largest database for violent crimes in the United States. This was a mistake.

But I knew that all of the mistakes put together would not be able to stop this squall that had broken free and was about to land hard. Not the Feds, not the Charlottesville PD, not even teams of forensic techs would be able to go down the trail of following psychic breadcrumbs that I could and that I soon would.

Chapter Thirty

It was hard for me to leave my personal horrors alone. I would pick at them like a scab that I refused to let heal. It was the thing that had ruined my life. It was the incident that made me withdraw from every relationship that grew too close. It was the area that I never wanted to see with my eyes wide open. Instead, it would seep into my sleep, invading my deepest dreams. And now I watched as someone else was slipping into that same terror. Jennifer would be his next victim. I could easily be her. Truth be told, I was her.

Libby did not understand my reticence. She could strike out further than I. That explained our relationship and the roles in our professional lives as well. It was the undercurrent for most of our fights. She wanted me to fight back. I wanted to find the nearest tree and hide there; or as I grew older, a stack of books would do. I did not want to be surrounded by raw evil again. And now Jennifer needed me to be strong, to face him. I could see that it was true and that it was the only truth that mattered.

Libby, Kravitz and Princey marched to their police procedures. I held on to what I knew to do. I was now more at peace with my demons. I walked outside to be with my own thoughts and hopefully, heightened perceptions. It was the time for me to reach out to Jennifer.

It started out as a faint sensation. I could feel that Jennifer was thirsty so I was thirsty. Often, it began that way. I would mimic the one that I was psychically entwined with in such a way that my perceptions and theirs commingled. There were no barriers to emotions or sensations.

Jennifer seemed to whisper, "Is that you? Are you really here? It is you! You did find me!" Her elation was electric. She had a light illuminating her black hole - me.

"Yes, it's Tess! I'm here with you." I walked a bit further from the house and found a spot of thick grass to sit on so that I could close my eyes and more easily stay with the connection.

"It's the sound of the stream that makes me so thirsty. I can hear the water but I can't get there." She was parched and so riveted on the water.

"Is is a big stream or a little one?" I tried not to be too excited but to remain calm. I was determined to keep our connection; this time I was going to find her.

"It's small I think. I'm on a small hill. The little stream is below it. There was a bunny drinking there earlier. I like bunnies, do you?" She had a dreamy quality to her voice.

"Yes, I do. They're so cute. Jennifer are you alone? Is he there?"

"No." She did not elaborate or care to think of him.

I wasn't sure if I should push or not, her extreme emotions might get in the way of being able to locate her. I played with a piece of damp grass, ripping the stalk to shreds trying to make my decision.

"What else is around you? Are there any other animals? Or maybe houses? Are you all right?" I had so many questions that picking out the ones that I wanted answered first, was a challenge now that I knew she was alone.

"I'm in a magical forest. The trees are very, very tall and they all have names, I am sure of it! I heard an owl earlier. Did you? Oh, I can hear a police car far away..." she paused in her narrative to squirm with the ties that cut into her wrists.

I knew that she was doing her best to describe her surroundings to me. But I knew that being in the dark woods, with only a sliver of the moon would not allow her to perceive much. It was then that the sirens grew even louder.

"Tess, I can hear them getting louder too." Jennifer was following my every thought.

"Yes, it's too loud," I was distracted by the noise, "it makes it hard for me to think." I felt a foot slightly kick me. Looking up I saw it was Libby, I mouthed the word Jennifer. She kept quiet and kept everyone else away from me.

"Mine aren't as loud as yours." Jennifer pronounced with certainty. She said that she heard more sirens coming but mine were the biggest ones." She was enjoying her telepathic ability. I realized then that she no longer felt it was strange, more that it was the natural way to talk to someone. Jennifer could not wait to try this out with her best friend, Audrey. "Tess, do you think that I could talk to some of my friends the same way that I do with you?" She was hopeful that I would say yes.

"I hope that you can, dear. Often people are more receptive when they are young." I did not want to lie to her or tell her that hardly anyone could do it as easily as we both could. We were an oddity in today's world.

" The sirens must go away soon. They are scaring the bunny away!" Jennifer was enamored with her little rabbit that lived in the magical woods.

The woods! I finally got it. She was experiencing the same situation that I was at the same time and that meant that she must be nearby. Louis Lanzac had not taken her too far away. How could I be so slow! "Jennifer, I think that you must be fairly close. Let's try to use the sirens as a guide. Okay?' She agreed. I pulled Libby down to me. "She is nearby, close. She is hearing the sirens come to this place." Libby's eyes got bigger as she understood the ramifications. She went inside to Ed and pulled him aside, explaining the situation that the sirens were the smoke signal for Jennifer to follow. He went outside and ordered the men to turn the sirens back on. He was going to make this sound like an unholy symphony from hell.

"Tess, they are so loud! What if the noise makes him come back and get me?" The terror was creeping into her voice. It shoved me into my memories of the past with the monster. Strong, be strong, I admonished myself for my weakness.

"No, I will reach you first. Can you tell me what direction you hear the sirens coming from? Are they deeper into the woods or away?"

"I don't, I can't..." Then I heard her giggle. "It's ahead of the moon!" Jennifer was delighted with the little moon looming large in the big forest.

My chin slumped down. I bit my lower lip trying to decide how to guide her with a psychic sonar that she could somehow attach to these sirens. I came up empty.

"Tess I know exactly where you are." The tone of her voice reminded me of children playing hide and go seek. " I know that you are right outside the house!"

"You know that... how?" My head reeled as I attempted to stretch out my perceptions to find her even with more of a pinpoint location. And once again, I struck out.

"It's the bunny! It's the bunny! Don't you get it? Oh, he's right near you now, look in the bushes. The bunny found you!" Her pure delight could not be put down.

"Okay sweetie, okay. I need to find him, the bunny. I'll be gone for just a little while."

"Yep." Jennifer was hopeful now for a true rescue. The

bunny, she was most certain, would come through for her as she had asked him to do so.

I got Libby's attention, "This is going to sound odd but there is a bunny out in those bushes near the front of the house and the bunny knows where Jennifer is. I need to find him without scaring him. You can help me."

"What do I do? Libby decided that this was not maybe the weirdest request that I had ever made but it was at least in the top three.

The sirens were deafening. I considered asking her to have them turned off but thought better of it. A change might scare the rabbit more than just leaving them on. He could be hiding in the bushes as his way of being safe from the god-awful racket that they made.

"We need to find the rabbit." I shrugged my shoulders and looked up at her.

Libby motioned for us to split up. Yew bushes had grown tall around the house. They were overgrown and thick. The yews evergreen branches had stubbornly entwined with one another encircling the entire perimeter. This, I realized, was a perfect bunny hide-a-way. I stayed three feet away from the wall of green and walked slowly by. I barely heard Libby call for me over the din of the sirens.

"Tess, Tess, Tess," her voice grew more urgent with each Tess. "I think I found him. Over here, he's over here!" She shone her flashlight straight out to the bottom of one bush and then moved the bottom branch with her foot ever so slightly.

I rushed over to her. I held my index finger over my mouth to signal for her to be quiet. Libby picked that moment to sneeze one of her bone-rattling sneezes. A small dark form bolted out from the bushes. "It's a tabby cat. I thought it was the rabbit, sorry."

"Libby, you have got to be quieter okay? I know that the

sirens are loud but they are a constant loudness. When we are noisy, it's more of a threat. I think that we should walk together this time. I'll try to find him and see what I can get, and you make sure that he doesn't get away. You could throw your jacket over him if he takes off." I was whispering by the end of the sentence.

"Glad to see that you've got this all worked out." She dismissed my comment as an obvious choice that did not need to be said. Libby did not want to waste any more time with logistics or big-sister logic. She was right. We had no time to fritter away.

We followed around the perimeter, beginning from where the cat spooked. Not too far away I felt the bunny. He was chomping on some grass, well hidden by the evergreen's unchecked growth. I pointed to him and Libby nodded. She stepped back behind us and took off her jacket. This explained why the cat would endure the noise, he smelled the rabbit. Squatting close to the ground I rested my palms on the grass and mentally touched the rabbit. He was quite content and feeling sleepy. Feeling more confident that he would stay put, I sat down. I had not tried to communicate with many animals since childhood. My thoughts were occupied with my grownup world. But I recalled that in order to talk to the animals I could not use words as I did with people. I could emote to them and also I could perceive their emotions. I could place my attention within them and I often felt their intent. But the most effective way to get information was to try to look at their pictures of their environment that they made with their mind. This was the most difficult way to go about it as different animals perceive the world using different quality of senses and often mine was not as good as theirs, or it was just different. Cats can't perceive color but birds can. The world looks much different to a snake than it does to a goldfish. So as I debated what would be the best way to communicate with the bunny, the rabbit decided that he wanted to talk to me. He sent me an image of an apple. The apple was large and cut into several pieces. The bunny wanted an apple! This rabbit must have been someone's pet at one time. He wiggled his nose attempting to smell the apple in the gentle breeze.

"Libby," I called to her over my shoulder. "The bunny wants an apple. Get me an apple."

She started to use some colorful curse words in response to my request, but bit back her words, and went back inside the house. There was not one apple in the kitchen, only a limp piece of celery could be found. Just as she was about to give up, one of the forensic specialists remembered that she had an apple in her van. Soon Libby was standing next to me with the desired fruit.

"Thanks," I whispered. "Do you have a knife or something that I could cut this up with?"

"Yeah." She reached in her back pocket and pulled out a pocket knife. I took it and cut up the apple just like the rabbit wanted it. Sitting back down on the ground I held my hand out with a piece of the apple in the middle of my upturned palm. Libby stepped back.

Very timidly the rabbit poked his head out from the shrubbery. He could smell the desired apple was near and moved cautiously towards the scent. I let him take the first piece and chew it completely before my negotiation began.

The rabbit looked up. His weakness was apples. I sent him a string of mental pictures of Jennifer with a trail of apple bits leading to her. The rabbit was not a Rhodes Scholar and did not understand my plan for him to lead us to Jennifer. Attempting to be brilliant and to make some kind of an amazing idea pop out about turning rabbits into trackers, I felt lost, as nothing presented itself to me. I was wrestling with this defeat, when I felt Jennifer's presence. She was communicating to the bunny!

Libby, feeling Jennifer, crept over to me and squatted down. She telepathically said to me that she had never felt anyone that loudly before. I agreed.

The rabbit left the bush and hopped past us. He wasn't scared by us, he was just on a new adventure led by Jennifer. We got up and followed. I still did not know what the exact terms were that she and the rabbit agreed to, but some deal had been worked out. So just like Alice in Wonderland, we were off chasing a rabbit down the rabbit hole, hopefully to a better end.

Chapter Thirty-One

The rabbit would go for about ten yards and then stop to demand another piece of the ever shrinking apple. After thirty or so feet, the pieces got cut in half again. I hoped that this would be enough to reach Jennifer. I tried to stretch the distance but the rabbit was having none of that! So every ten yards, the rabbit stopped, looked straight ahead and wiggled its nose, anticipating the next delightful bite. I would drop a precious piece of fruit, plop, the bunny would scurry over. We repeated this over and over. Libby grew impatient.

Our strange parade marched into the gloomy spring woods. The blaring sirens grew distant but still remained a reminder that help was not far away. Libby took her flashlight out of her pocket. I reached over and took it away. "No light." I told her silently. We heard the bunny scamper into a low undergrowth. The forest was thick here. Our path went straight through a patch of wild raspberry brambles with spiky thorns that caught on the sleeves of my jacket. Happily, we came out into a clearing. The rabbit, unperturbed from the journey through the brambles, looked over to find me picking out a few of the most annoying thorns and waited for the last piece of the fruit. I looked over to Libby, not sure about what to do. She saw the one lone piece of apple. We both eyed our furry guide.

"I guess that this is the moment of truth. You can give him the apple and we will get another ten yards out of him or we could try to nudge him a bit further before he gets it. I don't think that he is the nudging kind though. Do you?" Libby asked.

In my estimation, she was quite right. This bunny did not like to be pushed around. He had been a very spoiled pet before his big escape and he had not lost his glutinous habit formed by the help of a band of brothers. "I better give him the apple." I bent down and offer him our last piece. He chomped it down and then took off. The rabbit scooted down a narrow deer run. We followed his shimmering white tail down the uneven trail. Old roots, gnarly and weathered-scarred, seemed to spring forward with each step. The rabbit lead us down a steep incline, he seemed to be flying with all of his paws flung out in front and behind, as we stumbled to keep up. The rabbit flew over a large rock and then stopped as quickly as he started. I tried to not topple into Libby as we both had put on our brakes. I felt my heart racing and heard Libby catch her breath.

Libby drew her gun. She felt him first. Not too far off was the monster. I heard her take off the safety. "It's him." She whispered. And then she sent the rest of the message telepathically, 'He's nearby, over to the right, about thirty feet.'

I got a fleeting impression of someone holding their breath. And then I felt his eyes move. I could feel him looking directly at us. He did not hesitate or wonder who we were. He knew.

Libby placed her free hand on my forearm and gently squeezed. Her instincts and training demanded her to be quiet, alert for the kill. We stayed frozen in that moment with him. I became consumed, feeling his sick joy. Libby heard him. She broke the trance first and shot her gun at the monster. I realized that the shot in the dark could have hit Jennifer, "Jennifer!

Jennifer!" I called out in anguish. There was no response. I did not feel her. Libby and I stood in the encompassing silence thinking the worst.

We grew scared but the monster grew bolder. I felt him sneer and then blow kisses in the dark. I could feel his heavy, silver keychain in his left hand. He tossed it up two feet in the pitch blackness and caught it. He wanted me to know that he had no trouble seeing at all. He was most certain that he would win at this game; that's when I put it together. "It's Hannigan!" I called out to Libby.

Libby never saw it coming. He threw the knife expertly, hitting his target's upper right arm. She screamed at the unexpected pain, dropping her Glock as it discharged. The bullet's path was concealed in the heavy darkness of the forest. It struck a boulder and careened wildly down the path, hitting the bunny. Jennifer screamed in horror as the bloody rabbit fell into her lap. Libby reached down for her weapon and clumsily held it with her left hand. We helplessly listened as Jennifer's cries reverberated through the forest. "Oh my god! Did you hit her?" I cried out. This was a nightmare that left Libby speechless. We heard her scream out again. Libby took off after the sound. I ran as hard as I could, making it ten feet when my right foot was swallowed up by a hole. I heard the sound of my right ankle cracking as pain exploded in my foot and leg. My ankle went numb. I crashed like a tall tree taken down by a lumberjack, now sprawled helpless on the forest floor, twisted and useless.

Hannigan ran down the path. He knew where Jennifer was and was intent on snatching her up. The branches bent and broke as he made his way to her. His expensive Italian loafers became scuffed on the sharp edges of the rocky trail as he unerringly found firm footing on one rock to the next rock. He smacked and splashed his way down the hill. Libby could not feel the pain in her wounded arm. Adrenaline helped her fly unhesitatingly down the dim path; down to the monster.

And that is when I lost control. I felt like I was floating, seeing them all move from above, seeing the foggy shadows of the tops of their heads in the sliver of moon light. I saw each shadow. The nuance of every shade of gray became vivid as I lifted further away from my body and watched the scene play out. Each motion became clear to me; the creek trickling over the stoney stream bed, Libby and Hannigan in a mad chase, and Jennifer's heaving chest as she sobbed wildly. My perceptions were heightened and uncontrollable. The world was forcefully spinning without my agreement and I whirled with it. There were no edges left to my reality as I unwillingly crashed into my own thick blanket of unconsciousness and hid within its depths.

Kravitz stopped digging through Louis's things long enough to notice that Libby and Tess were gone. He walked over to Princey to ask him if he knew where they were. He didn't, but he tried reassuring Ed that the girls had to be somewhere close by. Kravitz's instinct tugged uncomfortably with this thought, so he decided to go and make sure that Libby's car was still there. The helpful forensic technician stopped him. She heard him ask about the girls.

"Detective, you're looking for Officer MacGregor and her sister?"

"Yeah, do you know where they are?" He moved a bit closer so that he could hear her over the blaring sirens.

"Officer MacGregor asked for an apple. She said it was important so I gave her the one I had in the van. I saw her go over to her sister. Then after a little while I saw them walking towards the formal garden. If we go outside I can show you."

They both walked out into the noise. The tech pointed to a

path that Kravitz had already been on once tonight. "I see, so I think that I know where they're off to." Kravitz silently cursed, thinking of them wandering off alone. "Thanks, I appreciate it."

"It's alright, isn't it? I mean, they're okay, aren't they?" She became concerned seeing his worried face.

"Sure, they are just going over an area that we went over before. They're probably looking for new clues." He said it in his most convincing tone possible. Ed was almost convincing himself.

Princey now stood behind him. "Hey Ed, I think that we can wrap this thing up and follow them. Detective Freeman is just a couple of minutes out, I'll let him know. Lets see what they've found, huh?"

"Right." Ed smiled at the tech as she went back inside to continue her work and then spoke to his partner.

"Princey, I don't like this. They've been gone for at least ten minutes, maybe longer. Libby knows better than to take off without backup." Kravitz was working himself into being mad so that he wouldn't have to be concerned that something had happened to them.

"Yeah," Princey said with a slow drawl, contemplating the situation. "How about if we don't make the same mistake they made, I'll tell Detective Freeman where we are headed off to."

"Are you crazy? We say something and the feds will blast it all over and we'll end up like a herd running wild. Every living creature will know that the invasion is happening. And you know, they will all want to be the one to get this guy. Each SOB will have a gun drawn, too ready to shoot and make their mark. So it's you and me. I'll grab a radio."

Princey grabbed Ed's arm. "Okay, I get it, but you know that Libby is not just wandering around in the woods aimlessly. She's not stupid, but she should have told us her plan. So the deal is, I don't want us to be stupid, we have to tell someone."

Kravitz saw the wisdom and relented. They told one of the uniformed cops where they were headed. They also told him not to blab it to the feds. Kravitz got his radio and they struck out.

Each step through the gardens grew more urgent. By the time that they had made it through the boxwoods and saw the woods across the meadow, they were jogging. Princey was breathing hard. He stopped at the edge of the woods. They heard a muffled cry coming from the heart of the forest.

"Yeah, I heard it." Kravitz unconsciously rested his hand on the butt of his revolver.

"Radio it back Ed."

"Can't do that yet. We've got to not put them in more danger. Just think of fifty cops and feds storming down there with their guns flopping around like a bunch of loose dicks. It's too dangerous until we know more. You know I'm right. I am right about this." Kravitz intended to hold his ground.

A piercing scream broke the tension between them and made both men run blindly into the woods. They stumbled into the eerie spring forest, the partial moonlight hung and danced on the bare branches with their small, early leaves. I was climbing up from the black-velvet depths. I could see their forms taking shape. They were running and tumbling forward into a blind rage that belonged to Stefan Hannigan. I saw that Stefan's steady footing was dead set on his doll.

Chapter Thirty-Two

Colleen was having an easier time getting information now. The reality of the earthquake and its consequences had sunk in with most people. They were not as confused and dazed as earlier that evening. She felt that a sense of normalcy was coming to the forefront.

"Agent Sexton," the disembodied voice coming from a small speaker on her desk said, "there is someone from the Charlottesville Police Department on the phone for you. Do you want to take this call?" It was Elizabeth, the only secretary left in her department that late Sunday night.

Colleen was ready to tell her no, get a message, when fate moved into the picture. A small yellow bee climbed up to the top of her trash can, watching Colleen's foot swing back and forth. As usual, she had kicked off her high heels. The bee saw the splash of red on her big toe and believing it to be a crimson bloom, made an expert landing and stung her toe. She cried out in pain, and her cursing sounded to a distracted Elizabeth, that she wanted to take the call.

Angeline's voice was now on her speakerphone. "Agent

Sexton, I am Officer Jefferson, Abigail MacGregor is my partner." She waited for an acknowledgment.

"Damn it!" She clearly heard Agent Sexton curse and then straining, she thought Agent Sexton might be kicking around a trash can in a frantic fashion.

"Agent Sexton, are you alright? Should I contact 911?" Angeline was seconds away from calling for help.

"No, he just stung me!" Colleen was still in pain and incensed.

"Excuse me?" Angeline was perplexed.

She now had her inflamed toe in her hand. "The damn bee came out of nowhere and stung my toe! Geez, you'd think that you would be safe from the great outdoors in an office, wouldn't you?" She sighed and then said, "Sorry," Colleen was calming down, "you said that you are Libby's partner?"

"Yes I am. Too bad about the bee sting. It's been warmer than usual so I guess they are out now."

Getting a bit of sympathy, Colleen felt better. "What can I do for you Officer Jefferson?" She asked while she bent over to put her shoes back on.

"This is out of left field but I overheard Tess MacGregor mention your name. I am working on the kidnapping of Jennifer Stark. I have Stefan Hannigan down as my federal contact but I would like to speak to someone else. Could you help me or point me in the right direction? I hope I haven't put you in an awkward situation."

"No, not at all." Colleen said as the pain of the bee sting was instantly forgotten.

"You know we don't, I mean we are not hooked up to VICAP so I wasn't sure what to do. I mean, who to contact." Angeline sounded apologetic.

"Really, it's okay to talk to me. In fact, I am the perfect person for you to be talking to, really." Colleen was going to take this lead and hopefully make her mark in the FBI hierarchy with this information. As a woman, she knew that she needed every break that would come her way.

"Good, because I have something that is very odd." Angeline paused, trying to organize her thoughts so that she would be taken seriously. "I haven't been able to reach my team, Detective Noble, Detective Kravitz or Officer MacGregor. They are all unavailable." She cleared her throat and then went on. "We found the house that Jennifer had been held captive in. There were photos of her on the computer there. Forensics is gathering evidence now."

"Am I the first federal contact for your department on this?" Colleen held her breath.

"Correct." Angeline could hear Detective Kravitz's warning about releasing the hounds. She hoped that this was the right thing to do.

"What is the location?" Colleen was all business now.

"It is 335 Riverside Avenue, Charlottesville."

"Got it," her voice bubbled with ebullience. She was anxious to get off.

"But Agent Sexton there is more that I should tell you."

Colleen realized that Officer Jefferson never told her why she had not contacted Hannigan. "Yes, of course. What else do you have for me?"

"I had requested a photo ID for Louis Lanzac, he is the man that rents the house, and I got a familiar photo back from them. I also have a police sketch that was done for a possible murder suspect. Both of them strongly resemble Agent Hannigan."

"Huh?" Did you say Agent Hannigan? You mean Stefan Hannigan?" Colleen did not believe it.

Angeline could feel the ice that had just formed on the line. "Yes it is a puzzle to me but I've met him and although there was an attempt at a disguise, I believe that its him. I compared his facial features, one to the other, I don't have the latest software on biometrics, but I have a strong likelihood that it is him. He is a good suspect if not our perpetrator."

"Have you gotten forensics to check this out?" Colleen's disbelief would only be taken away with hard evidence. She knew that Hannigan was ruthless in his career advancement, not really a team player, but a psychotic killer? No, that was not believable for a man that qualified for a CARD agent. She could not believe that he was that rotten. She began to tap nervously at her bottom tooth and unconsciously slipped off her high heels, now contemplating that maybe he *was* that rotten to the core.

Chapter Thirty-Three

Jennifer broke her fabric restraints reaching out to grab her friend. She was desperate to hold her bunny. She had never seen anyone or anything that was shot before. The blood pooled on her lap. Behind her raced the devil and her avenging angel. Crashing through the trees, snapping branches loudly, Hannigan was only a few seconds away from her. Jennifer clutched the wounded bunny to her chest, anticipating his arrival.

Libby ran faster than she had ever run before. She flew over the twisted roots and jutting rocks. She believed that Jennifer's life depended upon her speed. Hannigan was close. She could feel the warmth from his body trailing out in front of her, taunting her to fly even faster.

I saw them all from above. The world looked less solid, more dreamlike, yet each separate fragment of the puzzle glowed. It made the objects more real, the motions more lively, the intentions quite plain, all of it was intensely clear. I was watching a secret world unfold.

Kravitz and Noble followed the sound. Both flashlights

bounced up and down as they ran on the deer trail. Princey's light illuminated my leg. He ran towards me.

"Ed, Ed, it's Tess. Over there!" He motioned with the light.

I was far away from my body. I was focused on Hannigan and his rage. His anger exploded with black balls of mental confusion that made the night even darker around his torso. Oh God, it was *him*! I did not want to know this. I was not prepared to face this. The anguish overwhelmed me and I pushed myself away from the monster, I could not control it as I slammed back into my body.

"Tess, Tess," Ed was holding me in his arms.

"Is she okay?" Princey was next to us.

I attempted to raise my eyelids but they were heavy and uncooperative. I felt Ed shake me. My eyes popped open as I sucked in the cool night air. "Libby! you've got to get to her! She almost has him, she almost has the monster. Don't let her touch him, don't let her!" I sat up on my own. My throat was hoarse and I was disoriented.

"Where are they?" Princey asked.

I pointed ahead, down the steep path to the stream. "Jennifer is there, next to the stream."

They both rocketed up and headed down the hill, full-on, into the abyss. My heart was beating as fast as a hummingbird's wings.

Hannigan reached down and easily grabbed his prize. Jennifer screamed; the monster was back. She dropped the injured bunny as he leapt over the stream. Libby was right behind him. She stretched her arm out as far as it would reach and caught the bottom edge of his jacket. It tore as he took the next long stride. Jennifer wriggled and kicked to be free. Stefan momentarily lost his balance. Libby tackled his legs with her good arm. She landed on a mat of fallen leaves, fiercely hanging on to his calf. Hannigan broke free of her grip, turned and kicked her hard in the jaw. Jennifer howled into his jacket and then bit his chest. Her cries cut through my confusion. He was getting away with her. I couldn't believe it and I couldn't stop it. Or could I? This time my journey would be under my control. I told myself that I could do it, I had to do it.

I laid back down on the forest floor and closed my eyes. I wasn't sure what to do. I thought of Jennifer and the terror that would rain down on her. I tried to picture where Ed and Princey were and got nothing. This was going nowhere and time was disappearing. I felt a stem from a dry leaf poking through my sweater. I squirmed, attempting to find a comfortable spot so I could concentrate on a solution. Then I saw it! "The leaf..." I said aloud. "I need to be one with the leaf, and with the motion, stop resisting the situation, stop trying to control each movement and action." My realization was profoundly simple, as, in retrospect, all truths are simple. Letting go so tightly, my space seemed to expand and I now felt myself growing bigger and bigger. My perceptions soared, I saw the outline of the woods, I tasted the water in the stream, and felt Princey's knee absorb the shock from his foot slamming down on the trail. I was with them all and at the edges of my awareness was the monster. He had Jennifer held firmly to his chest. Her face was pressed tightly into him. She could hardly breathe. Libby was face down in the mud. I was startled to see her like that, I began to tense up and felt myself moving backwards. I made myself think of the leaf, think of the leaf, don't resist, just be in the present; and then I was with him again. The black masses and mental confusion were recognizable. I was with his dark, death-filled, painful existence again. Evil sat naked within him. He felt my life force there and mistakenly thought that I was Jennifer.

Kravitz stopped to get his bearings. The sirens were still blaring. Princey jostled him as Ed stood silent. "Shh, I can't tell which way to go." Ed strained to hear the sound of the stream." Shit Princey, I don't hear it."

"Don't hear what?" He panted.

"They're at the stream but I don't hear any water. Do you?"

"Take my word for it, the stream would run downhill. Just keep going down." The naturalist made his point and took off downhill. Ed followed. The pitch of the land grew steep. Ed had a hard time maintaining his balance as the rocks rolled and flew, making a noisy descent.

Princey heard the clumsy footfalls. "Ed, watch me. Don't run straight down!" He called out to him over his shoulder. Kravitz shone his flashlight on Princey' feet as they navigated securely downwards and saw that his partner was going down the hill with a sideways motion. Necessity made him a quick study. He imitated Princey and went down the hill with surer footing. Clumps of dirt spun out from under their feet as they made a rapid descent. In less than two minutes they stood next to the stream. No one was there. Ed shone his light in the water and saw that there was blood on the rocks. He thought of Libby. "God damn it! I knew that she shouldn't go off by herself." Kravitz rubbed his eyes, thinking about having to tell Tess.

Princey looked down at the blood on the rock. The blood made him feel queasy. "Is it Jennifer?"

He pulled out the radio and started to call for back up. They needed someone to stop Louis Lanzac from leaving the woods. If he got out on the street it would be simple for him to disappear in the panic of the city. Ed pushed down the button on the radio now ready to call it in.

Princey grabbed his elbow. "What's that? I hear someone moaning...over there!" He pointed ahead.

Kravitz heard it too and splashed through the stream. He found Libby lying on the ground behind a pile of rocks, a knife protruding from her bicep. She was not moving. Princey knelt down and found her pulse. They turned her over and looked for more holes, none were found.

"Hey, so far, so good." Kravitz's diagnosis in the dark would have at least noticed any large wounds.

"Oh...hurts." Libby found consciousness but could not say another word. The knife wound was not fatal but her jaw was deeply bruised and her cheekbone was fractured. She gallantly tried to speak but her words were muffled and indecipherable, leaving her to make hand gestures with her good arm for them to go. That was all the nudging that it took.

The monster had Jennifer and they were soaring through the woods. I felt her falling away. Hope had left her heart. Hannigan's steel grip to his chest was forcing her small face into his jacket. He was suffocating her. Jennifer was no longer conscious. The monster seemed to stampede up the hill, feeling victorious after capturing his prize and eluding the idiot cops. I hated to be with his thoughts. They drained me. Far in the distance I perceived Ed and Princey. They were too far away!

Louis was becoming more powerful with each step. His memories of Stefan became hazy and slipped under the surface. It was Louis that had her now, he pushed Stefan away, banished to the background of his life.

Louis only had a short distance to go and he would be on the street. He raced up the last incline and broke through the woods, both feet slamming onto the black top. He sneered and paused, lost in his illusions of his supposed lush life. This would be the satisfying end to his story once again. He had his doll.

"He's up there!" Kravitz called out to his partner. Princey had stopped to call for help. Help was coming, just not in the way he expected.

Louis couldn't feel feel the lightness that surrounded him. He was cocky now that he was out of the woods. Louis saw a car parked close by. He recognized the silhouette, it was an old

Honda Civic, one of the easiest cars to break into and hot-wire. He confidently strode over to it and placed Jennifer on the road. She took in a large mouthful of oxygen. It flooded into her nose and soon was rocketing through her blood. The monster pulled out his screwdriver and put his large, muscular hand on the car's door handle.

I drilled the last of my intention straight as an arrow to her, "Wake up!" I mentally screamed.

My sleeping beauty woke. The terror clung to her throat, she was unable to make a sound, her muscles were limp. "I'm here. You have to run. Run back into the woods. Run now!" I pleaded with her.

Jennifer was frozen in fear, she did not want to move, she did not want him to touch her again. She remained still, hardly letting herself breathe. "Run, run to the bunny!"

Without thinking about it, or feeling her fear, Jennifer jumped up and blasted straight back towards the trees. Back to save her furry friend.

"No, no, you can't go!" Louis lunged after his moving target. He would rather see her dead than let her escape. No one had ever escaped from him. He confidently held the screwdriver tight and dove after his doll.

Jennifer barely touched a leaf of the first tree as Kravitz's sure hands grabbed her into the woods. I felt her safe with Ed's arms tight around her as the jet-black unconsciousness swallowed me up.

Epilogue

The city was back to normal. The latest gossip revolved around the hometown boys, DMB, as they were called in Charlottesville. For the uninitiated it had to be spelled out, The Dave Matthews Band. I took a great deal of comfort in sitting in my chosen mussiness in my cramped office with a cup of delightful coffee from Shenandoah Joe and the latest copy of C'ville in my hand. I was newly determined not to take these simple comforts for granted.

Libby wanted us to take time off together and go for a vacation. She thought that maybe Scotland would be fun. Lots to see, attractive men with great accents in kilts, and a place where we could understand, mostly, what everyone was saying. She could go surfing off their rocky beaches and I could scuba dive or maybe go to one of thousands of historical sights. "Lose yourself in guide books!" This was one of Libby's arguments that did seem particularly appealing to my academic soul. I admitted that it sounded good but I wasn't interested in leaving then. For the first time as an adult, I wanted to enjoy my life, not run away from it.

I put down my now empty coffee cup and peered outside the small window. Spring was in full bloom; the daffodils, hyacinths and tulips made colorful patterns on the edge of the walkway. It was a beautiful campus. Staring at a stack of students' research papers, I considered sneaking out for another cup. I was tempted by my discount card and a large selection of home-made muffins and cakes. After all, it was only a short walk away. But a greater temptation won out. My new Mac Book Air, a reward to myself for facing the monster, sat smiling at me. I popped open the rose gold lid and quickly got online. There were two new personal emails. One was from Ed. We had become quite the internet friends. I hoped that our schedules would finally mesh and this would be a confirmation for an in-the-flesh date but then I noticed that the address of the other email was mine and the subject line was, Go Ask A Bunny. I sat perplexed, maybe it was Libby playing a joke? Curiosity got the better of me, so I opened that one up first.

I was one click away from my very own personal *haunted house*. This is how I would think of Louis. I had heard this description from a Texas Ranger. It is how he described escorting a serial killer through Texas while he identified the many dump sites of his victims. The Ranger's description stuck. I pictured Casper-like ghouls popping out of a decrepit mansion as I read his email.

"Howdy doll, sometimes these things happen...long time till I see you again? Kisses. Love, Louis.

PS. glad, glad, glad to be on my own again!"

His words seemed to fly off the digital page, dirtying my office, attacking my peace with a message that made no sense, one that he wanted me puzzle over, one that seemed to contain a not so covert threat. I breathed ten deep breaths, closed the rose-gold lid and went searching for solace by way of a lovely spring walk to a hot, flavorful cup of coffee. Scotland, I just decided, would definitely be in the near future.

THE END

Read on for an excerpt of
Yesterday's Time

The next novel of suspense
with Tess MacGregor

by VIRGINIA WATSON

Chapter 35

Chapter 1

I had been sitting alone all day. There wasn't much for me to do on a beach in Orkney, Scotland, except watch and think. I was now bored from enduring my long, complex thoughts. Libby, my younger sister, seemed to be tired of hearing them as well. She had escaped my worries by bobbing up and down like a blond ball in the vast ocean.

The beach stretched out forever. The walk I took on the warm, coarse sand seemed endless. The kind of endless that belonged on the fringes of time. I liked to hang on the fringes. It was a comfortable place to be with no demands. I had made the past my profession as well, teaching for the last two years at the University of Virginia's Archeology Department. I enjoyed being a professor in a quiet department that only attracted book-worms and geeks. It was a safe, comfortable existence; perfect for my wary soul.

Libby, being the opposite of me, chose to be a cop. Facing danger head-on was her life's pursuit. She wanted nothing to do with the fringes of anything.

She was enjoying hitting each wave that came to her. As they say in Scotland, she loved the "now." Being pummeled about by the North Sea didn't give her a second thought. I watched her carefully and then sat down to look at his unwanted and thoroughly creepy e-mail one more time.

Psycho Louis had sent a message a few weeks before. It was not a threatening email, as emails go, but anything from him made your pulse quicken. I reread his message, then putting my laptop down, I wondered why an ability would always feel more like a disability to me. I was reintroduced to Louis, the psycho, because I was psychic. Funny that both words had to do with the soul, as neither were spiritual in my book. He had stabbed my sister and kidnapped me, scaring us both so badly that we were now on our first vacation together as adults. Libby had suggested that we leave the country, and get as far away from Charlottesville, Virginia as one could reasonably get and still speak English. I didn't argue with her this time, Louis was still on the loose.

Everyone has various perceptions available to them. Some only dream in black and white, while others have high definition and a whole 64 crayon selection of colors to fill in their view of reality. My world had all of the crayons plus an added feature that I was not able to delete, the thoughts and unspoken intentions of those around me. Actually, I could read thoughts from far away, but that was something that only my close family, the FBI, psycho Louis, and until recently, a few detectives in the Charlottesville Police Department, knew.

The so-called brand new science of psychometry- reading the memories on objects, really a very old spiritual practice, was the next label given to my photo in the government's file. Nice to know that you are filed in alphabetical order somewhere with all of the appropriate boxes checked. But they had omitted one box, can talk to animals, nope, no one, not even the FBI would buy that one. Should have had a box though.

So here I sat, with the wind swirling uncontrollably around

me, while my beach neighbors gave no notice to what I thought was a threatening situation. Libby seemed fiercely happy fighting with the ocean. I could feel the joy radiating from a most primitive part of her being. White water smacked her hard in the chest. The cold waves crashed loudly on the rocky shore as the birds' piercing cries danced with the untamed ocean. I looked to see if anyone else on the beach was worried about the swimmers being tossed about in the rough sea. Nope, no one gave a damn. That is what I enjoyed most about the Scots more than any other quality; after many centuries of British rule, they knew when to not give a damn; I was learning this also.

We were comfortably settled in our self-catering cottage. The Orkney Isles, north of mainland Scotland, were home to several civilizations that left their mark on the scattered bits of land. The Vikings had claimed them as their own at one time, but I felt that Orkney belonged to the Picts. They were the mysterious, woad-painted people, whose legend stood in antiquity as strong as the standing stones that they carved with their hidden messages. Not one of their symbols had ever really been deciphered. Their meaning had only been guessed at by some not-so-knowledgeable, trendy, New Age types, whose hodgepodge philosophies spouted out blended beliefs of old and new. None of it made much sense to me. I had spent too many years in countless libraries and museums researching history and the philosophies of man, to take it seriously.

Here in the prehistoric splendor of Orkney I enjoyed being with the stones and feeling their strength and age. So while the quiet stones stood as witnesses to the beliefs of an ancient world, I was soon to face the truth of the present.

Chapter 36

Chapter 2

Lost to the exactness of a razor's edge was Richard's creative desire to carve beautiful pictures on her breasts. The picture seemed come alive as the blood appeared in his mind to gently wash over the tiny spirals. The spirals circled the dark areolas and grew larger the further out that they went. Her blood was not flowing now. The breath had left the empty shell, and all that remained had no vivid colors left. Those would come later, as the bruising would show in a few hours from now. She would be a prop for the next group of stones or perhaps, a neolithic site; maybe the new one, the Tomb of the Eagles, or an old favorite, Mine Howe. Outside, the wind howled and the waves rocked in time to an ancient rhythm. Richard pulsed with the sacred flow. He felt that he had no time to spare, as well as having all the time in the world. His time ebbed and then rushed in with the ghosts of the past.

Richard's senses came alive when what he was touching was dead. The intensity of feeling her made the center of his skull glow with warmth. The warmth spilled out and down his arms, making each capillary that it crossed dilate to deal with the rushing blood flow. Lost to the ecstasy of the moment, his pleasure took him to his private world of the dead. "Never shall I leave you!" He called out to his ancestors as his body shuddered one last time. The lack of sensation soon brought him back to the unemotional present. He withdrew from her cold shell and washed his hands in an old, lime-stained basin.

The black house, a three-roomed stone cottage, lay mostly in ruins, except for the kitchen area and the middle section that was a bedroom and sitting room of sorts. A well-worn sofa was placed next to the sooty fireplace; nappy sheepskin rugs were scattered about the cold stone floor. The honey-colored rocks, moist with ocean air, were raw and unyielding. They defined the room as they were the chunks of the cliff that the cottage clung to. No one cared for the remnants of the place since the last crofter left 150 years earlier. It was a secluded pile of forgotten scree, hidden in brambles, beaten up by the ocean's winds and claimed by Richard as his very own.

He turned his attention back to the woman. She had long, dark brown hair. Her nose was fairly straight and she was average in height and weight. She had been his nondescript neighbor. Her equally dull family, at least that was how he saw them, was soon to have a good cry after seeing the condition of their wayward daughter. Heaving breasts and their lone wolf cries would pierce the summer sun nights with the thought of her mutilated body. Having her carved like an Iron Age Pict would be of no consolation for them. Richard believed that he was giving her a place in history, something that would turn her inconsequential life energy into an impressive end. It was a grander death than her meager existence would have accomplished alone. She would have just to have been another fat hen on a nest; raising a brood of boorish, slovenly chicks that in turn would breed and create more foul stench on his island. He had saved her.

Twilight hung on the roof top, finally slipping into the swell of the dark ground. The summer sun did not set until near midnight. It was a long day with a short-lived night that glimmered with light in varying degrees. His private time with her would end. The dawn's golden radiance shimmered and filtered the earth's colors until they blended into a harmonious scheme. The soft light shone through Richard's bare window now. It illuminated his handiwork and gave an unholy glow to her skin. There was absolutely nothing better for him than being next to her. He stroked her belly and sighed deeply. Nothing would ever touch that place in his heart; no one would ever fill that void in his longing as death could. His nostrils flared as he breathed in her smell. This is what drove him to create his great masterpiece - a Pictish warrior woman. Richard's longings gave birth to great works of art. He was certain that his ancestors would wake up, their death cobwebs and bones of sand would vanish, and he would stand with them again. Words of praise would be bestowed and his halo of genius would remain intact. The past spoke to him in charming tones, beguiling to his rotten core. He was certain that these creations would be loved forever; he would be loved forever. It was all about forever for him; forever to live, forever to die, it was all the same to him.

Richard brought himself out of his reverie and took the small knife circling her belly, making sure to have the spirals trail downwards, dancing towards her pubic bone. The knife easily cut each line as he contemplated the next design. An infinite amount of time floated around him. He took the blade, and with a steady hand, skillfully cut his most intricate patterns. He happily hid himself within the designs. The swirls poked their way back and forth, up and down, on her cold skin. Richard's stomach grumbled with hunger but was ignored. He was lost in the spiral's pathway as it became a connected canvas. This, he decided, would look like the main lintel at Maes Howe. His ability to duplicate the design was uncanny. He believed that a hand from long ago guided him. The world was a vast array of connections for him. One thing would touch and influence another. This is what the spirals showed him; the cycles of life were everlasting, one flowing into the next. His essence flowed on that stream.

Summer's dusky dawn would be daylight soon. He pondered where to take her. He spiraled down to her left ankle just as a rat ran across one of the mangy sheepskin rugs. The rat stopped abruptly and looked back at Richard. The rodent's nose twitched as he smelled meat. He wondered if it would be shared. Richard's look fell heavy on the vermin's head. The rat realized the futility of his desire and vanished with lightning speed into a crack in the stones.

Richard took the handle of the replica of the stone age tool and twirled it in his palm. He had not used that blade yet, but the thought to christen it with her was tantalizing. A local craftsman had made the blade many years ago and now they were being sold by a local potter in Harray. His store sold many reproduction flint knives to the tourists that ventured down the single track road, so who could tell whose knife made these marks, he mused. The knife had been made in the same tradition of those from five thousand years ago. The blade honed sharp, its chisel marks gleaming on the grayish-black edge. He loved the antler handle as it fit perfectly into his palm. While holding the knife it became part of his body.

He took her right foot and propped up the bottom of her sole to cut a rune. It was the Viking rune for protection, an elk symbol. He was now quite satisfied that his blade had been used properly for its virgin cut. Reaching up, Richard tugged a wall hanging made of soft, felted wool, down from a chipped peg and wrapped her in it. He tossed her over his shoulder, and carried her out to the barn. There was just one last preparation to make before her debut.

An old oak table, too valuable to throw away, stood in the middle of the grimy walled barn. He placed his Pict on an improvised altar and reached for the day old, mold-caked bucket of lime. Contemplating that cutting off her hair would add a new level of horror for the parents was an added thrill. Richard savored the thought of her mom and dad squinting hard to recognize who she was because they would have to look through what she had become.

Her body fit nicely on the table top, Richard thought as he unwrapped the body and then pulled her long hair out from around her head. The sheep shears were cold and heavy in his hand. He held her head up and began to cut her hair. The foot-long tresses fell on the dirt floor. Richard methodically sectioned pieces of her scalp and cut each section in turn. He hummed a lament while he played with his toy. Her chopped hair stood only two inches in length when he was done with it. He put down the rusty scissors, and began coating sections of her hair with the lime. He grabbed about a square inch each time. It took a bit of effort to twirl each piece into twisted tubes, covered in globs of lime, but the effect was stunning.

The final step and he felt the most spiritual step, was application of the woad on his designs. Meticulously, each cut was covered in a lavender-scented potion of the darkest-blue woad. Richard used his favorite sable brush and savored the design as it came alive. Done, he rolled her back into the decrepit felt tapestry and loaded her in the trunk of his small car. Her body was a tight fit. Richard watched the sun begin to take ownership of the sky again, as he snaked his way along the coast road to the Tomb of the Eagles. This was his latest gift to his line and was the most creative design that he had ever done. This was his first human offering.

The trail that Richard chose was not the official one that was easily traversed by the tourists; instead, he cut through the pot-holed cow field and made his way to the remains of the Bronze Age home. The midden pile, an ancient stack of garbage now valued for its obscure history, was on the western side of the site. His first impulse was to put her there, with the lichen-covered, stoney debris. But providence made him choose another place. Richard lost his balance, the bite of a sharp rock hidden in the tall grass surprised him. He strained his shoulder muscles clutching on to her torso as she dove downwards. Grabbing the warrior Pict from her descent into mud, Richard furtively looked behind, as a cow's deep moo startled him, and the waking sun warned him to go, to leave that place. But Richard was on a sacred mission. It was a task that would guarantee his life forever, one to appease all of his critics. His graceful hands carefully placed her body on the nearby stone slab bed from thousands years ago. There were fewer steps to that spot; fewer marks to explain. His Pict was now home.

The golden sun lit the fields of Orkney, a new morning took hold of the land.

About the Author

Virginia Watson has made her living for over 35 years as a costume designer. Her design work can be seen at potomacwolfstone.com. Her first novel is one of a series, the second, "Yesterday's Time",will be released soon. In it, Tess and her sister, Libby, visit Orkney Scotland and become enmeshed in a one of the most unique murder mysteries that terrifies the small community and threatens the very essence of the island's culture. Was it death in the standing stones or death becoming the standing stones? Read on to find out.

Feel free to send an email to vwatsonwriter@gmail.com or visit www.vwatsonwriter.com for more information on upcoming projects and to subscribe to a newsletter.

Made in the USA
Middletown, DE
23 September 2023

38734943R00161